SHADOWS IN PARADISE

ABOUT THE AUTHOR

Tory Swedlund: A Life Journey to Writing

Tory Swedlund is a 46-year-old full-time single father who has made a name for himself as a writer. He raised two daughters, Dacey, and Ozzie, who are now 10 and 8 years old, respectively.

Tory has been honing his craft as a writer and note-taker for years, finally leaping to put his thoughts into books. His writing style is top-notch, leaving readers craving for more.

Tory has written several amazing books, including "Final Swipe," "Eating Death," and "Devils Highway." These thrilling stories are set to captivate readers, leaving them stunned.

Tory grew up in a small town in South Dakota where not everything was easy. He had to make difficult decisions that taught him valuable lessons. These experiences have shaped him into a resilient and introspective individual.

Tory is a recovering alcoholic and drug addict who has been sober for an incredible 24 years. His journey has been filled with ups and downs, but it has brought him closer to his true potential as a writer.

Tory brings a wholeheartedness to his writing, infusing it with insight and passion. His past and thought process adds depth and authenticity to his stories, leaving readers on the edge.

Tory Swedlund's writing journey is a testament to the power of perseverance and self-discovery. His ability to create captivating and thought-provoking stories is a testament to his talent and drive. With several amazing books under his belt, Tory is a force to be reckoned with in the world of writing.

CONTENTS

CHAPTER 1

Sunkissed Nightmares

A thin sliver of sunlight filtered through the gap in the living room curtains, casting a warm glow on Edward Kingsley's meticulously groomed features. The middle-aged man stood confidently as he addressed a potential tenant—a young woman with a curious, wide-eyed gaze.

"Welcome to your potential new home," Edward said, his voice smooth and persuasive. "As you can see, the open floor plan creates a spacious environment for entertaining guests or simply unwinding after a long day."

The young woman nodded appreciatively, her eyes scanning the room, taking in the polished hardwood floors and high ceilings.

"Come, let me show you the rest of the house," Edward urged, guiding her towards the gourmet kitchen. He gestured towards the stainless steel appliances and granite countertops, his attention to detail evident in every word. "These finishes are not only aesthetically pleasing but also designed for ease of use and durability."

"Wow, you've thought of everything," the young woman marveled, running her fingers over the sleek surface of the counter.

"Indeed," Edward replied, a sly smile playing at the corners of his mouth. "After years in the rental business, I pride myself on ensuring that each of my properties meets the highest standards."

They continued their tour, Edward pointing out subtle touches like the soft-close cabinets and energy-efficient windows. It was clear that he had invested a great deal of time and effort into crafting an idyllic living space for his tenants.

As they ascended the staircase, Edward could sense the woman's growing enthusiasm. She was captivated, drawn in by the allure of the property and the charm of its proprietor. It was a familiar scene for Edward, one that played out time and again in his successful career.

"Here we have the master suite," he announced, pushing open the door to reveal a large bedroom bathed in natural light. "I find that the vaulted ceilings and picture windows create a serene atmosphere, perfect for relaxation."

"Stunning," the woman breathed, her eyes widening in admiration.

Edward watched her reaction with a mixture of satisfaction and anticipation. He knew he had won her over, that she would soon be another tenant under his control. And yet, as the shadows lengthened and their tour drew to a close, Edward couldn't help but feel a sense of unease—a nagging reminder of the dark desires that lurked just beneath the surface, threatening to shatter his carefully constructed facade.

Edward led the potential tenant back to the main living area, his charm and attentiveness never wavering. The late afternoon sunlight streamed through the wide glass doors, casting golden rays across the polished floor.

"Shall we discuss the rental agreement?" Edward asked, gesturing toward the elegant dining table. As they sat down, he produced a crisp, neatly folded contract from his jacket pocket.

"Of course," the woman replied, her eyes scanning the document as Edward outlined the terms. He made a point to emphasize the flexibility of the lease, as well as the numerous amenities included in the rent. It was crucial to make every tenant feel they were getting the best possible deal.

"Normally, the rent for this property is set at $3,500 per month," Edward explained smoothly, "However, I'm willing to offer a discounted rate of $3,200 if you sign a twelve-month lease."

The woman hesitated, her eyes darting back and forth between the contract and Edward's expectant gaze. She seemed to be weighing her options, and for a moment, Edward worried that she might slip through his grasp. But then, with a decisive nod, she agreed to the terms.

"Fantastic!" Edward exclaimed, concealing his relief behind a warm smile. "I'll need your signature on the last page, please." As she signed, Edward allowed himself a moment of satisfaction. Another successful negotiation was another tenant under his control.

Samantha Kingsley strode through the doors of the police station, her tall figure cutting an imposing silhouette against the fading light outside. The officers on duty snapped to attention, their postures straightening and voices lowering as she entered. She acknowledged them with a curt nod, her sharp brown eyes conveying authority and respect.

"Evening, Chief Kingsley," one officer greeted her, stepping forward with a handful of reports.

"Thank you, Johnson," Samantha replied, taking the documents and scanning them with practiced efficiency. As she walked down the hall to her office, the murmurs of the station subsided, replaced by the steady hum of diligent work.

"Another long day?" a voice asked from behind her as she settled into her chair. It was Detective Roberts, one of her most trusted subordinates.

"Seems like they're all long days lately," Samantha sighed, rubbing her temples. She glanced at the stack of case files on her desk, each one demanding her attention. "But that's the job, isn't it?"

"True enough," Roberts agreed, his tone sympathetic but firm. "Speaking of which, we've had some developments in the Thompson case. I think you'll want to take a look."

"Alright, bring it in." Samantha steeled herself for another late night, her focus shifting from the burdens of her marriage to the responsibilities of her role as chief of police. Little did she know, somewhere across town, her husband Edward stood over a signed rental agreement, reveling in the dark thrill of his latest conquest.

Samantha's eyes narrowed as she poured over the documents spread across her desk, pen scribbling notes in the margins of each case file. Her office was dimly lit, casting an eerie shadow on her face that only heightened her intensity.

"Chief, we've identified a potential suspect in the Thompson case," Detective Roberts announced as he entered, holding a photo in his hand. Samantha looked up, her brow furrowed in determination.

"Let's see it," she demanded, snatching the photo from him and studying it closely. "Have we got a location on this man?"

"Working on it," Roberts replied. "Our team is tracking down leads as we speak."

"Good. Keep me updated." Samantha's mind raced with possibilities, and strategies to apprehend the suspect and bring justice to the victims. Her thoughts were suddenly interrupted by the vibration of her phone.

"Hey, it's me," Edward's voice chimed through the speaker, light and charming as ever. "Just checking in. How's your day going?"

"Busy, as usual." Samantha sighed, forcing a smile for her husband's sake. "But I'm making progress. How about you? Did you close that deal?"

"Indeed, I did," Edward boasted, his tone oozing with pride. "Seems like we both know how to get things done, don't we?"

"Of course. It's why we make such a great team." Samantha paused, trying to suppress her growing unease at the contrast between their worlds. While she fought to maintain order and justice, her husband reveled in the thrill of sealing deals, his charm disarming those he encountered.

"Listen, I've got to run," she said, struggling to keep the strain from her voice. "I'll see you later tonight, okay?"

"Sure thing," Edward replied, his voice laced with affection. "Take care, Samantha. I love you."

"Love you too," she echoed before ending the call, her eyes returning to the case files across her desk.

As Samantha delved back into her work, she couldn't help but feel a churning in her stomach – a discomfort that had been growing stronger with each passing day. She knew her husband's charm could be intoxicating, but deep down, she feared it held a sinister edge, one that threatened to engulf them both.

"Chief?" Roberts called, snapping her out of her thoughts. "You alright?"

"Fine," she replied tersely, forcing herself to refocus on the task at hand. With a deep breath, she plunged once more into the dark underbelly of the city, determined to bring light and justice where shadows festered, unaware of the darkness lurking within her own home.

Edward Kingsley stood in the doorway of one of his rental properties, his eyes scanning every inch of the pristine living room. The smell of fresh paint and polished wood filled his nostrils as he adjusted his cufflinks, a subtle sign of his perfectionism. He felt a sense of satisfaction knowing that every detail was in order – from the perfectly aligned picture frames to the immaculate arrangement of furniture.

"Everything looks perfect, as always," he said aloud, his voice rich and velvety, echoing through the empty room. As he prepared to leave, his phone buzzed with an incoming text message. Samantha's name appeared on the screen, her words terse and to the point: "We need to talk."

A flicker of irritation crossed Edward's face as he tapped out a quick response. "Of course, dear. I'll be home soon." He locked up the property and made his way to his car, his mind racing with possible reasons for Samantha's sudden urgency.

As he drove, Edward couldn't help but notice the stark contrast between their worlds. While Samantha fought to maintain order and justice in the city, he reveled in creating order within his domain – an empire built on charm and meticulous attention to detail.

Upon arriving home, Edward found Samantha waiting for him in the living room, her arms crossed and her expression steely.

"Edward, we need to discuss something important," she began, her tone laced with tension. "I've been noticing some... discrepancies in our finances lately."

"Discrepancies?" Edward replied smoothly, his brow furrowing in feigned concern. "What sort of discrepancies?"

"Large sums of money being transferred without explanation," Samantha continued, her eyes narrowing. "I trust you, Edward, but I need to know what's going on."

"Ah, that," Edward said, waving a dismissive hand. "It's all above board, Samantha. I've been making some investments in new properties – nothing to worry about."

"Then why didn't you mention it to me?" she pressed, her voice strained.

"Because I wanted it to be a surprise," he replied, his eyes locked on hers. "I know how hard you work, and I wanted to show you that I'm doing my part to contribute to our future."

Samantha hesitated, her resolve wavering momentarily as she searched his face for any hint of dishonesty. She saw only sincerity, and with a sigh, she relented. "Alright," she murmured, the tension dissipating. "But please, keep me informed from now on, okay?"

"Of course," Edward agreed, pulling her into an embrace. As they stood there, wrapped in each other's arms, he couldn't help but feel a twinge of guilt. He knew his charm could disarm even those closest to him. And yet, beneath the surface, his dark desires threatened to unravel everything they'd built together.

The sun dipped below the horizon, casting long, menacing shadows across the city streets as Edward Kingsley adjusted his cufflinks and surveyed the room. He had just finished preparing one of his rental properties for a new tenant – everything was in perfect order, down to the last detail. The scent of fresh linen lingered in the air, mingling with the faint aroma of lemon-scented cleaner.

"Another satisfied customer," he murmured, his lips curling into a self-assured smile.

As he locked the front door behind him, Edward's mind drifted to Samantha. Despite their earlier tension, he couldn't help but admire her dedication and commitment to justice. She made him want to be a better man, to suppress the dark urges that threatened to consume him. But the temptation was a persistent foe.

"Excuse me, sir?" A timid voice pulled him from his thoughts.

Edward turned to see a young woman standing at the end of the driveway, her arms wrapped around herself as her brown eyes stared nervously at him. "I, um, I think someone broke into my car."

"Ah, well, that is unfortunate." Edward forced a look of concern onto his face as he approached her. "What seems to be the problem?"

"Someone smashed my window and took my purse." The woman's voice trembled slightly, hinting at her vulnerability.

"Let's take a look then, shall we?" Edward offered, fighting back the sudden urge to exploit her weakness.

As they walked over to her vehicle, Edward lamented the fact that Samantha was not here to handle this situation. It would have been the perfect opportunity for her to showcase her skills as a police officer. However, she was investigating another minor crime across town, leaving him to deal with this issue.

"Here," said the woman, pointing at the shattered glass littering the ground.

"I see," Edward replied, his eyes narrowing as he inspected the damage. "It seems like a fairly amateur job if you ask me."

"Can you help me?" she asked, her voice wavering with desperation.

"Of course," he said, reaching for his phone to call Samantha's department. As he did so, his gaze lingered on the woman, tracing the curve of her neck and the way her hair framed her face.

"Edward, focus," he admonished himself silently, struggling to suppress his dark desires. But the sight of her vulnerable state stirred something within him – a hunger that demanded satisfaction. With great effort, he tore his eyes away from her and dialed the number.

"Hello, this is Edward Kingsley," he began, his voice steady and professional. "I'd like to report a break-in."

As he spoke with the dispatcher, Edward's mind waged a fierce battle between his commitment to Samantha and the sinister urges gnawing at his soul. The shadows of the night seemed to beckon, whispering promises of power and control. And for a moment, he wondered whether he could resist their call much longer.

"Thank you," the woman said once Edward finished the call. "I don't know what I would have done without your help."

"Think nothing of it," he replied, forcing a smile. "It's the least I could do."

As the young woman thanked him again, Edward's heart raced with an unsettling mixture of fear and excitement. He knew that sooner or later, his dark desires would threaten everything he and Samantha had built together. And as the night closed in around them, he couldn't help but wonder how long he could keep those malevolent urges at bay.

The sun dipped below the horizon, casting a blood-red glow across the sky as Edward stood on the balcony of their beachfront home. He took a deep breath, inhaling the salty air that always seemed to soothe his restless spirit. After dealing with the break-in earlier that day, he desperately needed some peace.

"Edward?" Samantha's voice called from behind him, her tone warm and gentle.

He turned to see his wife standing in the doorway, holding a tray laden with an array of mouthwatering delicacies—freshly shucked oysters, chilled champagne, and a single red rose.

"Surprise," she said softly, a loving smile gracing her lips. "I thought we could use a romantic evening after such a long day."

Edward's heart swelled with gratitude and affection, momentarily pushing away the shadows that had been haunting him. "You have no idea how much I needed this," he admitted, pulling Samantha into a tender embrace.

As they settled down onto the plush outdoor sofa, sipping champagne and exchanging loving glances, Edward found himself able to forget about the darkness that threatened to consume him. For a fleeting moment, he was simply a man in love, sharing an intimate connection with his soulmate.

"Here's to us," Samantha toasted, raising her glass. "No matter what challenges we face, we'll always have each other."

Edward clinked his glass against hers, silently praying that her words would prove true.

Suddenly, his phone buzzed in his pocket, jolting him out of their cherished bubble. With a sinking feeling in his gut, he pulled it out and glanced at the screen.

"Who is it?" Samantha asked, curiosity flickering in her eyes.

"An unknown number," he replied, hesitating for a moment before opening the message. And there, amidst the glowing embers of their romantic evening, Edward read the cryptic words that sent a shiver down his spine:

"Your secret is not safe. I know what you desire, and I can offer you all the power and control you crave. Meet me at the old warehouse on 8th Street tomorrow night, and you'll see just how far the rabbit hole goes."

Edward felt a cold dread clawing its way up his spine. He stared at the message, his mind racing with questions and possibilities. Who could know about his dark urges? And what did they want from him?

"Edward?" Samantha's concerned voice broke through his thoughts. "Is everything okay?"

"Y-yes," he stammered, quickly deleting the message and forcing a smile onto his face. "It's just a wrong number. Nothing to worry about."

But as the sun vanished completely, plunging their world into darkness, Edward knew deep down that this mysterious message was anything but harmless. And as he held Samantha close, savoring her warmth and love, he couldn't help but wonder if this was the beginning of the end for them both.

Edward stood at the window, his reflection staring back at him with a hollow gaze. The sun was setting, casting long shadows across the room and painting the sky in shades of crimson and gold. The eerie silence hung heavy around him, the weight of unspoken secrets threatening to crush him beneath their burden.

"Hey, Mr. Kingsley!" A cheerful voice called out, shattering the stillness. Edward turned to see one of his tenants, an energetic young woman named Lisa, waving enthusiastically from her porch next door.

"Good evening, Lisa," Edward replied, forcing a smile as he stepped outside to greet her. "How are you enjoying your time in the rental?"

"Loving it!" she gushed. "It's so beautiful here. We couldn't have picked a better place for our vacation."

"Excellent, I'm glad to hear that," he said, maintaining his professional demeanor despite the turmoil churning within him. "If there's anything you need or if you have any questions, please don't hesitate to ask."

"Will do! Thanks again, Mr. Kingsley!" She waved goodbye and disappeared into her rented home.

As Edward closed the door behind him, he couldn't shake the gnawing feeling that something was off. He knew he had to tread carefully, but the temptation lurking within the shadows felt overpowering. His thoughts raced with anticipation and fear, a twisted cocktail of emotions that left him both exhilarated and terrified.

Samantha, who had been observing the interaction from the kitchen doorway, furrowed her brow in concern. In the days following their romantic evening, she couldn't help but notice subtle changes in her husband. His once-warm eyes seemed distant, his laughter strained, and his touches lacked the familiarity they once held. She could sense the darkness creeping in, wrapping its cold tendrils around Edward's heart and pulling him further away from her.

"Edward, are you alright?" she asked gently, her voice laced with worry.

"Of course," he lied, the words coming out more like a plea than a reassurance. "I've just been busy with work, that's all."

"Is there anything I can do to help?" she offered, her love for him evident in her eyes.

"Everything's under control, Sam. I promise." The words felt hollow even to him, but he couldn't bring himself to reveal the truth. Not yet.

"Alright," she replied, unconvinced but unwilling to push further. "Just remember that I'm here for you, okay?"

"Thank you," he murmured, his heart aching with guilt and longing. As Samantha retreated to their bedroom, Edward knew that the clock was ticking. The shadows were closing in, threatening to consume him whole, and he had to make a choice: let them swallow him, or find a way to escape their grasp before it was too late.

The rain spattered against the windows of the community hall as Samantha Kingsley, chief of police, strode confidently to the podium. The room was crowded with concerned citizens, their faces a mixture of apprehension and determination. Tonight's meeting was called in response to the recent uptick in crime – minor incidents, mostly – but enough to warrant action. As she looked out at the sea of faces,

Samantha steeled herself, determined to provide answers and reassurance.

"Good evening, everyone," she began, her voice strong and authoritative. "Firstly, I want to thank you all for coming out tonight. Your involvement is vital to the safety and well-being of our community."

"Chief Kingsley," a man in the front row interjected, his brow furrowed in worry. "What are you doing about these crimes? People are scared."

Samantha nodded, acknowledging his concern. "I understand your fears, and I assure you that my team and I are working diligently to investigate and resolve these matters. We've increased patrols in the affected areas and are actively pursuing leads."

Her mind briefly wandered to Edward, wondering if he had any knowledge of these incidents. She shook the thought away, unwilling to entertain such suspicions.

"However," she continued, "I must emphasize the importance of cooperation from all of you. If you see something, say something. Your vigilance is crucial in our efforts to maintain a safe and secure community."

A woman stood up, her voice trembling slightly. "But Chief, what if the criminals come back? What can we do to protect ourselves?"

"Great question," Samantha responded, her tone empathetic yet firm. "Remember that there is strength in unity. Look out for one another, and consider forming neighborhood watch groups. Additionally, take precautions to secure your homes and properties, such as installing alarm systems or motion-activated lights."

As Samantha addressed the crowd, she could feel their anxiety subside. Her words were a balm to their fears, instilling confidence in her ability to lead and protect them. And yet, as the community's worries dissipated, her unease grew.

"Lastly," she concluded, "I want to remind you all that we are a resilient community. We will face these challenges together and emerge stronger for it. Thank you for your time, and please do not hesitate to contact my office with any concerns or information."

The room erupted in applause, and Samantha offered a final nod before stepping down from the podium. As she made her way through the crowd, accepting handshakes and words of gratitude, her thoughts returned to Edward and the darkness she sensed within him.

"Please don't let him be involved," she thought, her heart heavy with dread. But deep down, she knew that the truth would eventually reveal itself – one way or another.

CHAPTER 2

The Tenant's Peril

The sun was setting on the Floridian coast, casting a golden hue over the luxurious beachfront home. Edward Kingsley stepped out of his pristine black sedan, his polished shoes sinking slightly into the sand as he approached the property. He took a moment to admire the view, allowing himself a small smile before entering the house. As a successful property owner, Edward knew the importance of maintaining appearances and ensuring every detail was perfect for his vacationing clients.

"Never let them see what's beneath the surface," he murmured to himself, pausing at the entrance to adjust his cufflinks.

Edward unlocked the front door and stepped inside the airy, open-concept living room. The scent of saltwater and fresh linen greeted him, reminding him of his duty to maintain the illusion of perfection for his clients. He pulled on a pair of white gloves and began his inspection, his eyes scanning the room with the intensity of a hawk.

"Good evening, Mr. Kingsley," said the automated voice from the smart home system. "Welcome back."

"Thank you, Alice," Edward replied smoothly, adjusting the collar of his crisp, tailored shirt. "Begin prepping the house for our next guest. The temperature at a comfortable 72 degrees, soft lighting, and some ambient music, please."

"Of course, Mr. Kingsley," the system responded, immediately setting the atmosphere to Edward's precise specifications.

As the soothing sounds of classical music filled the air, Edward moved from room to room with a determined stride. Each space was subjected to his meticulous scrutiny, from the placement of decorative pillows to the alignment of cutlery in the kitchen drawers. His expert eyes could spot even the smallest imperfections, and he made sure to correct them before moving on.

"Let's see... Master bedroom, clean and orderly," Edward thought to himself as he adjusted a picture frame that had been ever so slightly tilted. "Next, the guest room."

He continued his thorough examination of the property, ensuring every corner was immaculate and ready for the next tenant. As he moved through the house, Edward's mind began to wander, thoughts of power and control teasing at the edges of his consciousness. He shook his head, forcing himself to refocus on the task at hand.

"Control," he muttered under his breath, straightening a bath towel in the pristine bathroom. "Everything must be perfect."

The final room Edward inspected was the home office, a space that served as both a workspace for his clients and a hub for the smart home system. He tapped on the screen embedded in the wall, ensuring all settings were functioning correctly and reviewing the schedule for upcoming tenants.

"Sarah Collins...arriving tomorrow," he noted, his eyes lingering on her name for a moment before he forced himself to move on. Edward took a deep breath, attempting to quiet the dark desires that threatened to overtake him.

"Focus, Edward," he whispered to himself. "You are in control. You must maintain the facade."

With one last sweep of the office, Edward was satisfied with the state of the house. Each room had been meticulously prepared, and every detail was in order. He knew that when Sarah arrived the following day, she would be none the wiser to the darkness that lurked beneath the surface of this beautiful beachfront paradise.

As Edward descended the staircase, he noticed a flurry of movement in the living room. Emily, the previous tenant, was packing her belongings into a suitcase, her blonde hair tied back in a messy bun. She glanced up as Edward approached, her eyes wide with surprise.

"Mr. Kingsley! I didn't realize you would be coming by today," she said, quickly wiping her hands on her jeans.

"Please, call me Edward," he replied, flashing a warm smile that made his eyes crinkle at the corners. "I'm just here to make sure everything is for the next guest." He gestured towards her suitcase. "I see you're preparing to leave."

"Unfortunately, yes," Emily sighed, folding a floral dress, and placing it carefully into her luggage. "My vacation time is over."

Edward leaned against the doorway, his gaze roaming the room as he mentally cataloged each item left behind. "Did you enjoy your stay?" he asked, his tone casual but his mind alert for any potential issues he might need to address.

"Absolutely," Emily enthused. "This place is stunning, and the beach is incredible. I wish I could stay longer." She paused, a thoughtful expression crossing her face. " I've been thinking about moving to Florida permanently. Do you know any good neighborhoods?"

"Really?" Edward inquired; his interest piqued. He took a step closer, his eyes locked on Emily's. "For work, or...?"

"Work, mostly," she explained, tucking a strand of hair behind her ear. "But also, because I fell in love with the area. It's so different from where I grew up."

"Where might that be?" Edward asked, feigning nonchalance as he edged closer still.

"New Jersey," she replied, a slight grimace on her face. "It's nice, but I'm ready for a change."

Edward chuckled, the sound low and soothing. "I understand completely. Florida can be quite alluring." He paused, considering her question. "As for neighborhoods, it depends on what you're looking for. Some people prefer the excitement of the city, while others enjoy the peace of a more secluded area."

"Secluded sounds perfect," Emily mused, her eyes lighting up at the thought.

"Interesting," Edward murmured, his mind already racing with possibilities. "Well, I happen to know a few spots that might suit your needs. If you ever decide to take the plunge, don't hesitate to give me a call."

"Thank you, Edward," she said, grinning widely. "I appreciate that."

"Of course," he replied, offering her a polite nod. As he turned to leave, Emily's voice stopped him in his tracks.

"Hey, Edward?" she called out, her tone hesitant.

"Yes?" he asked, turning back to face her.

"Did you...did you ever find yourself feeling like you were meant for something more? Like you just needed a fresh start to truly discover who you are?"

Edward stared at her for a moment, his mask of charm momentarily faltering as the question resonated within him. He swallowed hard, pushing down the darkness that threatened to spill over. With practiced ease, he plastered a smile on his face and nodded.

"Change can be a powerful thing, Emily," he said softly. "Sometimes, it's exactly what we need to find our true selves."

"Thank you, Edward," she whispered, her eyes shining with gratitude.

"Take care, Emily," he responded, his voice steady even as his thoughts roiled beneath the surface. And with that, he left her to finish packing, his mind already spinning with plans.

Edward let the door click shut behind him, leaving Emily to her packing. He stood in the spacious living room, his gaze lingering on the young woman as she moved about the room, folding clothes and placing them into suitcases. There was something about her - an innocence, a vulnerability - that stirred a dark hunger within him. He pushed back against the feeling, trying to focus on the task at hand.

"Emily," he called out, drawing her attention. She looked up, smiling warmly at him. "I almost forgot to mention, there's a fantastic little café nearby you might want to try before you leave. Great coffee."

"Thanks for the tip," she replied, seemingly unaware of the predatory glint in his eyes. "I'll check it out."

"Excellent choice," Edward said, forcing a smile. He watched as Emily returned to her packing; his thoughts consumed by the unsettling desires that clawed in his mind.

With a deep breath, he tore himself away from the scene, stepping out of the beachfront house and making his way toward his car. He slid into the driver's seat, gripping the steering wheel tightly. The thin veneer of control he maintained threatened to crack, but he refused to allow himself to succumb to the darkness within.

Arriving at his office, Edward locked the door behind him and settled into his plush leather chair, surrounded by the trappings of his success. He pulled open a drawer, revealing a stack of rental applications for his other properties. He began to review them with practiced efficiency, searching for the perfect tenant among the hopeful vacationers.

His mind wandered back to Emily, her youthful energy and zest for life igniting a fire within him that he could no longer ignore. Frustration bubbled beneath the surface as he struggled to maintain his composure, the line between his public persona and private desires becoming increasingly blurred.

"Focus, Edward," he muttered under his breath, scanning the applications, and trying to drive away the haunting image of Emily's trusting smile. "Business first."

The sunlight filtering through the blinds cast an eerie pattern on the stack of applications piled high on Edward's mahogany desk. He couldn't help but notice how each application seemed to pulse with a life of its own, beckoning him to indulge in the forbidden fruit they presented. The haunting memory of Emily's gaze lingered in his mind, her innocence fueling his obsession.

"Damn it," he muttered, shaking his head, and trying to refocus on the task at hand. But as he flipped through the rental applications, he couldn't stop himself from lingering on the photographs and personal details of the single women who hoped to rent his homes. Each new face brought with it the tantalizing promise of control, the temptation to surrender to his darkest desires growing increasingly stronger.

"Edward," a voice said, startling him. It was his secretary, Susan, standing just outside his office door. "I have some additional applications for you to review."

"Thank you, Susan," he replied, his voice strained. "Please, leave them on my desk."

As she complied, Edward found himself studying her as well – the curve of her neck, the way her hair framed her face. The fire within him burned brighter, threatening to engulf him.

"Is everything all right, sir?" Susan asked, sensing his unease.

"Everything is fine," he snapped, his frustration boiling over. "Now, if you'll excuse me, I have work to do."

"Of course," Susan said, quickly retreating. "Sorry to disturb you."

Alone once more, Edward closed his eyes and clenched his fists, willing himself to regain control. He was a successful businessman, respected by his peers and envied by many. He couldn't afford to let his twisted cravings consume him, to destroy everything he had built.

"Focus," he whispered, attempting to center himself. "You can do this."

As he opened his eyes, the sun dipped below the horizon, casting the room in a cold, ominous light. The shadows seemed to close in around him, mirroring the darkness that threatened to engulf his very soul. With a newfound resolve, he forced himself back to the task at hand, determined to hold onto the facade that hid his true nature.

But deep down, Edward knew that the battle was far from over. The hunger within him refused to be silenced, and as the night wore on, the line between his public persona and private desires became ever more precarious. He would have to tread carefully, lest everything he had worked so hard to achieve crumble beneath the weight of his depravity.

The door creaked open, casting a sliver of light across the dimly lit office. Edward's heart skipped a beat as he recognized the silhouette in the doorway. Samantha Kingsley, his wife, and the local chief of police, stood before him, her stern features softened by the warm glow of the hallway.

"Evening, Edward," she said, her voice betraying a hint of exhaustion. "I didn't mean to startle you."

Edward quickly closed the folder he had been obsessing over and turned to face his wife. "No harm done," he replied, his voice dripping with charm. "What brings you by?"

Samantha hesitated, her gaze sweeping the room as if searching for something amiss. "I need to discuss an ongoing investigation with you. There have been some... unsettling developments."

"Of course," Edward said, his pulse quickening. He gestured towards the plush leather chairs positioned in front of his desk. "Please, have a seat."

As Samantha settled into the chair, Edward couldn't help but study her. Though her uniform was immaculate, there were dark circles beneath her eyes, and the lines around her mouth seemed more pronounced than usual. She carried the weight of her responsibilities heavily, and it showed.

"Thank you, Edward," Samantha began, her voice tense. "As you know, we've been dealing with a series of break-ins at various rental properties throughout the area. The perpetrator seems to be targeting young, single women."

Edward's stomach churned at the mention of his twisted obsession, but he kept his expression neutral. "Yes, I've heard about that," he replied evenly. "Terrible business."

"Indeed," Samantha continued, her brow furrowing in concern. "The latest victim reported that she felt like she was being watched before the break-in occurred. This is the third such case in as many weeks."

Edward's mind raced, searching for a way to steer the conversation away from his dark desires. "What do you need from me?" he asked, feigning ignorance.

"Given your extensive knowledge of local rental properties, I was hoping you could help us identify any potential patterns or connections between the victims," Samantha said, her eyes narrowing as she studied him.

"Of course," Edward said, struggling to maintain his composure. "I'll do whatever I can to assist with the investigation."

"Thank you, Edward," Samantha replied, though her eyes remained locked on his as if she were searching for some hidden truth within them. "I knew I could count on you."

As the door closed behind her, Edward let out a long, shaky breath. He had narrowly avoided arousing suspicion this time, but he couldn't afford to let his guard down. The tension between them had been palpable, and he knew that it would only be a matter of time before the thin veneer of their relationship began to crack.

"Focus," he whispered to himself, his hands trembling as he clenched the edge of the desk. "You must stay in control."

But as the night wore on, and the shadows in the room deepened, Edward couldn't shake the growing dread that his carefully constructed world was beginning to unravel. And with each passing moment, the line between his public view and private desires blurred further, threatening to expose the darkness within.

The flickering glow of a dying candle cast eerie shadows across Edward's face as he stared at the door Samantha had just exited. The silence that filled the office seemed to amplify his racing thoughts, each one teetering dangerously between control and chaos.

"Edward," Samantha called out from the hallway, her voice catching him off guard. "I left my case file on the desk. Can you hand it to me?"

"Sure," he replied, trying to keep his voice steady as he picked up the file and handed it to her. As their fingers brushed, he couldn't help but wonder if she could sense the turmoil that raged within him.

"Thanks," she said curtly, her gaze lingering for a moment before she turned away. For a split second, it seemed as though she might have seen through his carefully crafted facade, but he quickly dismissed the thought. He was too good at this game; she wouldn't catch him so easily.

"Call me if you find anything," Samantha reminded him as she disappeared down the hall.

"Of course," he muttered to himself, clenching his fists until his knuckles turned white. He couldn't afford to make mistakes. Not now, not ever.

Hours later, Edward slipped into the darkness outside the beachfront home, his breath fogging in the chilly night air. Lit only by the moon reflecting off the waves, the property took on an ethereal quality, a sinister beauty that seemed to call to him. As Sarah's car pulled into the driveway, he watched intently from the shadows, his heart pounding in anticipation.

"Welcome home," he whispered under his breath, his eyes never leaving her silhouette as she stepped out of the car and began to unload her luggage.

"New beginnings," he mused, momentarily lost in his dark desires. But there was work to be done, and he couldn't afford to let his emotions get the better of him. With one last glance at Sarah, he retreated further into the shadows, his hunger for control only growing stronger.

"Patience," he reminded himself as he silently stalked the perimeter of the property, taking note of every potential vulnerability. "All in due time."

As the first light of dawn began to creep over the horizon, Edward knew that he had won another battle against his inner demons. But as he retreated to the safety of his own home, the war within him raged on, threatening to consume him whole.

"Only a matter of time," he thought grimly, steeling himself for the challenges that lie ahead. For now, however, Sarah was blissfully unaware of the danger that lurked just out of sight, and Edward would do everything in his power to keep it that way.

"Control," he whispered, the word both a promise and a curse. "It's all about control."

CHAPTER 3

Obsessive Shadows

Edward Kingsley's dark eyes flickered in the dim glow of his computer screen, surrounded by shadows that seemed to creep ever closer as he delved deeper into the abyss. His heart raced with anticipation, a sick thrill coursing through his veins as his fingers tapped on the keyboard, searching for answers to questions best left unasked.

"Finally," he muttered under his breath, his gaze locked onto the screen as he found a forum dedicated to the macabre. "The information I've been seeking."

His breathing quickened as he scrolled through thread after thread of grisly content, his twisted desires growing stronger with each discovery. He couldn't help but marvel at the depravity on display, feeling a sense of camaraderie with these faceless strangers who shared his morbid fixation.

"Ah, this looks promising," he said to himself, clicking on a link that led him to an article about body disposal methods. As Edward read through the chilling details, he took meticulous notes, jotting down every bit of information that could prove useful in his dark endeavors.

"Interesting... The pig farm method might work well here in Florida," Edward mused, his mind racing with possibilities. "But then again, there's always the old standby of dismemberment and acid."

He organized his notes carefully, categorizing them by type of murder and level of risk. Each new piece of data fed his obsession, driving him further into the depths of his darkness.

"Edward, what have you become?" he asked himself, pausing for a moment to reflect on the path that had led him to this point. But the answer eluded him; he couldn't even remember when his fascination with death had first taken root. All he knew was that it consumed him now, threatening to swallow him whole if he didn't find some way to satiate his perverse cravings.

"Focus," he commanded himself, shaking off the momentary doubt and returning his attention to the screen. "You need more information on murder techniques."

With renewed determination, Edward continued his research, poring over articles about various methods of killing and how to avoid leaving behind evidence. He studied each technique with the same intensity he brought to his successful property business, his keen mind absorbing every gruesome detail.

"Silent and efficient," he whispered, making a note about a particular type of garrote that had caught his eye. "I like that."

Edward understood he stood on the precipice of a dangerous abyss, yet he couldn't resist the allure of the darkness that beckoned him. As he immersed himself in the grisly world of death and destruction, he felt alive in a way he never had before. And as his heart pounded with the thrill of his newfound knowledge, Edward Kingsley knew that there was no turning back from the path he now walked.

The flickering glow of the computer screen cast eerie shadows across Edward's face as he delved deeper into the rabbit hole. His eyes darted back and forth, greedily devouring the morbid information that flooded his vision: the subtle, lethal poisons that left no trace; the art of strangulation, with its cold efficiency; even the use of chloroform to render his prey helpless.

"Ah, I see," Edward muttered, a sinister smile playing at the corners of his lips. "So many possibilities."

His fingers danced across the keyboard, tapping out the names of deadly chemicals and lethal combinations. With each discovery, Edward felt the darkness within him growing stronger, the insatiable hunger for power and control building like a storm inside his chest.

"Enough research," he whispered under his breath, finally tearing himself away from the screen. "It's time to gather my tools."

Edward's hands were steady as he navigated through various online marketplaces, carefully selecting the items he would need for his dark journey. He chose disposable gloves to leave no fingerprints, rolls of heavy-duty plastic sheeting to contain the mess, and industrial-strength cleaning supplies to erase any lingering traces of his gruesome deeds.

"Can't be too careful," he murmured, feeling a thrill of excitement course through him as he clicked 'Add to Cart.'

As he finalized his purchases, using multiple shipping addresses and opting for discreet packaging, Edward's mind raced with anticipation. He imagined himself donning the gloves, wielding the garrote he'd read about earlier, the power coursing through his veins as he held life and death in his hands.

"Is this really what you want?" a small voice in the back of his mind questioned, but Edward silenced it with a cold, decisive thought: Yes. It is.

With his preparations complete, he leaned back in his chair, a predatory gleam in his eyes. He felt both invigorated and terrified by what lay ahead, the thrill of the hunt mingling with the fear of the unknown.

"Let the journey begin," he whispered into the darkness, a twisted sense of satisfaction settling over him like a shroud. And as Edward Kingsley allowed himself to become fully consumed by his dark desires, he knew that there would be no turning back.

An eerie silence hung in the air, broken only by the creaking of Edward's footsteps as he descended the basement stairs. The dim glow of a single lightbulb cast shadows on the walls, revealing a hidden workspace tucked away from prying eyes. This would be his sanctuary, a place where he could indulge in his darkest fantasies without fear of discovery.

"Everything must be perfect," he whispered to himself, his voice barely audible.

Edward set to work organizing his tools with meticulous precision. The gloves, plastic sheeting, and cleaning supplies he had ordered online were arranged neatly on a table, each item within easy reach. Alongside them lay a collection of sinister implements: a coil of rope for strangulation, a bottle of chloroform for incapacitation, and an array of knives gleaming wickedly in the low light.

"Patience," he muttered, forcing himself to focus on the task at hand. "Precision is key."

As if to underscore his commitment to perfection, Edward spent hours practicing his techniques on inanimate objects scattered around the room. He looped the rope around a wooden post, feeling the fibers tighten around his fingers as he pulled it taut. The sensation sent a shiver down his spine, the anticipation of control coursing through him like an electric charge.

"Focus," he told himself, honing his movements until they were swift and seamless. "This will all be worth it."

Edward practiced draping plastic sheeting over furniture, imagining it enveloping the lifeless form of a victim. He visualized every step, every movement required to carry out his plans with flawless precision. His determination was unwavering, fueled by the intoxicating power that lay just beyond his grasp.

"Time to test the chloroform," he said, his voice cold and detached. He dabbed a cloth with the liquid, holding it to his face for a brief moment to gauge its potency. Satisfied, he set it aside, knowing that it would be a vital part of his arsenal.

"Everything has its place," Edward thought, surveying the organized chaos of his macabre workspace. "And soon, I will take mine."

As the hours passed, Edward continued to practice his dark craft, stopping only when he was confident in his abilities. He knew that his journey had only just begun, but with each passing moment, his resolve grew stronger.

"Let them come," he whispered into the darkness, embracing the fear and excitement that swirled within him. "I am ready."

And as Edward Kingsley stood among the tools of his twisted trade, an unsettling sense of calm descended upon him – the calm before a storm that would leave devastation in its wake.

The sun dipped below the horizon, casting long shadows across Edward's workspace. He stood at the edge of a dense forest, map in hand, pinpointing the locations he had scouted earlier that day. The chirping of crickets and the rustling of leaves provided a macabre soundtrack to his grim task.

"Secluded areas... Check," Edward muttered, marking off an old abandoned farmhouse on the outskirts of town. "Bodies of water... Check." He traced a finger along the winding river that cut through the dense woodland, its dark waters promising to conceal his gruesome secrets.

"Remember, Edward, timing is everything," he reminded himself as he studied the routines of his potential victims. His mind filled with images of the people who would unknowingly cross his path – their lives hanging by a thread, dictated by his twisted desires. He envisioned each step they would take, calculating the precise moment to strike.

"Monday, 10:00 PM. She'll be alone, her husband is out of town on business," Edward whispered, his voice dripping with anticipation. He began plotting his meticulous timeline, ensuring that no detail was overlooked. "Tuesday, 8:30 PM. The family will be out for dinner, leaving their teenage daughter vulnerable."

"Alright, it's time to put this plan into motion," Edward said, folding the map and tucking it into his pocket. He walked back to his car, feeling a cold thrill run down his spine at the thought of what lay ahead.

"Stay focused, stay sharp," he repeated like a mantra, his hands gripping the steering wheel tightly. He felt a sense of power coursing through him, a deep satisfaction in knowing that he held the fate of others in his very hands.

"Everything will go according to plan," Edward assured himself, picturing the intricate web he had woven in his mind. "No one will ever know."

And as he drove into the night, a sinister smile spread across Edward's face. The darkness that had consumed him was now unleashed, ready to claim its first victims in the shadows of the moonlit streets.

Edward Kingsley stood in the shadows of the night, his eyes narrowed as he observed the living room window of one of his tenants. Clutching a pair of binoculars, he peered through them, noting every detail of their lives as they unfolded before him. The voyeuristic thrill coursed through him like an electric current, heightening his anticipation.

"Mother's home late from work again," Edward muttered to himself, watching as she hurriedly entered the house and tossed her keys on the counter. "She's been having an affair with that coworker, I'm sure of it."

He scribbled down the time of her arrival in a small notebook, adding it to the list of comings and goings he had been studying for weeks. Each routine, each habit, a piece of the puzzle that would lead to their ultimate undoing.

"Edward, my man, you are truly a master of deception," he whispered to himself, feeling a cold satisfaction wash over him.

The following day, Edward sat at his desk, browsing through various articles on home maintenance. He needed to find the perfect ruse to gain access to his tenants' homes without arousing suspicion. That's when it hit him; plumbing issues were something everyone dealt with, and who wouldn't trust their landlord to fix a problem?

"Leaky faucet, broken toilet, clogged drain... Perfect," Edward thought, smirking as he began drafting fake maintenance requests.

"Dear Tenant," he typed with feigned sincerity, "We have received a report of a possible water leak affecting some units in the building. As your landlord, I will be conducting inspections and repairs starting tomorrow. Your cooperation is greatly appreciated. Sincerely, Edward Kingsley."

With the emails sent, Edward spent the evening practicing his role as the trustworthy landlord. He rehearsed lines in front of the mirror, smiling warmly and assuring his reflection that he was simply there to help.

"Good evening," Edward said smoothly, brushing imaginary lint from his shirt. "I'm just here to conduct a quick inspection of your plumbing. Nothing to worry about, I assure you."

He could hear the imaginary tenant thanking him for his prompt attention and inviting him in. The door would close behind him, sealing their fate as the predator stepped into their home.

"Once I'm inside," Edward mused, relishing the power he felt surging through him. "It's only a matter of time before they're mine."

As he lay in bed that night, sleep eluded Edward. Instead, he was consumed by thoughts of the dark journey he was about to embark upon. Each tenant, each victim, meticulously planned and studied. He knew their lives, their secrets, and soon, he would control their very existence.

"Let the games begin," Edward whispered, his eyes gleaming with sinister anticipation. "My reign of terror is only just beginning."

The dim light from a single bulb illuminated Edward's hidden workspace, casting eerie shadows on the walls. A small animal, trembling in fear, was trapped within a makeshift cage. Edward's eyes gleamed with perverse satisfaction as he stared at his captive, the power he held over this innocent creature intoxicating.

"Let's see how you handle this, little one," he said softly, donning a pair of latex gloves before reaching for a syringe filled with an experimental concoction.

With cautious precision, he inserted the needle into the animal, monitoring its reaction to the substance. It winced and squealed in pain, its body convulsing as the poison took effect. Edward's heart raced as he observed the results, the success of his morbid experiment fueling his dark desires.

"Remarkable," he thought, making a mental note of the dosage and reaction time. "A little more refinement and this will be perfect."

Over the next several days, Edward continued his twisted experiments, testing different methods on a variety of small animals. Each new piece of information he gathered only served to strengthen his resolve, pushing him further down the path he had chosen.

"Struggle all you want," he whispered to a dying creature, its labored breaths filling the air. "Your suffering is my education."

As Edward disposed of the remains, he felt the darkness within him growing stronger, consuming him entirely. The line between his outward persona – the charming, successful property owner – and the monster lurking beneath was beginning to blur.

"Everything is in place," he murmured to himself, reviewing his meticulous notes one final time. "The tools, the techniques, the timelines... It's time to put my plan into action."

Standing at the precipice of his dark journey, Edward's mind swirled with a mixture of excitement and trepidation. He knew that once he crossed this line, there would be no turning back.

"Am I truly prepared for this?" he wondered, his heart pounding in his chest. "Can I carry out these heinous acts and maintain the facade of normalcy?"

But as he looked around his hidden workspace – at the collection of tools, supplies, and notes that represented his twisted desires – Edward knew that there was only one path forward.

"Embrace the darkness," he whispered to himself, a sinister smile spreading across his face. "It's time to begin."

And with that, Edward Kingsley, the seemingly charming and successful property owner, stepped into the abyss, leaving behind any semblance of humanity as he embarked on his dark journey.

CHAPTER 4

The Killing School

Edward Kingsley sat alone in his well-appointed study, the soft hum of his computer filling the silence of the room. The screen's eerie glow illuminated his face, casting deep shadows across his perfectly groomed features. He leaned in closer, squinting at the text on the monitor, as he navigated the dark corners of the internet, searching for others who shared his twisted desires. As a successful property owner in Florida, Edward's life appeared perfect from the outside – but few knew about the darkness that dwelled within him.

"Finally..." he muttered under his breath, his fingers hovering over the keyboard with anticipation.

The cursor blinked expectantly on the screen as Edward stumbled upon an online forum that seemed promising. A mix of excitement and apprehension coursed through his veins, making his heart pound like a jackrabbit. He hesitated for a moment, considering the risks involved in exposing his innermost thoughts to strangers, even if they were anonymous.

"Is there anyone out there like me?" he thought, taking a deep breath before plunging into the virtual abyss.

Clicking on the link, Edward found himself submerged in a world where his darkest fantasies seemed commonplace. The words on the screen danced before his eyes, tantalizing him with the promise of understanding and camaraderie.

"Welcome to the Forum," the screen announced, its cryptic message inviting him to explore further. "Please introduce yourself."

"Here goes nothing," Edward whispered, his fingers tapping away on the keys as he composed his introduction.

"Hi, I'm EK35," he typed, choosing a simple pseudonym to protect his identity. "I'm new here, and I'm looking for... guidance."

"Guidance" was an understatement, but Edward hoped it would be enough to pique the interest of like-minded individuals lurking in the shadows of the forum. Almost immediately, he received a response.

"Hello, EK35. You've come to the right place. We're here to help," came a reply from a user named DarkOracle.

Edward's pulse quickened as he read the words on the screen. He had been searching for this kind of connection for years, and now it seemed as though he had finally found it.

"Thank you," Edward typed, his fingers trembling slightly with excitement. "I've been struggling with some... desires. It's hard to find people who understand."

"Believe me, EK35, we know what it's like," DarkOracle responded. "It can be lonely out there when you're different. But you're not alone."

"Like-minded" might not have been the best term to describe the denizens of the forum, but it was close enough for Edward. He had found a place where he could share his thoughts without fear of judgment or reprisal. It was a strange sensation, both liberating and terrifying, like standing at the edge of a precipice and staring into the abyss.

"Let's see where this takes me," Edward thought, feeling a shiver of anticipation crawls up his spine.

Edward's eyes fixated on the screen as he delved deeper into DarkOracle's posts. Each word seemed to resonate within him, igniting a fire that had been smoldering inside for years. The mentor's knowledge of murder techniques was vast and chillingly precise – a morbid symphony crafted from the darkest recesses of human imagination.

"An instrument of death is like a painter's brush," one post read. "You must choose the right one for your canvas. A swift stroke across the throat with a razor-sharp blade can create a beautiful crimson spray, while a slow, deliberate twist of a wire garrote brings about an agonizing dance of life slipping away."

Edward's heart thundered in his chest as he continued reading, each post more sinister than the last. His fingers hovered over the keys, itching to type out questions and seek further guidance.

"DarkOracle," he began hesitantly, "your knowledge is extraordinary. I'm constantly haunted by these thoughts...how did you learn so much?"

"Years of study and dedication, EK35," came the reply. "I've spent my entire life honing my craft. But it's not just about the techniques themselves. It's also about understanding the nuances of control and power. They are intoxicating, addictive forces that few truly comprehend."

As Edward absorbed these teachings, a transformation began to take hold. He felt a newfound sense of empowerment coursing through his veins, a hunger for control that threatened to consume him entirely. The once meticulous and cunning property owner now found himself entranced by the macabre world laid before him.

"Control," Edward whispered, his voice barely audible. "That's what I've been craving all this time."

"Exactly," DarkOracle responded. "And once you've tasted true control, there's no turning back. It becomes an obsession, a driving force that propels you toward greatness – or, in our case, infamy."

Edward's eyes widened as he considered the implications of his mentor's words. He could feel the darkness within him churning and expanding, eager to be unleashed upon the world.

"Teach me," he typed feverishly. "I want to understand this power, this control. I want to become a master like you."

"Patience, EK35," DarkOracle cautioned. "The path you seek is long and treacherous. But if you're willing to learn and dedicate yourself to the art, I will guide you."

Edward stared at the screen, feeling a shiver of anticipation crawl up his spine. He had finally found someone who understood his twisted desires, someone who could help him harness the power that had been gnawing at the edges of his consciousness for years.

"Thank you," he typed, his fingers steady and determined. "I'm ready to begin."

In the dim glow of the computer screen, Edward's eyes darted across the words that seemed to dance in front of him, like shadows playing on the walls of a darkened room. He could almost feel the breath of DarkOracle on his neck as they typed back and forth, their conversation growing more intense with each passing moment.

"Remember," DarkOracle wrote, their words laced with an unsettling sense of authority, "the key to a perfect murder is meticulous planning. Every detail must be accounted for, every possible outcome considered."

Edward leaned in closer to the screen, his heart pounding as he absorbed the sinister wisdom flowing from this mysterious figure. He felt both thrilled and terrified by the power that now lay at his fingertips.

"Of course," he replied, his mind racing with possibilities. "I understand the importance of being thorough. But where do I begin?"

"Start with your target," DarkOracle instructed. "Study them carefully – their habits, their routines, their weaknesses. The more you know about them, the easier it will be to manipulate the circumstances around them."

Edward nodded, his fingers flying across the keyboard as he jotted down notes. Though the prospect of stalking someone and learning their every move chilled him to the bone, he couldn't deny the thrill that coursed through him at the thought of wielding such control over another person's life.

"Once you have gathered sufficient information," DarkOracle continued, "you can begin to construct your plan. Be creative in your approach – the more unexpected, the better. And always ensure that you leave no trace behind."

"Understood," Edward typed, his breathing shallow but steady. "But what if something goes wrong during the execution?"

"Ah," DarkOracle responded, their words dripping with malevolent glee. "That is where the true artistry lies, EK35. A master craftsman knows how to adapt, to turn even the most disastrous situations to their advantage. Remember, chaos can be a powerful ally."

Edward felt a shiver run down his spine as he pondered the implications of DarkOracle's guidance. The thought of turning chaos into control, of bending even the most unpredictable circumstances to his will, filled him with a sense of both dread and exhilaration.

"Thank you," he typed, his resolve hardening with every word. "I won't disappoint you."

"Good," DarkOracle replied, their presence on the screen seeming to loom larger by the moment. "I have great expectations for you, EK35. Do not squander this opportunity."

As Edward sat back in his chair, he could feel the weight of DarkOracle's influence settling upon him like a cloak of shadows. He knew that he was venturing into uncharted territory, guided only by the sinister wisdom of his unseen mentor. But despite the darkness that lay ahead, he couldn't help but feel a twisted sense of excitement at the thought of finally unleashing his inner demons upon the world.

The glow of the computer screen flickered over Edward's face, casting eerie shadows as he continued his exchange with DarkOracle. It appears his mysterious mentor had an uncanny ability to peer into his very soul, tapping into the darkest recesses of his mind and drawing out desires that had long lain dormant.

"EK35," DarkOracle typed, their words appearing on the screen like a sinister incantation. "There is a primal hunger within you, a thirst for power and control that has gone unquenched for far too long."

Edward felt a chill run down his spine as if the words had been spoken directly into his ear. He hesitated for a moment before typing back, "How do you know me so well?"

"Because I have walked this path before you," DarkOracle replied, their message tinged with an unsettling air of familiarity. "I, too, was once a man of wealth and success. But beneath the veneer of my respectable life, there lurked a darkness that could not be denied."

As Edward read the words, he couldn't help but feel a strange kinship with his mentor, a sense that they were kindred spirits bound together by their shared cravings. His heartbeat quickened, fueled by excitement and a hint of fear, as he allowed himself to imagine the possibilities that awaited him under DarkOracle's guidance.

"Listen closely, EK35" DarkOracle's words commanded attention, "Embrace your destiny. The world will tremble at your feet, and you will revel in the chaos you sow."

A surge of adrenaline coursed through Edward's veins, igniting something deep within him. He could no longer deny the truth – he was destined for greatness, and the time had come to seize it. As he contemplated the dark path that lay before him, he found himself invigorated by the thought of applying his newfound knowledge to his twisted machinations.

"Thank you, DarkOracle," Edward typed with trembling fingers. "Your guidance has opened my eyes to my true potential."

"Remember, EK35" DarkOracle's response was swift and authoritative. "With great power comes great responsibility. Use your talents wisely, and your name will become a legend in the realm of darkness."

As Edward absorbed his mentor's words, he felt an unshakable resolve take root within him. He would not squander this opportunity; he would rise to the challenge and prove himself worthy of DarkOracle's tutelage. With each passing day, he would hone his skills and craft the perfect plan, ensuring that every detail was meticulously executed.

He took a deep breath, feeling the weight of his newfound purpose settle onto his shoulders. As he closed his laptop, Edward Kingsley, property owner, and charming entrepreneur caught a glimpse of the man he was destined to become – a ruthless predator who would stop at nothing to feed his insatiable hunger for power and control.

Edward's fingers danced across the keyboard as he eagerly awaited DarkOracle's next message. The dim glow of the computer monitors cast eerie shadows on the walls of his study, enveloping him in a cocoon of darkness. He couldn't help but shudder at the chilling instructions that appeared on screen, each word etched into his mind like a haunting melody.

"Remember, EK35," DarkOracle typed, their words cold and calculated. "The key to a successful kill is precision. You must strike with surgical accuracy, leaving no room for error or hesitation."

As Edward read the detailed descriptions of various murder techniques – from the swift severing of arteries to the careful administration of lethal poisons – he felt both repulsed and captivated. These were the teachings he had long sought, the forbidden knowledge that would grant him the power he craved. And yet, there was something undeniably unsettling about the ease with which DarkOracle discussed such gruesome acts.

"DarkOracle," Edward typed, swallowing hard as he confronted his inner turmoil. "How can you speak so casually about taking another person's life?"

"EK35, you must understand," came the reply, laced with sinister wisdom. "In our world, death is not an end, but a means to an end. It is a tool we wield to shape our destinies, to create the lives we desire."

Edward's heart raced as he considered the implications of his mentor's words. No longer would he be shackled by society's expectations, forced to hide his true nature behind a veneer of charm and success. He would forge his path, unbound by the constraints of morality or conscience.

He spent countless hours poring over DarkOracle's teachings, consuming every scrap of knowledge they offered. Each grisly detail, each twisted musing, served to fuel his dark fantasies. No longer was he merely a passive observer, gazing longingly into the abyss; he was an active participant, ready to leap headfirst into its depths.

"DarkOracle," Edward typed one late night, his fingers trembling with anticipation. "I am ready to take the next step. I have studied your teachings and committed them to memory. It is time for me to put theory into practice."

"Very well, EK35," came the reply, accompanied by a sense of foreboding that sent shivers down Edward's spine. "Proceed with caution, for the path you now tread is fraught with danger and uncertainty. But remember greatness awaits those who dare to seize it."

As the exchange continued, Edward felt a newfound confidence surging through him. He was no longer just Edward Kingsley, property owner and entrepreneur – he was the master of his dark destiny. With each keystroke, he took another step closer to unleashing his terrible desires upon the unsuspecting world. As he immersed himself in the twisted wisdom of his enigmatic mentor, he could feel the boundaries between fantasy and reality begin to blur, ushering in a new era of darkness and depravity.

The flickering reflection of Edward's face on the polished blade of a hunting knife seemed to leer back at him as if it too was eager to taste the thrill of its first kill. He studied his own eyes in the steel, noting how they glittered with an unsettling mix of anticipation and fear.

"Remember, EK35," came DarkOracle's voice through the computer speakers, each syllable echoing within the walls of Edward's mind. "Precision is key. Too shallow a cut, and they won't bleed out fast enough. Too deep, and you risk losing control."

Edward nodded, gripping the knife handle more tightly as he practiced the slicing motion DarkOracle had instructed. The air itself seemed to shudder in response to the deadly arc traced by the gleaming weapon.

"DarkOracle, what if... What if I can't go through with it?" Edward stammered, his voice barely more than a whisper.

"Then you are not the predator I believed you to be," replied the mentor, the coldness in their tone sending a chill down Edward's spine. "But I have faith in you, EK35. You possess a darkness within that yearns to be unleashed. Do not let your fear hold you back."

As Edward continued to practice his deadly art, the world outside his window seemed to fade away. No longer did he hear the laughter of children playing on the beach or the gentle lapping of waves upon the shore. All that existed now was the pounding of his heart and the sinister guidance of his enigmatic mentor.

"Good," DarkOracle finally said. "Now, choose your target wisely. Remember the lessons I've taught you, and strike when the time is right. Soon, you will know the ecstasy of taking a life – and once you've tasted that power, there will be no turning back."

Every ounce of Edward's being felt electrified as if he were a coiled spring waiting to be released. As he closed his laptop, the sinister smile that played on his lips seemed like something foreign and alien – yet it belonged there, a testament to the darkness that now consumed him.

"Thank you, DarkOracle," he murmured, placing the hunting knife into its sheath with reverence. "I won't disappoint you."

And with those words, Edward Kingsley took the first step towards embracing his grim new destiny, leaving behind the veneer of normality that had once defined his life. Fueled by the insidious tutelage of his mentor, he prepared to embark on a dark journey that would forever alter the course of his existence.

Chapter 5

Fatal Infatuation

Sunlight filtered through the swaying palm trees, casting dappled shadows on the pristine white sand. Waves lapped gently at the shore, creating a serene backdrop for the picturesque vacation home that served as Lara Reynolds' temporary sanctuary. She stood on the terrace, sipping her morning coffee and admiring the view of the azure ocean before her.

Lara was a young aspiring writer in her late 20s, with wavy blonde hair that tumbled over her shoulders and a warm smile that drew people in. Despite her kind-hearted and open-minded nature, she had difficulty trusting others, a trait instilled by past experiences. Her cautious demeanor led her to be vigilant in her surroundings, always alert to potential threats.

"Stunning," she murmured to herself, her fingers tapping against the ceramic mug.

As she soaked in the beauty around her, Edward Kingsley watched her from a distance, hidden behind the tinted windows of his sleek black car. Inconspicuous as it sat among the other vehicles parked along the quiet street, it was the perfect vantage point to observe his first chosen victim.

"Beautiful… so very beautiful," he whispered, his eyes fixed on Lara. His obsession with her grew with every passing moment, his thoughts consumed by desires far darker than anything her innocent mind could conjure. He longed to possess her, to take control of her life and bend it to his twisted will.

"Ah, Lara," he muttered under his breath, "you have no idea what awaits you."

Edward's hands trembled with anticipation as he gripped the steering wheel, sweat beading on his forehead despite the air conditioning blasting cold air into the cabin. He knew he should leave, return to his office, and maintain the façade of a successful property owner. But he couldn't tear himself away from the sight of Lara enjoying her morning ritual, blissfully unaware of the danger looming nearby.

"Mr. Kingsley, are you there?" A voice crackled through the car's Bluetooth speaker, snapping Edward back to the present.

"Y-yes, what is it?" he stammered, struggling to regain his composure.

"Ms. Reynolds called about a minor issue with the property," the voice on the other end informed him. "She said it's not urgent, but she'd appreciate it if you could take a look."

"Of course," Edward replied, his mind racing. This was the

opportunity he had been waiting for—to be alone with Lara under the guise of a helpful landlord. "I'll head over there as soon as I can."

"Thank you, Mr. Kingsley. Have a great day," the voice concluded, and the line went dead.

Edward turned off the car's engine, his heart pounding in his chest. He glanced at the house one more time, savoring the sight of Lara before steeling himself for the twisted task that lay ahead.

"Brace yourself, my dear," he murmured, his voice filled with dark intent. "For our dance has only just begun."

Edward Kingsley sat alone in his dimly lit study, surrounded by the musty aroma of leather-bound books and the faint sound of a ticking grandfather clock. His eyes darted back and forth across the screen of his laptop as he researched the most efficient methods of murder and body disposal. He had always been a man who prided himself on his attention to detail and his ability to plan, and this twisted task was no exception.

"Ah, now that's interesting," he murmured under his breath as he read about a particular method of killing that would leave little trace, a lethal injection of air into the bloodstream. The information sent a shiver down his spine, a mix of excitement and dread building within him.

"Edward, are you sure about this?" he whispered to himself, the voice of reason attempting to break through the darkness that consumed his thoughts. But it was too late; the seed had been planted, and Edward knew there was no turning back.

When the day finally arrived for Edward to put his plan into action, he dressed in all black, donning gloves and a dark cap to conceal his identity. With each calculated step, he felt a sense of tension and suspense taking hold of him, but it only fueled his determination to see this through.

Lara Reynolds had been so cautious, so vigilant in her surroundings, but Edward knew that even the most careful person couldn't anticipate every danger lurking in the shadows. As he watched her from a distance, he marveled at the cruel irony of fate: an aspiring writer whose own life was about to become the ultimate tragedy.

"Beautiful day, isn't it?" Lara said to a neighbor as she stepped outside her rented home, her golden hair glistening in the sun. She smiled warmly, completely unaware of the sinister figure watching her every move.

"Indeed," the neighbor replied, returning the smile before continuing on their way.

"Such a shame," Edward thought, his cold gaze following Lara as she strolled down the sidewalk with a sense of carefree joy. "But fate has chosen you, my dear."

As he stalked her from afar, he felt a thrill run through him, like a conductor commanding an orchestra of fear and anticipation. He moved like a shadow, unseen by those around him, waiting for the perfect moment to strike.

"Patience, Edward," he told himself, his breath shallow and controlled. "Wait for the right opportunity."

And so, with each carefully calculated step, Edward Kingsley drew closer to fulfilling his dark desires, inching ever nearer to the unsuspecting Lara Reynolds. The game had begun, and only one could emerge victorious.

The sun dipped below the horizon, casting long shadows across the Florida coastline. Edward Kingsley stood in the gathering darkness, his heart pounding with anticipation as he watched Lara Reynolds retreat into her rented home – a beautiful property he owned.

"Power," Edward whispered to himself, lost in his thoughts. "That's what this is all about." He clenched his fists, feeling the weight of his sinister intentions pooling within him. "Control over life and death, having the ultimate say in someone else's existence."

He knew that what he was planning was wrong – society would condemn him for it – but he couldn't resist the allure, the thrill of holding another person's life in his hands. The temptation gnawed at him, consuming him until he could think of nothing else.

"Tonight's the night," he murmured, his breath fogging up the glass door of the beachside property. "Everything's led me here."

The setting of the murder seemed almost too perfect: the gentle crash of waves against the shore, the salty breeze rustling through palm trees, and the hypnotic dance of the moonlight on the water. It was as if nature itself were conspiring with him, urging him forward in his twisted pursuit.

"Such beauty," Edward mused, "and yet such darkness lurks beneath the surface." His gaze drifted from the idyllic scene to Lara's silhouette, visible through the curtains. "A fitting backdrop for the end of one story and the beginning of another."

As Edward prepared himself for the moment that had been building inside him for so long, he felt a strange mix of elation and fear. This was something new, uncharted territory – a game he had never played before. But he relished the challenge, the excitement of pushing himself beyond his limits.

"Are you ready, my dear?" he whispered, his voice barely audible over the sound of the waves. "Are you ready to become part of something much greater than yourself? To be immortalized in the annals of my dark desires?"

Closing his eyes, Edward drew in a deep breath, savoring the taste of the salty air. He knew that once he crossed this line, there would be no going back – and yet, the thought only served to fuel his anticipation.

"Let the games begin," he murmured, taking a step toward the house. And with that, Edward Kingsley disappeared into the night, leaving only the sound of the wind and waves to bear witness to his dark deeds.

The moon's reflection glistened on the ocean's surface, casting an eerie glow as if nature itself was aware of the horrors unfolding. Edward Kingsley stood in the shadows; his hands clad in tight-fitting gloves. He watched Lara through the window, her silhouette framed by the glow of her laptop screen. She appeared so vulnerable, so innocent – yet soon, she would become a monumental part of his twisted desires.

"Such a fleeting existence, my dear," he thought, his heart racing with anticipation. "But I shall ensure your impact is everlasting."

As Lara stood up and walked towards the bedroom, Edward seized his opportunity to enter the house. The door's lock yielded easily under his expert touch, a testament to his meticulous research and practice. Silently, he made his way to the kitchen, retrieving the sharpened knife he had hidden there earlier. His pulse quickened at the sight of it, its smooth blade reflecting the moonlight that filtered through the window.

"Precision, Edward. Precision and patience," he reminded himself, feeling the chilling thrill of control course through his veins. His eyes narrowed, focused intently on every detail of his surroundings as he stalked toward the bedroom.

Lara was standing by the bed, folding her clothes neatly before placing them on a chair. Edward marveled at her diligence, even in such mundane tasks. "A kindred spirit in thoroughness, but sadly, our similarities must end here tonight," he mused.

Edward stepped closer, his movements deliberate and calculated, each step a measured dance of death. He could feel his heartbeat thumping in his ears, his breath deep and steady. The knife felt like an extension of his arm, its weight perfectly balanced.

"Goodbye, Lara," he whispered, a perverse intimacy shared only between predator and prey.

With swift precision, he struck, his blade finding its mark flawlessly. The act was over in a matter of seconds, but for Edward, it felt like an eternity of ecstasy. The power he wielded, the control he exerted – it was intoxicating.

As Lara's life slipped away, her eyes met Edward's – a mixture of confusion and terror. He savored that moment, the ultimate expression of his dominance. With each fading breath she drew, Edward felt a surge of elation, a euphoria unlike any he had ever experienced.

"Your story ends here, my dear," he thought, watching as the light left her eyes. "But mine has just begun."

He pulled the knife from her body, wiping it clean with calculated efficiency. Every fiber of his being buzzed with satisfaction, the thrill of the kill still pulsing through him. At that moment, Edward Kingsley knew that he had truly become a master of death – and there was nothing more exhilarating than that knowledge.

"Tonight," he whispered, gazing at Lara's lifeless form, "I have transcended beyond the realm of mere mortals. Tonight, I have written my legacy in blood."

And with that, Edward began the meticulous task of erasing any trace of his presence, his mind already racing ahead, plotting the next chapter in his twisted tale.

The heavy scent of death hung in the air as Edward, like an artist wielding his brush, began the intricate process of removing any trace of his presence from Lara's final resting place. He moved with a deliberate elegance, each action calculated and precise.

"Such a shame," he mused, carefully folding her limp body into a large canvas tarp. "We barely had the time to get acquainted." His voice was laced with ice-cold satisfaction, a smirk playing at the corners of his lips.

Edward paused for a moment, pondering the logistics of disposing of Lara's remains. The challenge invigorated him, entwining itself with the thrill of his recent kill. He relished the thought of outsmarting anyone who dared to cross his path, leaving no clues behind.

"Ah, the perfect spot," he finally decided, recalling a secluded area deep within the nearby woods. It would provide ample cover for his macabre task – one that he approached with the same intensity and dedication he applied to every aspect of his life.

With a strained grunt, Edward hoisted Lara's wrapped body onto his shoulder. He could feel the weight of her lifeless form pressing down on him, a physical reminder of the power he now held over her. As he trudged through the underbrush, each step brought a renewed sense of accomplishment, further solidifying his belief that he was untouchable.

"Death is but a game," he thought, his heart pounding with exhilaration. "And I am its grandmaster."

Upon reaching the chosen location, Edward lowered Lara's body to the ground, taking a moment to admire his handiwork. The careful placement of the tarp ensured that no blood would seep into the soil, and the remote location guaranteed that it would remain undisturbed until he deemed otherwise.

"Rest well, sweet Lara," he whispered, patting the tarp affectionately. "You have served your purpose, and in doing so, you have granted me a most precious gift – the knowledge that I am truly unstoppable."

Edward's eyes gleamed with dark satisfaction as he gazed upon the makeshift grave, his mind already racing ahead to future conquests. The line between life and death had become but a blur to him, an intoxicating elixir that only fueled his hunger for control.

"Never again will I be shackled by the mundane," he vowed, feeling a thrill of excitement course through his veins. "From this day forth, I shall write my destiny – one kill at a time."

As Edward left the desolate spot, Lara's lifeless body hidden beneath the earth, the shadows seemed to embrace him. He felt alive, invigorated by the power coursing through him, and eager to begin his next hunt.

"Let them try to catch me," he thought, a sinister smile spreading across his lips. "I am the unseen hand that guides the reaper, the harbinger of death itself. And I am just getting started."

Edward stood on the balcony of his luxurious beachfront property, the salt-laden breeze caressing his face as he sipped on a glass of fine whiskey. The sun dipped below the horizon, casting an eerie glow upon the crashing waves. Beneath this charming facade, however, lay a sinister darkness that had taken root in Edward's soul.

"Mr. Kingsley?" a voice called from inside the house, jolting him from his thoughts. "There's a Detective Ramirez here to see you."

"Thank you, Helen," he replied smoothly, his tone betraying none of his inner turmoil. "Please send him out to join me."

As the detective stepped onto the balcony, Edward appraised him with a practiced eye. He was a middle-aged man with a hardened expression, the kind that only years of working in law enforcement could bestow.

"Detective Ramirez," Edward greeted him, extending a hand. "To what do I owe the pleasure?"

"Mr. Kingsley," Ramirez said, shaking his hand firmly. "I'm here about one of your tenants, Lara Reynolds. She's been reported missing."

"Missing?" Edward feigned concern, his heart pounding in his chest. "But she just checked in a few days ago. Is everything all right?"

"Her family hasn't heard from her, and they're growing worried. We've searched her rental, but there's no sign of her or any belongings." Ramirez paused, eyeing Edward carefully. "We'd like to ask if you've seen anything unusual around your properties lately."

"Unusual? No, not at all," Edward lied, his mind racing with calculations. "But please, let me know if there's anything I can do to help. This is most distressing."

"Thank you, Mr. Kingsley. We'll be in touch if we need anything more from you," Ramirez said, giving a curt nod before departing.

Once the detective was out of sight, Edward's heart rate slowly stabilized. He leaned against the railing, his mind a whirlwind of thoughts and emotions. A sense of dread began to claw at him, gnawing at the edges of the satisfaction he had felt only moments prior.

"Did I leave something behind?" he wondered, his grip on the glass tightening. "No... No, I was careful – meticulous. There's no way they could trace anything back to me."

Yet, as the night continued its descent upon the Florida coast, doubt crept into Edward's heart, sowing seeds of unease. He pondered his next move, the thrill of the hunt now tainted by the specter of capture.

"Perhaps it's time to change my scenery," he mused, gazing out at the dark ocean. "A new location, fresh prey...and even more devious methods."

Edward downed the last of his whiskey and smiled a wicked smile, feeling an ominous thrill at the thought of what lay ahead. As he stared into the heart of darkness, a chilling realization settled over him – the game had only just begun. And in the shadows, unseen forces were gathering, preparing to unleash a storm of terror that would sweep through the lives of all who crossed Edward Kingsley's path.

CHAPTER 6

Invincible Insanity

The dim glow of the computer screen cast eerie shadows on Edward Kingsley's face as he perused through every scrap of information about Rebecca Sinclair he could find. The hum of the cooling fan was the only sound in the room, providing a fittingly sinister soundtrack to his meticulous research.

"Ah, Rebecca," he murmured, his fingers dancing over the keyboard. "You are quite the enigma, aren't you?" He clicked on another link, revealing photos from one of her many social media accounts, showcasing her luxurious lifestyle and undeniable beauty. Her dark hair framed her striking green eyes, a seductive smile playing on her lips.

Edward leaned back in his chair, savoring the thrill that coursed through him as he imagined the fear in those captivating eyes when he finally confronted her. He knew that she was staying at one of his rental properties – the perfect opportunity to strike and indulge in his twisted desires. But first, he needed to learn everything about her. Every habit, every routine, every little detail that would bring him closer to his goal.

As the days went by, Edward continued his research, memorizing Rebecca's daily patterns. He noted the times she left for work, the places she frequented during her lunch hour, and whom she met after office hours. He even managed to discern her favorite brand of wine, which she often enjoyed on her balcony overlooking the water.

"Knowledge is power," Edward mused, his voice barely above a whisper. "And I will use it to control you, Rebecca."

With his plan formulated, Edward donned a pair of black gloves and embarked on the next phase of his hunt. He began stalking Rebecca, lurking in the shadows as she conducted her daily affairs. He felt an electric surge of excitement each time he spotted her leaving the house, her confident stride betraying nothing of her impending doom.

"Control," Edward reminded himself, suppressing the urge to strike immediately. "Patience, and control."

He kept his distance, observing Rebecca's interactions with others. He watched as she flirted with a bartender, her laughter like music that made his heart race. He saw the way men looked at her, their eyes lingering on her curves, their thoughts undoubtedly filled with lustful intentions – just like his own.

"Little do they know," Edward thought, his grip tightening around the binoculars, "that I am the one who will possess her completely when all is said and done."

As the days turned into weeks, the line between Edward Kingsley and the monster within him blurred further. The charming property owner that the world knew was gradually consumed by the predator lurking in the shadows, stalking his prey. And soon, he would be ready to strike.

The moon hung low in the sky, casting eerie shadows on the quiet street. Edward felt his heart pounding in anticipation as he stood outside Rebecca's rental home, watching the silhouettes of palm trees dance against the walls. He knew tonight was night – her friends had left early that evening, leaving her all alone and vulnerable. It was the perfect moment to strike.

"Patience," Edward whispered under his breath, his voice a mere echo in the still air. "Control."

As the clock struck midnight, Edward made his move. He expertly picked the lock on the back door, feeling the familiar thrill of breaking into a forbidden sanctuary. With each step he took deeper into the house, he felt his power grow, knowing that Rebecca was completely unaware of his presence.

"Rebecca," he murmured, savoring the taste of her name on his lips. "You have no idea what awaits you."

Edward moved silently through the dimly lit rooms of the house, using his intimate knowledge of the property to avoid detection. He could hear the faint sound of water running upstairs, and he crept closer, drawn by the promise of his prey.

"Who's there?" Rebecca called out suddenly, her voice echoing through the empty hallway.

Edward froze, his pulse quickening as he realized that she had detected something amiss. He pressed his back against the wall, cursing himself for his carelessness, but at the same time relishing the challenge she presented.

"Show yourself!" Rebecca shouted, her voice tinged with anger and fear.

"Interesting," Edward mused, his thoughts racing as he considered his options. "It seems our dear Rebecca is not as helpless as I thought. But that only makes this game more exhilarating."

"Fine! If you won't come out, then I'll find you myself!" Rebecca declared, her footsteps growing louder as she descended the stairs.

"Bold move, Rebecca," Edward thought, his excitement mounting. "But it's one you'll soon regret."

As Rebecca reached the bottom of the stairs, Edward seized his opportunity. He moved swiftly and silently, closing the distance between them in just a few strides. He could feel the heat of her body, the energy radiating from her like a beacon in the darkness.

"Such power," he marveled, his hands itching to touch her, to claim her as his own. "Soon, you will be mine."

"Who are you?" Rebecca screamed, her voice high-pitched and desperate. "What do you want from me?"

Edward stepped out of the shadows; his eyes locked on hers. "I am the predator," he whispered, his voice dripping with menace. "And you, my dear Rebecca, are my prey."

"Please," she begged, tears streaming down her cheeks. "Please, don't hurt me."

"Ah, the sweet sound of surrender," Edward mused, his heart swelling with satisfaction. "The moment I have been waiting for."

"Your fear fuels me, Rebecca," he said, his voice barely audible. "It gives me the power I crave."

As Edward stood before her, the thrill of the hunt reaching its crescendo, he knew that he had never felt more alive. This was the addiction that consumed him, the dark desires that drove him to unspeakable acts.

"Tonight, I feast," he vowed, his eyes gleaming with sinister intent. "And no one can stop me."

Edward's eyes bore into Rebecca's, taking in her fear and vulnerability. He reached out, his hand a vice around her slender wrist. She tried to resist, but he was too strong, too cunning.

"Did you think you could escape me?" Edward taunted, his voice low and menacing. "You've been under my watchful gaze since the moment you arrived. It's only fitting that I claim what's rightfully mine."

"Please," Rebecca choked out, tears staining her cheeks. "I don't know what you're talking about. Just let me go."

"Ah, the lies we tell ourselves," Edward mused, tightening his grip on her wrist. "But deep down, you know the truth. This is your fate, Rebecca."

Rebecca struggled against his hold, her desperation fueling her movements. But it was futile. Edward was methodical, calculating each move with precision as he overpowered her.

"Such resilience," he whispered, admiring her spirit even as he crushed it. "It makes this all the more satisfying."

"Please," she begged, her voice barely a whisper. "Don't do this."

Edward ignored her pleas, focusing on the task at hand. With practiced efficiency, he carried out his meticulously planned murder, using the method he had perfected over time. He felt a perverse satisfaction as the life drained from her eyes, knowing that he alone controlled her fate.

He's done it again, he thought, relishing the thrill of success. Another kill, another trophy. And just like before, no one will ever suspect a thing.

As Edward moved through the house, he erased any trace of his presence, ensuring that the authorities would be none the wiser. The thrill of the hunt still coursed through his veins, spurring him on as he readied himself to slip back into the world beyond these walls.

"Another flawless performance," he congratulated himself, the darkness of his twisted desires consuming him. "And soon, another unsuspecting victim will fall prey to my insatiable hunger."

With that thought lingering in the shadows of his mind, Edward vanished into the night, leaving behind only the haunting memory of his presence and the lifeless body of Rebecca Sinclair.

The moonlit sky cast an eerie glow over the abandoned industrial district as Edward parked his car, its headlights extinguished. The stench of decay and rust permeated the air, a fitting place for the vile deeds he had committed. He stepped out, his eyes scanning the desolate landscape, ensuring no witnesses would be privy to his gruesome task.

"Perfect," he muttered, opening the trunk to reveal Rebecca's lifeless body. Her once vibrant green eyes were now dull and vacant, her dark hair matted with blood. Edward felt a twisted sense of pride as he admired his handiwork.

"Time to make my mark," Edward said to himself, lifting her body from the trunk. He carried her to a nearby chain-link fence, positioning her in a gruesome display that would haunt those who stumbled upon it.

"Ah, Rebecca, if only you knew the part you're playing in my masterpiece," he mused aloud, stepping back to admire his arrangement. "A chilling reminder of my presence, indeed."

Satisfied, Edward returned to his car and wiped down the steering wheel, gearshift, and door handle with a cloth, ensuring he left no trace of his presence. As he drove away, his thoughts turned to the life he'd return to, the facade he maintained so effortlessly.

"Another kill, another victory," he thought, smirking at his reflection in the rearview mirror. "I am the puppet master, and they are all oblivious to the strings I pull."

Edward arrived home, the first light of dawn breaking through the darkness. He showered, washing away any lingering evidence of his crime, and changed into his usual attire – pressed khakis and a crisp, white button-down shirt. With meticulous care, he groomed himself, ensuring no hair was out of place.

"Good morning, Mr. Kingsley!" greeted his neighbor, Mrs. Thompson, as she collected her morning paper. "Such a beautiful day, isn't it?"

"Indeed, it is, Mrs. Thompson," Edward replied with a charming smile. "I hope you enjoy it."

"Thank you, dear," she said, returning his smile, blissfully unaware of the monster that lived next door.

As Edward walked to his car, he couldn't help but revel in the knowledge that he had successfully taken another life without arousing suspicion. He was untouchable, a predator hidden in plain sight.

"Rebecca was merely a stepping stone," he thought, the thrill of his most recent kill still coursing through his veins. "My insatiable hunger will not be satisfied until I've claimed them all."

With a renewed sense of purpose, Edward Kingsley, the charming property owner, drove away, leaving behind the darkness that consumed him – for now.

The flickering glow of a streetlamp cast eerie shadows along the quiet street, as Edward Kingsley watched his next victim from his parked car. The woman fumbled with her keys, finally unlocking the door to one of his rental properties. He studied her movements with rapt attention, his heart pounding in his chest – an intoxicating mix of excitement and anticipation.

"Welcome home, my dear," he muttered to himself, a sinister grin playing at the corners of his mouth. "You have no idea what awaits you."

Edward had become bolder since Rebecca's murder, his confidence soaring. He was a hunter, stalking his prey without fear of consequence, leaving behind a trail of terror that only fueled his insatiable hunger for power and control.

"Is it really this easy?" Edward mused, watching the woman disappear inside. "They trust me, let me into their lives, completely unaware of the darkness that lurks within."

He couldn't deny the rush he felt with each new kill, the thrill of asserting his dominance over these unsuspecting women. It was a high unlike any other, and he had become addicted to the terrifying taste of power.

"Tonight's the night," he whispered, gripping the steering wheel tightly as he considered his plan of attack. "I've studied her every move, learned her habits, her weaknesses... She won't even know what hit her."

As he sat there, contemplating his next move, Edward's phone rang, the shrill sound breaking through his dark thoughts. He glanced at the screen, an unexpected wave of irritation washing over him.

"Hello?" he answered coldly, not bothering to hide his frustration.

"Mr. Kingsley, there's been a last-minute booking for one of your properties," said the voice on the other end, a young woman from his rental management company. "A family of four, looking for a weekend getaway."

"Fine," he snapped, his plans momentarily disrupted. "Send them the details and make sure everything is in order."

"Of course, Mr. Kingsley. Have a good night," she replied before ending the call.

His irritation quickly gave way to a dark sense of amusement. "A family, hm?" he thought, his twisted desires already adapting to this new challenge. "A more complex game, but one I'm more than capable of winning."

Edward started his car, preparing to leave his current target for another night. While the unexpected change of plans had momentarily thrown him off, it only served to fuel his growing arrogance and addiction to the thrill of the hunt.

"Each life I take only strengthens my control," he thought, a wicked smile spreading across his face as he drove away from the scene. "And there's no one who can stop me now."

The stench of blood and sweat hung heavy in the air, a pungent reminder of Edward's latest conquest. He stood over his victim, his pulse racing with excitement as he reveled in the power he held over her lifeless form. The thrill of each new kill had become an intoxicating elixir, dulling the edges of his everyday existence and blurring the lines between the charming property owner and the sadistic monster that lurked within.

"Are you proud of yourself?" he muttered to his reflection in the mirror, the twisted grin on his face a stark contrast to the terror etched into the faces of his victims. "You've come so far, Edward. And who can stop you now?"

His arrogance swelled, bolstered by his belief in his invincibility. As he continued his grisly work, Edward's thoughts began to wander – not to the disposal of the body, but to the next victim who would inevitably fall prey to his dark desires. With each passing moment, the urgency of maintaining his façade waned, replaced by a growing obsession with the hunt.

"Edward, we're all waiting for you," called a voice from downstairs, startling him back to reality.

"Coming!" he replied, hastily concealing any traces of his latest crime. As he descended the staircase, Edward forced a smile onto his face, attempting to keep up appearances despite the raging storm of darkness within.

"Sorry for the lateness," he said, joining his friends at the dinner table. "I was just... dealing with some last-minute business."

"Always the professional, aren't you, Edward?" remarked one of his guests, chuckling as he raised his glass in a toast. "To our gracious host, who never lets anything get in the way of his success!"

"Cheers!" They all chimed in, completely oblivious to the sinister truth that lurked just beneath the surface.

As the evening wore on, Edward found it increasingly difficult to maintain his composure. Each laugh, each casual touch, and every shared story felt like a taunt – a challenge to see how long he could keep up the charade before succumbing to his twisted desires.

"Tell me, Edward," began one of his friends, leaning in close with a conspiratorial smile. "How do you manage to find such exquisite properties? I swear, each one is more beautiful than the last."

"Ah, well," Edward replied, struggling to keep his voice steady as the thrill of his crimes threatened to overtake him. "I have my ways."

"Indeed, you do, my friend," nodded another guest, raising his glass once more. "Here's to your continued success!"

Unbeknownst to them, a small crimson stain marred the pristine white tablecloth – a single drop of blood that had escaped Edward's careful cleanup. It sat there, a silent witness to unspeakable horrors, daring anyone to uncover the truth hidden behind the charming exterior of their gracious host.

"Thank you," Edward said through gritted teeth, clenching his fists beneath the table. The line between his normal life and his secret life as a serial killer was eroding, and his growing arrogance had begun to cloud his judgment, making him careless in his actions.

"Edward?" asked a concerned voice, snapping him from his dark thoughts.

"Sorry, I was just... lost in thought," he stammered, cursing himself for his recklessness. As the night drew to a close, Edward couldn't shake the feeling that the walls were closing in around him, threatening to expose the monster that lurked within.

But for now, he would continue to wear the mask and revel in the chaos he had wrought. After all, who could stop him now?

A soft, eerie laughter echoed through the darkness as Edward Kingsley stood alone on a deserted bridge, the cold wind whipping at his neatly combed hair. The local newspaper headlines screamed of yet another gruesome murder in his rental properties, and he reveled in the chaos and fear he had created.

"Untouchable," he whispered to himself with a wicked grin, his breath forming a misty cloud in the crisp night air.

In the shadows, Edward plotted his next kill, his hunger insatiable. Each murder became more brazen and audacious; he was no longer satisfied with merely stalking and killing his victims. He craved control – the power to manipulate their lives before snuffing them out.

"Edward," came a voice from behind, causing him to startle.

"Detective Harrison," he responded coolly, turning to face the man who had been hunting him for months. "What brings you here at this hour?"

"Can't sleep," the detective replied, maintaining eye contact. "Too many unsolved cases on my mind."

"Ah, yes," Edward said, feigning sympathy. "The recent murders must be quite troubling."

"Indeed, they are," Detective Harrison agreed, studying Edward's face for any sign of recognition or guilt. "We'll catch the bastard eventually, though. It's just a matter of time."

"Of course," Edward replied, trying to suppress a smirk. "I have every faith in your abilities, Detective."

"Appreciate that, Mr. Kingsley. Enjoy the rest of your evening," the detective said, nodding curtly before walking away.

As Edward watched him leave, a sinister smile crept across his face. "You'll never catch me," he thought, his confidence swelling. "I am the master of this game, and you are all my unsuspecting pawns."

With each new victim, Edward's obsession with control and power only grew stronger. The vulnerable women who rented his homes were nothing more than prey for him to toy with, manipulate, and ultimately destroy.

"Tonight's the night," Edward thought as he prepared for his latest conquest, checking the contents of his leather bag one last time before leaving his own home.

The darkness enveloped him as he silently approached his newest rental property, a quaint cottage tucked away in a secluded corner of town. He knew every inch of this house, having designed it himself to provide the perfect hunting ground.

"Welcome, my dear," he whispered into the night, knowing that his next victim was just inside, blissfully unaware of the nightmare that awaited her.

As Edward picked the lock and entered the cottage, all thoughts of caution and restraint evaporated. His arrogance blinded him, and he no longer feared capture or retribution. In his mind, there was no force on earth powerful enough to stop him.

"Your reign of terror ends tonight, Rebecca Sinclair," Edward thought, his heart pounding with anticipation as he moved stealthily through the darkened rooms. Little did he know that his sense of invincibility would soon become his greatest enemy, propelling him closer to the edge of discovery and potential downfall.

The moon, a pale and sinister crescent, cast its eerie glow on the lifeless body of Edward's 17th victim. He stood over her, admiring his handiwork, the intoxicating mix of fear and satisfaction coursing through his veins.

"Such a shame, my dear," he whispered to the corpse, a wicked smile curling at the corners of his lips. "You were so vibrant, but now you're just another statistic."

Edward wiped the blood from his hands with a monogrammed handkerchief, momentarily reflecting on how easily one could slip beneath the radar in this modern age. No one had suspected him, not even for a moment. They saw only the charming property owner, offering luxurious accommodations to unwitting prey.

"Mr. Kingsley?" A voice called from behind him, causing Edward to freeze mid-wipe. He quickly composed himself, hiding his bloody hands behind his back.

"Ah, Officer Carmichael," Edward replied, feigning surprise as he turned to face the uniformed man. "What brings you here tonight?"

"Reports of suspicious activity," the officer said, his gaze flickering between Edward and the lifeless body on the floor. "We've been working on tracking down a... serial killer." His eyes narrowed slightly, suspicion gnawing at the edges of his thoughts.

"Terrible business," Edward agreed, his voice steady despite the pounding of his heart in his chest. "I'm just as concerned as anyone else. But you'll find I've got nothing to do with it."

"Mind if we take a look around the property?" Officer Carmichael asked, his instincts telling him that something was amiss.

"Of course not," Edward responded, attempting to mask his growing unease with a confident smile. "But I assure you, there's nothing to see here."

As the police officer moved past him, Edward couldn't help but wonder if he'd finally pushed his luck too far. The thrill of the kill had blinded him to the possibility of capture, and now it seemed as though the noose was tightening around his neck.

"Is everything alright, Mr. Kingsley?" Officer Carmichael asked, noticing Edward's sudden pallor.

"Quite fine," Edward lied, forcing a laugh. "Just a bit shaken by all this, you understand."

"Of course," the officer said, unconvinced. "We'll be quick about our search."

As the police began combing through the property, Edward's thoughts raced. He knew that one misstep could bring his carefully constructed façade crashing down around him. But even with the weight of suspicion bearing down on him, he couldn't help but revel in the chaos he had unleashed upon the community.

"Seventeen victims," he mused internally, a twisted sense of pride swelling within him. "I've made my mark, and they still can't catch me."

But with every passing moment, Edward's confidence waned, replaced by a creeping dread that maybe, just maybe, his reign of terror was nearing its end. And yet, despite the fear gnawing at his heart, he couldn't deny the delicious thrill that coursed through his veins – a thrill that threatened to consume him entirely.

CHAPTER 7

Gruesome Gestures

The glow of the computer screen cast eerie shadows on Edward Kingsley's face, his ice-blue eyes locked on the gruesome images and articles that filled the dark corners of the internet. The room was silent, save for the tapping of the keyboard as Edward delved into the morbid world of body disposal. He was determined to learn the most effective and untraceable techniques for his twisted desires.

"Ah," he whispered, a sinister grin spreading across his lips. "This could be interesting."

Edward studied an article detailing the use of various chemicals and substances to dissolve flesh and bones without leaving a trace. As he read, he took meticulous notes, analyzing the strengths and weaknesses of each method. His mind raced with excitement at the thought of putting these newly acquired skills into practice, further fueling his addiction to power and control.

"Hydrofluoric acid... Sodium hydroxide... Potassium hydroxide... Hmm," Edward mused aloud, growing increasingly intrigued by the potential of these caustic substances. "The devil's in the details, isn't it?"

He leaned back in his chair, allowing himself a moment to revel in the macabre knowledge before him. This information – once applied to his grim experiments – would be the key to maintaining his carefully constructed façade and avoiding suspicion.

"Edward, you sly fox," he said to himself, chuckling darkly. "You've got this down to a science."

With renewed determination, Edward set about acquiring small amounts of the needed chemicals. He made sure to order from various online retailers, careful not to draw attention to his purchases. Each chemical arrived in unmarked packages, and Edward eagerly tore them open, eager to begin his clandestine experiments.

In the dead of night, Edward slipped out to a remote location where he had discreetly set up a makeshift laboratory. There, he began his grisly work in earnest, using the chemicals he had researched to test their effectiveness on pieces of meat that he had purchased from a local butcher shop. He methodically documented each reaction, taking careful notes and photographs to perfect his technique.

"Remarkable," he muttered as he observed the powerful reaction of hydrofluoric acid. "In mere hours, there's nothing left but a slurry of unidentifiable residue."

Edward's mind raced with excitement as he continued his experiments, refining his method until he was confident that he could effectively dissolve flesh and bones without leaving a trace. As he worked, he imagined his next victim – a young woman named Emily Thompson who was renting one of his properties. He felt a sick thrill at the thought of how effortlessly her life would be snuffed out and her body disposed of, all thanks to his meticulous research and planning.

"Sleep well, dear Emily," Edward whispered into the darkness. "Your time is drawing near."

And with that chilling promise, he packed up his tools and chemicals, erasing any evidence of his presence at the makeshift laboratory. As he drove back to his rental property, Edward's heart pounded with anticipation, knowing that his twisted desires were about to be unleashed once more.

A cloud of fog formed in front of Edward's face as he exhaled into the cold night air. He pulled his coat tighter around himself, the collar brushing against the stubble on his jawline. He had been methodically collecting the necessary materials for his twisted experiments, careful to avoid detection. Each purchase was made under a different name, using various payment methods and locations.

"Your total is $87.50," said the cashier, her fingers flying across the cash register with practiced ease.

"Thank you," replied Edward, handing over a stack of crisp bills. He adopted a friendly smile, the same one that had won over countless tenants and business partners. No one suspected the monster lurking beneath his charming facade.

As he loaded the chemicals and tools into the trunk of his car, Edward couldn't help but feel a thrill at the thought of what was to come. His research had been thorough, his methods perfected. Now, it was time to put them to the test.

Late that night, Edward descended the creaky wooden steps of the basement of one of his rental properties. The musty smell of damp earth filled his nostrils as he flicked on the overhead light, revealing a cluttered space filled with boxes and discarded furniture. It was here that he would create his makeshift laboratory, where he would conduct his macabre experiments.

"Let's get to work," he muttered to himself, his breath misting in the chilly air. He began unloading the supplies, organizing them with meticulous precision. Piles of plastic sheeting were stacked in one corner, while glass containers of various sizes filled another. A row of gleaming stainless-steel tools lay atop a sterile metal table, their sharp edges glinting menacingly in the dim light.

As Edward worked, he imagined the young woman named Emily Thompson, who would soon become his next victim. He could almost see her frightened eyes, the way her chest would heave as she struggled to draw breath. The thought sent a shiver of excitement down his spine.

"Edward, focus," he scolded himself, shaking off the distraction. He couldn't afford any mistakes, not now. Every detail had to be perfect, every step executed with precision.

Hours later, Edward stood back to survey his handiwork. The

basement had been transformed into a sterile and efficient workspace, each tool and chemical in its place, ready for use. A sense of satisfaction washed over him. He had spent countless hours planning, researching, and preparing for this moment, but it was all worth it. Soon, Emily Thompson's life would be snuffed out, her body disposed of without a trace.

"Sleep well, dear Emily," he whispered into the darkness. "Your time is drawing near."

And with that chilling promise, Edward turned off the light and ascended the stairs, leaving the makeshift laboratory behind. As he locked the door, the weight of his sinister intentions seemed to fade away, replaced by the familiar facades of a successful property owner and respected member of the community. No one would ever suspect the truth.

Emily Thompson's laughter floated through the air and carried on the warm Florida breeze. Edward watched her from a distance, hidden in the shadows as she chatted happily with her friends by the pool of the rental property. Her sun-kissed skin and carefree demeanor made her the perfect picture of innocence. It was this very innocence that had drawn him to her, like a moth to a flame.

"An ideal specimen," he mused, his eyes narrowing as he studied her movements. He had been watching her for days, learning her routines, her habits, her likes and dislikes.

"Edward, what are you doing here?" a voice called out, shattering his reverie. He turned to find one of his renters approaching.

"Ah, just checking on the property," he replied smoothly, slipping back into character. "Is everything to your liking?"

"Absolutely," the man said with a smile. "You have an eye for detail."

"Thank you, my friend," Edward responded, forcing a grin. "I take pride in providing a comfortable experience for my guests."

As they exchanged pleasantries, Edward's mind raced with thoughts of Emily. He couldn't shake the feeling that she was special, that her life would satiate his dark appetite in a way no previous victims had.

"Have a great day!" Edward bid farewell to his guest, eager to resume his observation of Emily. After ensuring that he was alone, he returned to the shadows and focused intently on the young woman.

"Patience, Edward," he reminded himself. "Wait for the right moment."

That moment came a few evenings later when Emily set out for her daily jog. As soon as she disappeared around the corner, Edward sprang into action. With gloved hands and silent footsteps, he moved towards her rental home, confident in his ability to enter undetected.

"Every detail counts," he thought, picking the lock with practiced ease. "No mistakes."

Once inside, Edward was careful to leave no trace of his presence. He moved through the house like a ghost, effortlessly avoiding any possible evidence that could link him to the crime he was about to commit.

"Emily will never know I was here," he mused, a sinister smile playing at the corners of his lips.

His heart raced as he surveyed the scene one last time, ensuring that everything was in order. As he closed the door behind him, he felt a rush of adrenaline-fueled by both his anticipation for the kill and the knowledge that he had successfully infiltrated Emily's sanctuary.

"Tonight," he whispered into the darkness, his eyes burning with malevolent intent. "Tonight, you will be mine."

A dimly lit room filled with an array of sinister-looking vials and syringes greeted Edward as he returned to his makeshift laboratory. The air hung heavy with the scent of chemicals, and in the silence, he could hear the faint hum of the ventilation system.

"Precision is key," he muttered to himself as he began to meticulously prepare the lethal dose of sedative. Every measurement had to be perfect; there was no room for error.

Edward's hands were steady as he filled a syringe with the powerful liquid. He looked at it, admiring the gleaming needle and the way the amber substance caught the light. This small instrument held the power to end a life, and that knowledge thrilled him.

"Swift and painless," he whispered, practicing the motion of injecting the drug into a piece of fruit. "No one will ever know."

As Edward continued to rehearse, refining his technique, his thoughts drifted to Emily. He imagined her running, her heart pounding in her chest, unaware that her final moments were fast approaching. The thought sent shivers down his spine, and he reveled in the anticipation.

"Tonight, she'll be mine," he repeated to himself like a dark mantra, fueling his twisted desires.

Outside, the night was moonless and still. Shadows clung to every corner, providing ample cover for someone to lurk unnoticed. It was in these shadows that Edward waited, clad in gloves and a mask to ensure no trace of his presence would remain.

"Patience," he reminded himself, his eyes fixed on Emily's home. "She'll return soon."

As minutes ticked by, Edward's excitement grew. His heart raced, and his fingers twitched with anticipation – each moment bringing him closer to the satisfaction he craved.

"Control," he thought, taking a deep breath to calm himself. "I am in control."

Finally, the sound of approaching footsteps reached his ears. Emily was returning from her jog, and Edward's body tensed, ready to strike. He watched as she unlocked the door, none the wiser to the fate that awaited her.

"Time to make my move," he murmured, his voice barely audible. With practiced stealth, Edward emerged from the shadows, his gloved hand gripping the syringe tightly.

"Tonight, Emily Thompson," he thought, a wicked grin spreading across his face. "You'll become a part of my dark masterpiece."

Emily's labored breaths echoed through the quiet night as she jogged toward her front door, sweat glistening on her skin. Edward's heart pounded in his chest, matching the rhythm of her footsteps. This was the moment he had been waiting for – the culmination of his meticulous planning and preparation.

"Focus," he told himself. "No mistakes."

As Emily fumbled with her keys, Edward closed the distance between them in a few silent strides. "Hey, Emily!" he called out with feigned cheerfulness.

Startled, she turned to face him. Her eyes widened with surprise, but before she could react, Edward plunged the syringe into her arm. The sedative worked quickly, coursing through her veins with lethal efficiency.

"Wha–" she mumbled confusion and fear mingling in her voice as her body went limp.

"Shh," Edward whispered, catching her before she hit the ground. "Sleep now, Emily. Soon, you'll be part of something greater."

He cradled her unconscious form, savoring the weight of her life in his arms. "Perfect," he thought, admiring his handiwork. "Not a single trace left behind."

As he carried her to his vehicle, parked discreetly down the street, Edward's mind raced with anticipation. He recalled the hours spent scouting the ideal location on the outskirts of town – a place where his dark desires could be fully realized without interruption.

"Control," he reminded himself, his grip tightening around Emily's lifeless body. "I am in control here."

The drive was quiet, save for the soft hum of the engine and the pounding of Edward's heartbeat. Every mile that passed brought him closer to the satisfaction he craved, fueling his resolve.

"Almost there," he murmured, his knuckles white as he gripped the steering wheel. "Soon, Emily, you'll be just a memory – a fleeting moment in my twisted symphony."

As he pulled into the remote location, Edward's excitement reached a fever pitch. He knew that tonight would be a turning point in his life, a step further into the abyss of his dark desires.

"Tonight," he thought, his eyes locked on Emily's unconscious form, "I become the master of my fate."

With meticulous care, Edward carried her from the vehicle, ensuring that no traces of their journey remained. The night was still, and an eerie calm settled over the remote location as Edward prepared to enact his plan.

"Welcome, Emily," he whispered into the darkness, a sinister smile playing on his lips. "Your time has come."

The moonless night embraced Edward as he stood over Emily's body, the darkness swallowing his silhouette. The air was thick with tension, anticipation hanging like a noose around his neck.

"Control," Edward whispered a mantra that had become second nature to him. "Control is power."

He reached into the duffel bag he'd brought along, retrieving the tools he'd carefully researched and acquired. Each instrument gleamed in the faint light of his headlamp, their cold metal surfaces reflecting his sinister intentions. He paused for a moment, taking in the scene before him.

"Time to begin," he said, more to himself than to the lifeless form lying on the ground. With practiced precision, he began the gruesome task of dismembering Emily's body. His hands moved confidently, guided by the knowledge he'd amassed during countless hours of research.

"Such a beautiful girl," he mused, pausing for a moment to admire his handiwork. "But beauty must be sacrificed for the greater cause."

His thoughts flitted through memories of other victims, each one fueling his insatiable appetite for control. As he worked, he reveled in the chaos that would inevitably follow the discovery of Emily's remains.

"Can you imagine their faces?" he asked Emily's lifeless form, a wicked grin spreading across his face. "The shock, the horror... The delicious confusion as they try to piece it all together."

As the last cut was made, Edward surveyed the carnage with a sense of pride. He methodically wrapped each body part in plastic, ensuring that any evidence would remain sealed away from prying eyes.

"An artist must take care of his masterpiece," he mused, focusing on the task at hand. "And I am nothing if not an artist."

With each wrapped parcel, he felt a surge of satisfaction. He loaded them into his vehicle, preparing for the final stage of his plan. As he drove from one location to another, burying pieces of Emily's body throughout the town, his anticipation grew. The thought of the fear and chaos that would engulf the community sent shivers down his spine.

"Let them tremble," he whispered into the darkness, a perverse pleasure coursing through his veins. "Let them fear the unknown, the unseen. Let them know that they are not safe, that I am in control."

His work complete, Edward took a moment to bask in the satisfaction of a job well done. He'd orchestrated a symphony of terror, each note perfectly tuned to send the town spiraling into chaos.

"Sleep well, Emily," he said, his voice fading into the night. "For you have become a part of something much greater than yourself."

The moonless night sky was a canvas devoid of stars, an inky blackness that cloaked Edward's return to the rental property. He parked his vehicle in the shadows, ensuring it was hidden from view before stepping out into the cool evening air.

"Showtime," he whispered, his breath forming a ghostly cloud in the darkness.

Edward approached the back door, sliding on a fresh pair of gloves as he unlocked it with Emily's spare key. Inside, he surveyed the scene: the immaculate living room, untouched since he'd last been there. He couldn't help but marvel at his cunning, the way he'd planned everything down to the smallest detail.

"Like clockwork," he mused, allowing himself a moment of self-congratulation before getting to work.

Edward began the meticulous process of cleaning up any trace of his presence. The efficiency and precision he employed were almost surgical, a testament to his intelligence and determination. He wiped down surfaces, vacuumed meticulously, and disposed of any potentially incriminating evidence.

"Nothing left to chance," he thought, a satisfied smirk creeping across his face.

As he worked, Edward replayed the events of the evening in his head, savoring each gruesome detail with perverse pleasure. He could still feel the weight of Emily's lifeless body in his arms, the sensation of power that had coursed through him as he dismembered her.

"Perfect execution," he murmured, his voice low and sinister.

With the rental property restored to its pristine state, Edward took one final look around, ensuring that nothing was amiss. He replaced Emily's key, locked the door behind him, and slipped away into the shadows, a phantom returning to the night.

"Another masterpiece completed," he congratulated himself, his heart swelling with pride.

Edward resumed his normal life, seamlessly blending back into the community as if nothing had happened. He attended neighborhood events, greeted fellow residents with a smile, and continued to manage his properties with the same charm and professionalism that had earned him their respect.

"Such simple creatures," he thought, smirking at their naivete. "How easily they are deceived."

In the quiet moments between public appearances, Edward found solace in the knowledge that he had once again successfully executed his twisted desires. He reveled in the power and control he held over the community, basking in the fear and chaos that would soon envelop them.

"Let them shudder in the darkness," he mused, his eyes glazed over with anticipation. "For I am the master of shadows, the puppeteer behind their nightmares."

As the days passed, Edward felt invigorated by his latest success, fueled by the thrill of his secret reign of terror. It was an intoxicating feeling, one that whispered seductively in his ear, urging him onward, deeper into the abyss.

"Sleep well, Emily," he thought, his voice a haunting echo in the recesses of his mind. "Your sacrifice was not in vain."

The soft glow of the computer screen illuminated Edward's face as he sat hunched over his desk in the shadowy corner of his study. He felt a shiver of excitement run down his spine, an electric current that sent goosebumps across his skin. The night was young, and he had work to do.

"Time to hunt," he whispered to himself, fingers dancing across the keyboard like a virtuoso pianist. His eyes darted across the screen, scanning various social media profiles, searching for any signs of vulnerability or patterns that could be exploited.

Edward paused on a photograph of a young woman with fiery red hair, her green eyes sparkling with life. Something about her intrigued him

– perhaps it was the way she smiled, a mixture of innocence and hidden depths, or the hint of sadness lurking behind those vibrant eyes.

"Hello there," he murmured, tracing the outline of her face on the screen. "What secrets do you hide, my dear?"

As the days passed, Edward's addiction to power and control only grew stronger. He knew he couldn't stop, not until he was finally caught, or his cravings consumed him entirely. Each new victim was a testament to his skill, his artistry, proof that he was the apex predator in this twisted game.

"Have you ever played chess?" he asked a fellow property owner at a community gathering, feigning casual interest. "It's all about strategy, anticipating your opponent's moves, controlling the board."

"Can't say I have," the man replied, scratching his head. "Never had the patience for it, I suppose."

"Ah, well," Edward said, a knowing smile playing on his lips. "You don't know what you're missing."

Late at night, after the rest of the world had gone to sleep, Edward would lose himself in fantasies, meticulously planning every detail of his next kill. He imagined the fear in his victim's eyes as he loomed over them, the helplessness they would feel as he took control. The thought sent a shiver of pleasure down his spine.

"Checkmate," he whispered into the darkness, a sinister grin spreading across his face.

Edward's mind raced with possibilities; each new idea more thrilling than the last. He was like an artist, and death was his canvas – a blank space waiting to be filled with blood and terror. As the days turned to weeks, his hunger for power grew insatiable, driving him ever closer to the edge of madness.

"Patience, my dear," he told himself, his fingers tapping a steady rhythm on the desk. "All great works of art take time."

With every passing day, Edward grew more cunning, and more meticulous in his planning. He knew that one wrong move could bring his reign of terror to an end, and he had no intention of letting that happen. If he remained in control, if he held the strings, he could continue to dance in the shadows, unseen and untouchable.

"Until we meet again," he whispered to the night, his voice a chilling promise of what was to come. "Sleep well, my darlings. Your time will come soon enough."

CHAPTER 8

Beneath the Shadows

Rain lashed against the police station's windows, a fitting backdrop for the grim task that lay ahead. Daniel Thompson, a local detective in his mid-30s, strode into the precinct with determination etched across his chiseled features. Today marked the beginning of his investigation into the string of mysterious deaths plaguing the city, and he had no intention of letting this case go unsolved.

"Morning, Thompson," greeted Officer Johnson from behind the front desk. "You ready to tackle these cases?"

"More than ever," replied Daniel, his deep voice steady as he approached the officer. "I won't rest until I find out who's responsible for these tragedies."

"Your dedication is commendable, as always," Johnson remarked, handing Daniel the first of several thick case files. "Good luck."

"Thanks," Daniel nodded before heading towards his workspace, his tall and athletic frame navigating through the maze of desks with ease.

As he settled into his chair, Daniel began poring over the case files, his keen eye for detail absorbing every piece of information, no matter how minute. The victims varied in age, gender, and occupation, but they all shared one commonality – their lives had been snuffed out in the most gruesome and inexplicable ways imaginable. It was a puzzle that needed solving, and Daniel felt the weight of responsibility bearing down on him.

"Alright," he muttered under his breath, starting to organize the files before him. "Let's see if we can find any patterns here." His fingers tapped the edge of his desk impatiently, reflecting his eagerness to delve into the heart of the matter.

Hours passed, with Daniel meticulously reviewing every aspect of each victim's life, searching for connections or clues that could lead him to the killer. One by one, he began compiling a list of potential suspects, scribbling down names alongside interrogation notes and alibis.

"Damn it," he cursed softly as he rubbed his temples, frustration mounting. "There has to be something I'm missing." Despite the growing pressure, Daniel's resolve never wavered. He knew that he had to find justice for these victims – it was not just an obligation, but a moral imperative.

As he continued to analyze the case files, Daniel couldn't shake off the nagging feeling that there was more to these deaths than met the eye. Each murder scene was meticulously staged, as if the killer was taunting him, daring him to connect the dots. And with every new piece of evidence he uncovered, the more he felt like he was on the cusp of a breakthrough.

"Thompson," called out Sergeant Mills from across the room. "You've been at this all day. Why don't you take a break?"

"Can't," Daniel replied curtly, without lifting his gaze from the files spread before him. "I need to find the person responsible for this." His voice held a quiet intensity, reflecting the fervor that fueled his investigation.

"Alright," conceded Mills, knowing better than to argue with him. "But remember, you're not in this alone. We're all here to help."

Daniel nodded absentmindedly, already diving back into the sea of information that threatened to consume him. With each passing moment, he became more and more determined to solve the case, even if it meant sacrificing his relationships and well-being. For in the shadows of the city, a monster lurked, and only Daniel could bring it to light.

Rain pattered against the windshield as Daniel pulled up to the home of the first victim's family. He watched as a single streetlamp flickered, casting eerie shadows upon the darkened house. Hesitating for a moment, he shook off his doubts and stepped out into the stormy night.

"Thompson," he muttered under his breath, gathering his resolve. "You're here to find answers, not to let fear take hold." With that, he strode towards the front door, his shoes crunching on the gravel beneath him.

As the door creaked open, a somber-faced woman greeted him. "Detective Thompson?" she asked hesitantly, her voice tinged with sorrow and anxiety.

"Mrs. Reynolds," Daniel replied, offering a sympathetic smile. "I'm here to discuss your daughter's case."

"Please, come in," she said quietly, stepping aside to allow him entrance.

As they sat down in the dimly lit living room, Daniel took a moment to observe his surroundings. The house was filled with pictures of happier times: family vacations, birthday parties, and holiday celebrations. It was a stark reminder of what had been stolen from these people.

"Mrs. Reynolds," Daniel began gently, "I understand how difficult this must be for you. But any information you can provide might help us catch the person responsible." He couldn't bring himself to utter the word 'killer,' not in this sanctuary of memories.

The woman swallowed hard, tears welling up in her eyes. "I... I don't know where to start," she whispered, her voice trembling.

"Take your time," Daniel reassured her, his tone soft and understanding. "We only need to go through this once."

As they spoke, Daniel listened intently, absorbing every detail and storing it away for future reference. He shared in Mrs. Reynolds' pain, her loss, and her desire for justice. And as he left the house that night, he felt a renewed sense of determination.

"Edward Kingsley," he mused to himself, pondering the man who had risen to the top of his list of suspects. "On paper, you seem like just another successful businessman. But I can't shake the feeling that there's something more to these murders." He couldn't quite put his finger on it, but something about Edward seemed off – too perfect, too calculated.

As Daniel drove away from the Reynolds' home, he resolved to keep digging, to explore every lead no matter how unlikely or far-fetched. For he knew that somewhere in this twisted web of clues and deception, the truth was waiting to be uncovered. And until he found it, the families of the victims would never truly find peace.

The sun dipped below the horizon, casting long shadows across the desolate streets. In the dimming light, Detective Daniel Thompson sat in his unmarked car, a steely determination etched onto his face. The cold air from the car's AC mingled with his warm breath as he gripped the steering wheel tightly, his focus unwavering.

"Damn it, Edward," Daniel muttered under his breath, his eyes locked on the figure emerging from the upscale bar up ahead. "What are you hiding?"

He watched as Edward Kingsley, impeccably dressed and exuding an air of confidence, made his way to a sleek, black sedan. The man seemed untouchable; yet, as the investigation progressed, Daniel couldn't shake the sinking feeling that Edward was somehow involved in the gruesome murders that had plagued the city.

"Alright, Mr. Kingsley," Daniel said to himself, starting the engine. "Let's see what secrets you've got buried."

As he tailed Edward through the winding streets, keeping a safe distance to avoid detection, Daniel's mind raced with possibilities. He'd spent hours poring over case files, searching for any shred of evidence that might link Edward to the killings. So far, all he had were small, seemingly insignificant details: a reservation at one of Edward's properties coinciding with a victim's disappearance; Edward's cryptic responses during their initial interview; and even the unnerving way his eyes seemed to dart about when discussing the case.

"Coincidences," Daniel thought. "That's all they are, right? But there are just too many..."

His thoughts were interrupted as Edward pulled into the parking lot of a rundown motel - a far cry from the luxurious accommodations he typically provided for his clients. Daniel parked across the street, watching intently as Edward exited the vehicle and approached Room 12. After a brief knock, the door swung open, revealing a young woman with a forced smile plastered on her face.

"Who the hell is she?" Daniel muttered, snapping a few quick photos with his phone. The exchange was suspicious, and he couldn't help but feel that he was getting closer to uncovering the truth.

"Damn it!" he growled in frustration as Edward slipped inside the motel room without so much as a second glance, leaving Daniel with nothing more than questions and mounting tension.

"Think, Daniel. What's the connection? Why is he here?" He raked his fingers through his hair, his mind working overtime to piece together the puzzle before him.

"Okay, Daniel," he whispered, steeling himself for what might lie ahead. "You've got one shot at this. Time to find out who this mystery woman is, what she knows about Edward, and if she's connected to the victims."

As he stepped out of the car and began his stealthy approach toward Room 12, Daniel's heart pounded in his chest, fear, and anticipation coursing through his veins. But despite the risks, he knew he had to press on – for the sake of the victims, their families, and the city he had sworn to protect.

"Justice will be served," he vowed silently, inching closer to the door. "No matter what it takes."

The dim light of the streetlamp cast a sinister glow on the cracked pavement as Daniel crouched behind the corner of the motel. He had spent hours following Edward, documenting every move he made – but so far, it was all circumstantial. Nothing concrete. Nothing that would hold up in court.

"Damn it," Daniel muttered to himself, clenching his fists in frustration. He couldn't shake the feeling that Edward was involved in the murders, but without solid proof, he couldn't make an arrest.

As he watched Edward's silhouette move about in the motel room, he pondered his next move. Should he bring this information to his colleagues at the police station? Or should he continue investigating on his own, risking not only his career but also his safety?

"Hey, detective?" a gravelly voice called out from behind him, making Daniel jump. He turned to see a middle-aged man with a scraggly beard and disheveled clothing leaning against the wall.

"Who are you?" Daniel asked warily, his hand instinctively moving towards his holstered gun.

"Name's Roger. I've seen you around here the past few days, watching that guy" – he nodded towards the motel room – "and I thought maybe I could help."

"Help? How do you know anything about this case?" Daniel eyed him suspiciously, unsure if he could trust this stranger.

"Let's just say I've been keeping an eye on things around here for a while," Roger replied cryptically. "And I've seen some things that might interest you."

"Like what?" Daniel asked, his curiosity piqued despite his reservations.

"First, tell me who you think he is," Roger said, gesturing towards Edward's shadow behind the curtains.

"Edward Kingsley," Daniel replied, his jaw clenched. "And I have reason to believe he's involved in the recent string of murders in this city."

"Kingsley, huh?" Roger mused, rubbing his chin thoughtfully. "Well, detective, I've got something that might just blow this case wide open."

"Spit it out, then," Daniel urged impatiently.

"Before I do, you should know that this information isn't exactly...

legal," Roger admitted with a smirk. "So, if you want it, you'll have to keep me out of whatever mess you're going to stir up."

Daniel hesitated for a moment, torn between his need for evidence and his duty to uphold the law. But ultimately, he knew what he had to do.

"Deal," he said, extending his hand to shake it.

The dim glow of the computer screen illuminated Daniel's haggard face, casting eerie shadows on the walls of his cluttered home office. He had been working tirelessly for days, fueled by a relentless determination to uncover the truth behind Edward Kingsley's veneer of charm and success.

"Edward must have slipped up somewhere," Daniel muttered under his breath, his eyes darting across the screen as he dug through public records, hunting for any connection between Edward and the victims. "There has to be something I'm missing."

As the hours stretched into the night, Daniel's phone buzzed with a text from his wife, Sarah. "Are you coming to bed anytime soon?"

Daniel glanced at the message, his thumb hovering over the keyboard before he finally typed out a response. "I can't. Not until I find something that links Edward to these murders." He knew his obsession with the case was taking a toll on their relationship, but the thought of another innocent life being snuffed out haunted him.

"Daniel, you're pushing yourself too hard," Sarah replied, her concern evident in her words. "You need to rest."

"Rest won't bring justice to those families," he shot back, his frustration mounting. "I'll sleep when this monster is behind bars."

With each passing day, Daniel became more consumed by the case, his personal life fading into the background as he delved deeper into Edward's past. He conducted interviews with old acquaintances and business associates, searching for any scrap of information that might shed light on Edward's true nature.

"Did you ever notice anything… off about Edward?" he asked one of Edward's former neighbors, a middle-aged woman named Claire.

"Off? Well, he always seemed so… perfect, you know?" she said hesitantly. "Like he was hiding something. But I never would've guessed he could do something like this."

"Neither did I," Daniel admitted quietly, his eyes narrowing as he scribbled down her statement in his ever-growing case file.

He spent countless hours poring over evidence, piecing together a chilling mosaic of Edward's life – one that bore little resemblance to the image he presented to the world. He could feel himself closing in on the truth, yet it remained just out of reach, taunting him like a shadow in the night.

"Dammit," Daniel growled, slamming his fist on the desk as another lead hit a dead end. "I know you're guilty, Kingsley. I just need to prove it."

The weight of the unsolved murders bore down on him, an oppressive force that threatened to crush his spirit. But even in the darkest moments, Daniel refused to waver in his pursuit of justice.

"Edward Kingsley, your days are numbered," he whispered into the darkness, his voice filled with steely resolve. "I will find the truth, and I will make sure you pay for what you've done."

Daniel's phone buzzed relentlessly on his bedside table, rousing him from a fitful sleep. He grasped blindly for the device, squinting at the screen as he registered the flurry of missed calls and messages.

"Jesus Christ," he muttered, scrubbing a hand over his face as he realized yet another body had been discovered. The killer was growing bolder, taunting him with their increasingly grisly displays. How many more innocent lives would be snuffed out before he finally cracked this case?

"Detective Thompson!" A reporter shoved a microphone in his face as he stepped outside the precinct, a sea of cameras and anxious faces waiting to capture his reaction. "Do you have any leads on the latest murder?"

Daniel fought the urge to snap at the intrusive journalist, instead plastering on a stoic expression as he fielded their questions. "We're following up on several promising leads, but I can't disclose any further details at this time," he said tersely, pushing past the throng of reporters and ducking into the relative sanctuary of his car.

"Damn it," he muttered under his breath, the mounting pressure gnawing at him like a persistent ache. His every move was now under intense scrutiny, and he could feel the community's collective gaze burning into the back of his neck. They demanded answers, and Daniel was determined to provide them – no matter the cost.

It was late when Daniel stumbled upon it: the thread that would unravel Edward Kingsley's carefully constructed facade. He'd been poring over crime scene photos for hours, searching for the elusive clue that would tie everything together. And there it was, staring him right in the face.

"Son of a bitch," he whispered, his heart hammering in his chest as adrenaline surged through his veins. The evidence was damning: a set of unique tire tracks found at multiple crime scenes, which matched the make and model of Edward's car.

"Finally," Daniel thought, his pulse racing with a mix of excitement and trepidation. "I've got you now, Kingsley."

But as the reality of his discovery sank in, so too did the understanding that this was just the beginning. The tire tracks were a crucial piece of the puzzle, but they wouldn't be enough to secure a conviction on their own. He needed more – irrefutable proof that would withstand the scrutiny of a courtroom and expose Edward for the monster he truly was.

"Alright, Kingsley," Daniel muttered, his eyes flashing with determination. "Let's see what else you're hiding."

The flickering light of the streetlamps cast eerie shadows across the abandoned warehouse, their shapes contorting and twisting like the dark secrets Daniel knew Edward was hiding. He crouched behind a stack of rotting wooden crates, clutching the damning evidence that would finally expose Edward Kingsley's sinister double life.

"Big mistake, leaving these tracks behind," Daniel muttered under his breath, his eyes never leaving the figure of Edward as he moved about inside the warehouse. He could feel the weight of the tire track photos in his jacket pocket – a constant reminder of the connection he'd made, and the pivotal role he now played in this deadly game.

"Alright, let's see what you're up to," he whispered, steeling himself for the confrontation that loomed ahead. He knew he couldn't wait any longer; every moment wasted was another opportunity for Edward to slip through his fingers.

"Kingsley," Daniel called out, his voice echoing through the space as he stepped into the dimly lit interior. "It's over."

Edward froze, his eyes narrowing as they investigated Daniel's unwavering gaze. "Detective Thompson," he replied with a sneer, his voice dripping with contempt. "To what do I owe the pleasure?"

"Cut the crap, Edward," Daniel growled, his fists clenching at his sides as anger surged through him. "I know what you've been doing. And I have the evidence to prove it."

Edward's eyes widened momentarily before he regained his composure, a sly smile spreading across his lips. "Oh? And what evidence might that be?"

"You left tire tracks at multiple crime scenes, Edward," Daniel said, his voice cold and controlled. "And they match your car. You're not as smart as you think you are."

"Is that all you've got?" Edward scoffed, his confidence seeming to swell by the second. "You'll need more than that to take me down, Detective."

"Then let's see how you like what I find in here," Daniel replied, his gaze never leaving Edward as he moved deeper into the warehouse. He knew he was playing a dangerous game, but he couldn't afford to back down now – not when he was so close to bringing Edward to justice.

"Go ahead and look," Edward taunted, his eyes glinting with malice. "But you won't find anything that connects me to those... unfortunate incidents."

"Unfortunate incidents?" Daniel echoed incredulously, his anger bubbling to the surface once more. "You're a sick bastard, Kingsley. You can't hide from the truth any longer."

"Let's see about that," Edward retorted, his voice dripping with menace as he took a step forward. "I've dealt with the likes of you before, Detective. And I have no problem doing it again."

As the two men faced off in the shadows of the warehouse, Daniel could feel the tension crackling between them like a live wire. It was only a matter of time before one of them snapped, setting off a chain reaction that would change the course of their lives forever.

"Bring it on, Kingsley," Daniel growled, his determination unwavering as he prepared for the confrontation that would either make or break his investigation. "I'm not going anywhere until I find the evidence, I need to put you away for good."

And with those words, Daniel sealed his fate, plunging headfirst into the darkness as he hunted for the proof that would finally expose Edward's twisted world – unaware of the horrors that awaited him just beyond the shadows.

The sound of footsteps echoed through the dimly lit alley as Daniel approached Edward's upscale townhouse. The moon, shrouded by clouds, cast an eerie glow over the scene, sending a chill down his spine. He could feel the weight of the evidence he had unearthed pressing heavily on him, and as he drew closer to Edward's home, his heart pulsed with equal parts anticipation and dread.

"Edward Kingsley," he muttered under his breath, the name leaving a bitter taste in his mouth. "Your time is running out."

As Daniel cautiously approached the front door, he took a moment to collect his thoughts, knowing that what happened next would be critical.

"Stay focused, Thompson," he told himself. "You can't afford any mistakes now."

Just as he raised his hand to knock, the door swung open, revealing Edward standing on the threshold, a smug grin plastered across his face.

"Detective Thompson," he drawled, looking Daniel up and down with a predatory gaze. "I was wondering when you'd show up."

"Cut the crap, Kingsley," Daniel snapped, his patience wearing thin. "I know what you've done, and I have enough evidence to prove it."

Edward's smile faltered for a moment, but he quickly regained his composure. "Oh, really?" he challenged, crossing his arms. "Why don't you come in and tell me all about it?"

Daniel hesitated, keenly aware that entering Edward's lair could put him at risk. But he couldn't let this opportunity slip away – not when so much was at stake. Steeling himself, he followed Edward inside, every sense heightened as he mentally prepared for the confrontation ahead.

"Make no mistake, Kingsley," Daniel warned as they entered the lavish living room. "This ends tonight. One way or another."

"Bold words, Detective," Edward replied, his tone icy. "But it'll take more than empty threats to bring me down."

"Empty threats?" Daniel scoffed, feeling his anger rising. "I have evidence that directly connects you to the murders. It's over for you."

Edward's eyes narrowed, and he leaned in closer, a sinister glint in his eye. "We'll see about that," he whispered, his voice dripping with menace. "You may think you have me cornered but remember – I'm not the only one with secrets."

Daniel clenched his fists, struggling to maintain control as the tension between them crackled like a live wire. He knew that every second counted, and yet, for all his determination, he couldn't shake the gnawing fear that Edward might still somehow slip through his grasp.

"Let's get this over with, Kingsley," Daniel growled, his voice filled with resolve. "You can't run from the truth any longer."

"Neither can you," Edward replied, his eyes boring into Daniel's, their two wills locked in a deadly dance of power and deception.

With that, the final battle lines were drawn, setting the stage for a confrontation that would determine the fate of both men and the lives they had so ruthlessly destroyed. As Daniel stared into the abyss of Edward's twisted soul, he knew that only one thing was certain: there could be no turning back now.

CHAPTER 9

Seduction of Silence

The dim glow of the computer screen illuminated Edward Kingsley's face, his eyes flicking back and forth as they devoured information about his latest obsession: Mia Evans. He had stumbled upon her by chance when she rented one of his luxurious seaside properties for a quiet getaway. But now, the once harmless fascination had morphed into a sinister fixation.

"Ah, an artist," Edward murmured, scrolling through Mia's online portfolio. The muted colors and fluid lines of her work resonated with him; it was as if each piece was a window into Mia's soul. "How fitting."

Edward clicked through photos from her social media profiles, taking careful note of the way she dressed, the friends she kept, and the places she frequented. It wasn't long before he found what he was looking for, a vulnerability to exploit.

"Lonely beach walks," he whispered, smirking at the discovery. "Perfect."

It seemed that Mia had developed a habit of wandering the coastal shore near the rental property every evening, just as the sun began dipping below the horizon. The thought of her slender form silhouetted against the dying light sent a shiver down Edward's spine. His mind churned with possibilities, painting vivid images of the unsuspecting woman falling prey to his carefully laid plans.

"Such a predictable creature," Edward mused, leaning back in his chair. "And so...vulnerable."

His heart raced with anticipation as he began to outline the perfect moment to strike. He imagined her soft footsteps on the wet sand, the salty breeze tugging at her hair, and the hypnotic crash of the waves drowning out any sound he might make as he approached.

"Tomorrow night will be the night," he vowed, unable to contain the excitement bubbling within him. "Mia Evans, you have no idea what you've walked into."

As Edward continued his research, he began to feel an intoxicating sense of power surging through him. He knew he held Mia's fate within his grasp, and the thrill of manipulating her actions from behind the scenes was electrifying.

"Such a delicate little thing," he thought, his eyes narrowing as they traced the curve of her cheek in one of her photos. "Soon you'll be mine, and there'll be no escape."

Edward closed his laptop with a satisfied snap, his mind already racing ahead to the following evening. The sun would set, casting shadows long enough to hide his sinister intentions, and he would finally have Mia Evans right where he wanted her.

"Sweet dreams, my dear," he whispered into the darkness. "Tomorrow night, your nightmare begins."

The setting sun cast an eerie orange glow over the shoreline, its light playing off the crashing waves as they licked the sand. Edward Kingsley watched from a distance; his eyes locked on the solitary figure of Mia Evans as she strolled along the beach. He had been observing her for days now, studying her movements and routines with the precision of a master predator.

"Such predictability," he mused to himself, his fingers drumming against the steering wheel of his parked car. "I wonder if you even realize how exposed you are."

Edward had carefully chosen his vantage point – far enough away to remain undetected, but close enough to keep a watchful eye on his prey. As Mia continued her walk, her long brown hair whipped around her face by the ocean breeze, he felt a twisted thrill run down his spine.

"Tonight," he whispered, his voice heavy with anticipation. "Tonight is the night I claim you."

Edward's mind raced as he considered every detail of his plan. The secluded spot he had selected was perfect – a small cove hidden from view by large rocks and dense foliage. It was just far enough from the main path that no one would hear Mia's cries for help, yet still within her usual walking route. It would be here that he would make his move.

"Time to prepare," he thought, his pulse quickening with excitement. He opened his glove compartment, retrieving a pair of black leather gloves and slipping them onto his hands. They fit snugly, like a second skin, ensuring that he would leave no trace of his presence.

As the sun dipped lower in the sky, Edward scanned the area once more, noting the positions of nearby houses and the comings and goings of their residents. Every detail was important; he couldn't afford to make any mistakes. With a final glance at Mia, who was now little more than a distant silhouette against the darkening horizon, he stepped out of his car and began to make his way toward the cove.

"Patience," he reminded himself as he moved silently through the shadows, mindful of every sound, every movement. "The perfect moment will present itself. Do not rush."

Edward could feel his excitement mounting with each step, but he forced himself to remain calm. He knew that one wrong move would jeopardize everything, and he was determined to see his plan through to completion.

"Control," he thought, his breaths coming in short, shallow gasps as he neared the spot where he would lie in wait for Mia. "Control is everything."

Upon reaching the cove, Edward took a moment to survey his surroundings, ensuring that nothing had changed since his last reconnaissance. Satisfied, he settled into his hiding place, his eyes trained on the path where Mia would soon appear.

"Any minute now," he whispered, feeling an odd sense of serenity settle over him as the sun dipped below the horizon, plunging the world into darkness. "Soon, you'll be mine."

Edward's heart pounded in his chest as he waited, the anticipation building with each passing moment. He knew that Mia was walking towards her fate, completely unaware of the danger lurking nearby.

"Come to me, my dear," he thought, a twisted smile playing at the corners of his lips. "Your nightmare is about to begin."

Beneath the flickering glow of a streetlamp, Edward's fingers tightened around the black leather bag housing his tools. The feeling of control surged through him, intoxicating and addictive. He had spent days carefully assembling each item, ensuring that he was prepared for every eventuality.

"Are you ready for this?", a voice inside his head whispered, as if taunting him. Edward responded with a smirk. "Of course," he thought, the words laced with venom. "I've never been more prepared."

He approached the beachside path, intent on studying the surroundings where he planned to strike. As he walked, the waves crashed against the shore, filling the air with a salty mist. It created an eerie atmosphere, heightening the sinister tone of his mission.

Edward paused, taking in the details of the area - the gnarled branches of a nearby tree, the abandoned lifeguard tower casting long shadows across the sand, and the jagged rocks lining the water's edge. He imagined Mia's terror as she stumbled across these hazards in her desperate attempt to escape his grasp.

"Such a perfect setting for our encounter," he mused, his eyes narrowing in satisfaction.

"Hey there! Out for a walk?", a cheerful voice called out from behind him. Edward turned to see a young couple passing by their laughter grating on his nerves as they continued down the path, unaware of the darkness lurking nearby.

"Idiots," he muttered under his breath, watching them recede into the distance. He sighed, irritated by the interruption but refocused on the task at hand. "Now, where would be the best place to hide?"

He surveyed the terrain, considering each potential hiding spot. He wanted Mia to feel safe, lulled into a false sense of security before he made his move. Finally, his gaze settled on a cluster of bushes near the base of the lifeguard tower. The shadows cast by the structure would provide ample cover, allowing him to watch Mia undetected.

"Perfect," he whispered, a fierce grin spreading. "The hunt begins."

Edward crouched behind the bushes, his heart pounding in anticipation. The sand beneath him was cold and damp, but he hardly noticed, consumed with thoughts of the moment when he would finally have her within his grasp.

"Patience," he reminded himself, eyes fixed on the path where she was sure to appear. "Control yourself, Edward. Your time will come."

As he waited, the wind carried the distant sound of laughter to his ears - a chilling reminder of the unsuspecting world that continued to exist just beyond his reach. But for now, none of it mattered. For now, only one thing held any significance: the impending culmination of his twisted plan, and the sweet taste of power that awaited him.

The sun dipped below the horizon, painting the sky with shades of red and orange as twilight crept in. Edward Kingsley stood at the edge of the beach, his eyes scanning the shoreline for any sign of Mia Evans. Despite the beauty of the setting sun, his thoughts were consumed by darker desires - a predatory hunger that could only be satisfied by the thrill of the hunt.

"Come on, Mia," he murmured under his breath, a cruel smile tugging at the corners of his lips. "Time to take your walk."

As if on cue, a figure appeared in the distance, her long brown hair fluttering in the breeze. Edward's pulse quickened, and he fought to control the excitement that threatened to overwhelm him.

"Stay calm," he told himself. "You've prepared for this. You know exactly what to do."

"Edward?" a voice called from behind him. He tensed, his heart skipping a beat before he recognized it as one of his tenants from a neighboring house.

"Ah, hello, Mrs. Thompson," he said, forcing a smile. "Enjoying the sunset?"

"Indeed," she replied, her eyes never leaving the vibrant colors of the sky. "There's something about it that just quiets the soul, don't you think?"

"Absolutely," agreed Edward, his mind already returning to the task at hand. "But if you'll excuse me, I have some business to attend to."

"Of course, dear," she said, waving him off. "Have a good evening."

"Thank you," he replied, moving swiftly towards the bushes near the base of the lifeguard tower. The shadows had deepened, providing perfect cover as he crouched down, his gaze locked on Mia's approaching form.

"Almost there," he whispered, his fingers tightening around the handle of the knife he'd brought along. "Just a little closer."

"Remember, Edward," he thought, his heart pounding in anticipation. "Control is everything. Savor the moment, but don't let it consume you."

Mia's footsteps grew nearer, her face illuminated by the last rays of sunlight. Edward could see the serenity in her eyes as she strolled along the beach, completely unaware of the danger lurking just a few feet away.

"Perfect," he whispered, his pulse racing. "Now, it's time to claim what's rightfully mine."

The setting sun cast an eerie glow on the ocean, painting the waves in shades of blood and fire. Edward's heart pounded in his chest as he watched Mia stroll along the shoreline from his hiding spot among the tall sea oats. Her long brown hair danced in the breeze, and she seemed lost in thought, her eyes gazing at the horizon.

"Beautiful, isn't she?" Edward whispered to himself, a sinister smile playing across his lips. "But so vulnerable."

He observed her every move, noting how she paused occasionally to admire the shells and seaweed that had washed ashore. She appeared to be completely alone, an easy target for his carefully laid plan.

"Keep walking, my dear," he urged silently, his fingers drumming impatiently against his thigh. "Just a bit further now."

As Mia drew closer to the predetermined location, Edward felt the tension build inside him like a coiled spring. He knew it wouldn't be long before he'd have her all to himself, and the anticipation thrilled him.

"Control yourself," he admonished internally. "You've waited this long; you can wait a bit longer."

Mia stopped suddenly; her attention caught by something in the sand. She bent down and picked up a small, delicate seashell, turning it over in her hands with a soft smile.

"Ah, an artist's eye," Edward mused, admiring her appreciation for the simple beauty of nature. "Such a shame that her talent will go to waste."

"Everything will go according to plan," he reassured himself, watching intently as Mia resumed her walk, drawing ever nearer to his trap. "She'll never see it coming."

"Almost there," he whispered, feeling the adrenaline surge through his veins. "Just a few more steps..."

His breath hitched as Mia reached the spot he'd chosen for their encounter, her demeanor still innocent and unsuspecting.

"Let the games begin," Edward thought, a wicked grin spreading across his face. And with that, he prepared to make his move.

The golden sun dipped closer to the horizon, casting long shadows that crept over the sand like grasping fingers. Mia's footsteps traced a winding path along the shoreline, her thoughts drifting peacefully with the ebbing tide. She was oblivious to the sinister figure lurking in the nearby dunes, his presence camouflaged by the deepening twilight.

"Patience," Edward reminded himself, feeling an unnerving blend of excitement and malice warping his features as he watched Mia from the darkness. He knew this moment had been meticulously orchestrated, and now it was finally time to strike.

"Beautiful evening, isn't it?" Edward stepped out from behind a clump of seagrass, his voice smooth and disarming.

Mia jumped in surprise, her hand instinctively gripping the strap of her bag. "Oh! I didn't see you there. Yes, it's lovely."

"Forgive me for startling you," Edward replied, his tone dripping with feigned concern. "I just couldn't help but notice how serene you looked, walking all by yourself."

"Thank you," Mia said hesitantly, her intuition warning her that something was off about this man. "I enjoy these solitary walks."

"Solitude can be a double-edged sword," Edward mused, taking a step closer. His eyes locked onto hers, searching for any signs of weakness. "It grants us peace yet leaves us vulnerable."

"Vulnerable?" Mia repeated, her heart rate quickening as she felt the undercurrents of tension in the air.

"Indeed," Edward responded, closing the distance between them. "One never knows what dangers may be lurking in the shadows."

As he spoke those words, Mia's instincts screamed at her to run, but her legs refused to obey. She was rooted to the spot, caught in the predatory gaze of a man whose intentions were far from benign.

"Please," she stammered, her voice barely a whisper. "I don't want any trouble."

"Trouble?" Edward feigned innocence, his eyes glinting with malicious intent. "Oh, my dear, you misunderstand me. I simply wish to offer some... advice."

"Advice?" Mia's heart pounded in her chest, her fear mounting with each passing second.

"Indeed," Edward said, his grin widening as he leaned in closer. "You see, there are those who would exploit your vulnerability, prey upon your kindness. It's a cruel world, and one must always be on guard."

With that, Edward reached out, his fingers brushing against the delicate curve of Mia's jawline. Her breath hitched, the chilling touch sending shivers down her spine.

"Wh-what are you doing?" she managed to choke out, her eyes wide with terror.

"Merely offering a warning, my dear," Edward replied, his voice low and menacing. "For there are far worse things out here than the darkness itself."

As his grip tightened around her wrist, Mia's mind raced, searching for a way to escape the nightmare unfolding before her. But before she could react, Edward pulled her close, his hot breath on her neck as he whispered, "Now, let's see what kind of artist you truly are."

In that instant, the world seemed to hold its breath, waiting for the outcome of this twisted encounter. The sun dipped below the horizon, plunging them both into darkness.

CHAPTER 10

The Chilling Deception

The dim flicker of a dying fluorescent light cast an eerie glow over the otherwise dark and empty police station. Samantha Kingsley, her eyes puffy from reading through countless case files, sat hunched over her desk. The weight of the unsolved murders in their city bore down on her shoulders, threatening to crush her once indomitable spirit.

"Damn it," she muttered under her breath, rubbing her tired eyes. Her hands trembled slightly as they reached for another file, the gruesome details of yet another life taken far too soon. "Why can't I find anything?"

Samantha's brow furrowed with concern as she scanned the pages before her. Each piece of evidence, every witness statement, seemed only to add to the growing mountain of chaos that loomed over her. It was as if the killer was taunting her from the shadows, daring her to venture further into the abyss.

"Chief?" A voice called out from the darkness, jolting Samantha from her thoughts.

"Detective Thompson, what are you doing here so late?" she asked, trying to mask the unease in her voice.

"Couldn't sleep, Chief. Thought I'd come in and see if there were any new leads on the case." Daniel Thompson, a seasoned detective with years of experience under his belt, approached Samantha's desk cautiously. His eyes narrowed in curiosity as he noticed the stacks of files surrounding her.

"Find anything interesting?" He inquired, leaning against the edge of the desk.

"Actually, yes." Samantha hesitated for a moment, unsure if she should share her findings just yet. But Daniel was a trusted colleague, and she needed someone to bounce ideas off of. "I've been noticing some similarities in the victims' profiles and the locations where their bodies were found."

"Really? What kind of similarities?" Daniel asked, his interest piqued.

"Most of the victims were young women, all found in or around vacation homes in the city. And it looks like they were all strangled." Samantha sighed, rubbing her temples as she struggled to make sense of the information.

"Strange," Daniel mused, his eyes fixed on the files before him. "Could be a coincidence, but it's worth looking into."

"Agreed," Samantha replied, her resolve strengthened by Daniel's support. "I'm going to keep digging, see if I can find any more connections."

"Good luck, Chief. If you need any help, just let me know." With that, Daniel retreated into the shadows, leaving Samantha to grapple with the horrifying implications of her discovery.

The silence of the police station seemed to close in around her, suffocating her thoughts and clouding her judgment. But Samantha knew she couldn't afford to lose focus now. The answers were out there, hidden amidst the chaos.

As she continued to pore over the files, a cold dread began to seep into her bones. The truth was drawing closer, its icy fingers reaching out for her, threatening to ensnare her in its merciless grasp.

Samantha stared at the map of crime scenes pinned to the wall, her heart pounding like a metronome in her chest. Cold sweat dripped down her brow as she realized that all the properties were owned by her husband, Edward Kingsley.

"Chief? You alright?" Officer Jenkins asked, his voice filled with concern.

"Fine," she lied, forcing a smile. "Just working on something important."

"Let me know if you need any help," he offered before returning to his desk.

"Thank you, Jenkins," she whispered, her voice barely audible even to herself.

Samantha turned back to the files and began to discreetly gather more information about the rental properties and their tenants. Her fingers trembled as she flipped through pages, struggling to find any connections or suspicious activities.

"Edward wouldn't do this... would he?" she wondered silently, her thoughts plagued by disbelief and horror. "We've been married for years, and I've never suspected anything like this."

"Hey, Chief, you still digging into those cases?" Detective Daniel Thompson asked as he approached her desk.

"Daniel, I need you to check something for me," Samantha said, her voice shaking with urgency. "These unsolved murders... they're all connected to my husband's rental properties."

"Are you sure?" Daniel asked, his eyes widening in shock.

"Look at the locations, the victims' profiles... it's too much of a coincidence," she replied, her voice wavering. "I need to know if there's anything else we've missed."

"Alright, Chief. I'll dig deeper," Daniel agreed, his expression serious and determined.

"Thank you, Daniel," Samantha whispered, feeling a surge of gratitude and relief. At least she wasn't alone in her suspicions.

As the hours passed, Samantha continued to sift through the files, her mind clouded by a storm of fear and doubt. The image of Edward's face haunted her, the warmth of his embrace now a chilling reminder of the secrets that might lie beneath his charming exterior.

"Focus, Samantha," she scolded herself, her grip on the files tightening like a vice. "You're a police officer first, and a wife second. You need to find the truth, no matter how painful it may be."

And with that grim determination, Samantha Kingsley descended further into the darkness, each step bringing her closer to the horrifying truth hidden within her own home.

The dim glow of a streetlight outside the rental property cast eerie shadows against the living room wall. Samantha Kingsley crouched behind the window, her pulse pounding in her ears as she watched her husband Edward approach the front door.

"Edward, what are you doing here?" she whispered to herself, her mind racing with fear and confusion. The timestamp on the surveillance footage she had acquired was undeniable – he was entering these properties during odd hours, long after any respectable landlord should have been asleep.

As she watched him fumble with his keys, Samantha couldn't help but wonder if this was just another maintenance visit, or something far more sinister. Her instincts as a police chief screamed that something was amiss, yet the woman who loved him desperately clung to the hope that there was a reasonable explanation.

"Enough," Samantha muttered under her breath, determination flooding her veins. She needed answers.

As Edward stepped inside, Samantha followed, her heart pounding like a drumbeat in her chest. The floorboards creaked beneath her feet, sending shivers down her spine as she made her way towards her husband.

"Edward?" she called out, her voice trembling ever so slightly.

Edward jumped, visibly startled by her presence. "Samantha? What are you doing here?"

"Isn't that my question to ask?" she countered, her eyes narrowing. "I've been reviewing security footage from your rental properties. You've been coming here late at night, claiming it's for maintenance."

"Of course," Edward replied smoothly, his charming smile slipping into place like a well-worn mask. "I'm just trying to be diligent in managing my business."

"Doing maintenance after midnight doesn't strike you as suspicious?" Samantha pressed, her gut twisting as she struggled to maintain her composure.

"Tenants appreciate that I don't interrupt their day with repairs," Edward explained, his eyes never leaving hers. "Besides, it's not illegal to work late, is it?"

"Edward, I'm worried about you," Samantha admitted, her voice cracking with emotion. "These visits... they coincide with the unsolved murders in our city."

"Are you accusing me of being involved?" Edward asked, his tone icy and defensive.

"Of course not," she lied, her heart shattering beneath the weight of her own words. "I just... I need to know that you're okay."

"Trust me, Samantha," Edward said, his voice softening. "I promise, there's nothing to worry about."

As she stared into his eyes, searching for any trace of deceit, Samantha couldn't help but feel a chill run down her spine. Her husband, the man she had loved and trusted for so long, was hiding something – something dark and twisted.

And she would do whatever it took to uncover the truth.

A shiver crept down Samantha's spine as she gazed at the moonlit rental property, the shadows dancing like ghosts across its facade. She knew that something was wrong, despite Edward's insistence that everything was fine. With every fiber of her being, Samantha knew that there was a dark secret lurking beneath the surface – and she would do whatever it took to uncover it.

"Mrs. Thompson?" Samantha called out softly as she knocked on the door of one of the tenants. The door creaked open, revealing an elderly woman with a warm smile. "I'm sorry to disturb you so late, but I was hoping to ask you a few questions about Edward Kingsley, your landlord."

"Of course, dear," Mrs. Thompson replied, her voice gentle and welcoming. "Come in, please."

"Thank you," Samantha said, stepping into the dimly lit living room. As she settled onto the worn couch, she couldn't help but feel a sense of unease, as though danger lurked just around the corner.

"Has Edward ever acted strangely towards you or any of the other tenants?" Samantha asked, trying to keep her voice steady.

"Strangely? No, not really," Mrs. Thompson said, furrowing her brow. "He's always been very polite and attentive. Why do you ask?"

"Have you noticed him visiting the property during odd hours, perhaps late at night?" Samantha pressed, her heart pounding in anticipation of the answer.

"Late at night? Well, now that you mention it, I did hear some noise outside my window one evening. It must have been around midnight," Mrs. Thompson recalled, her eyes narrowing. "When I looked out, I saw Edward entering another tenant's unit. He had a toolbox with him, so I assumed he was fixing something."

"Did he say anything to you about it afterward?" Samantha questioned, her mind racing with the implications of this new information.

"No," Mrs. Thompson admitted, shaking her head. "But like I said, he's always been very diligent about maintaining the property, so I didn't think much of it at the time."

"Thank you, Mrs. Thompson. You've been very helpful," Samantha said, forcing a smile. As she left the apartment, her thoughts were consumed by the chilling realization that her husband's late-night visits were more than just coincidences. They were a pattern – a terrifying connection to the unsolved murders that haunted her city.

Samantha spoke with several other tenants, each echoing similar sentiments about Edward's odd hours and seemingly innocent explanations. The weight of suspicion grew heavier with each conversation, crushing Samantha's spirit beneath its oppressive mass.

She leaned against the car; her breathing ragged as her mind raced with the grim possibilities. Every instinct screamed that something was wrong, but she needed concrete evidence before she could act. With a steely resolve, Samantha decided that she would uncover the truth, no matter the cost.

And with each step closer to the truth, she felt herself descending deeper into a nightmare from which there could be no escape.

The sun dipped below the horizon, casting ominous shadows over the once-vibrant tropical paradise. Samantha approached the door of Emily's first-floor apartment, her heart pounding in anticipation. The oppressive Florida heat mingled with the weight of her unspoken fears, forming beads of sweat that trickled down her brow.

"Who is it?" a timid voice called out as Samantha knocked on the door.

"Hi, Emily," Samantha replied, forcing a smile into her voice. "It's Chief Kingsley. I just wanted to have a quick chat."

There was a pause, and then the click of the deadbolt sliding back. The door opened slowly, revealing a young woman with wide, frightened eyes and sun-bleached hair. "Hello, Chief," Emily said nervously, her gaze flicking to the badge clipped to Samantha's belt. "What can I help you with?"

"Have you ever noticed my husband, Edward, visiting the property at odd hours?" Samantha asked, getting straight to the point. She tried to keep her tone casual, but there was an undercurrent of urgency she couldn't hide.

"Um, well, yeah," Emily stammered, glancing around nervously.

"There was this one time... I saw him outside late at night. He was just standing there, watching me through my window. It creeped me out."

Samantha's pulse raced as Emily's description echoed the chilling pattern of behavior exhibited by the killer in the unsolved murder cases. Her blood ran cold, and her mind reeled with the implications.

"Did he say anything to you or approach your apartment?" Samantha inquired, struggling to maintain her composure.

"No," Emily whispered, shaking her head. "He didn't come any closer. He just stood there for a while, and then he left."

"Thank you, Emily," Samantha said, her voice barely audible. "You've been very helpful." She turned to leave, feeling the walls of her world closing in around her as the darkness of the night enveloped her.

As she walked back to her car, Samantha's thoughts tumbled like a raging storm. The pieces were falling into place, painting a sinister portrait of the man she thought she knew. But despite the mounting evidence, Samantha knew she couldn't act without concrete proof. Her duty as a police officer and her love for Edward waged war on her, threatening to tear her apart.

"Can I do this?" she whispered to herself, her resolve wavering. "Can I bring down the man I love?"

She clenched her fists, determination flooding her veins. The truth would come to light, no matter the cost. And in that moment, she resolved to see this nightmare through to its bitter end.

The moon hung low in the sky, casting a haunting glow over the

Kingsley residence. The wind whispered through the trees as Samantha sat alone in her dimly lit office, a stack of case files spread out before her. She took a deep breath and began to sift through the grisly details, her instincts driving her to find the elusive truth.

"Victim one – strangled, found on Kingsley property number six," she muttered under her breath. "Victim two – stabbed, discovered in the woods behind property twelve." The list went on, each victim's fate echoing the same gruesome pattern. As the connections became clearer, Samantha felt her heart clench with dread.

"Edward," she whispered, his name tasting like poison on her tongue. "Could it be him?"

"Sam?" Edward's voice called from the hallway, a shadow appearing in the doorway. She hastily closed the files, feigning calmness as she turned to face her husband.

"Edward, I didn't hear you come in," she said, hoping her voice didn't betray her inner turmoil. "How was your day?"

"Long," he sighed, walking further into the room. "I had to check on some repairs at one of the properties. But enough about me, how was your day, sweetheart?"

"Fine. Just the usual," she replied, her mind racing as she tried to maintain her composure. Despite her growing suspicions, confronting him directly would only jeopardize her investigation.

"Sam, is everything okay? You seem...distressed," Edward asked, his eyes narrowing with concern.

"Everything's fine," Samantha assured him, forcing a smile. "Just a lot on my mind."

"Alright, if you say so," Edward replied, unconvinced but not pressing further. He leaned down to give her a brief kiss on the forehead before retreating from the room.

As soon as he was gone, Samantha's thoughts turned dark once more. Her loyalty to the law and her love for Edward clashed violently within her, tearing at her very soul. The thought of accusing her husband of such heinous crimes was unbearable, but she could not ignore the mounting evidence.

"First, I need proof," Samantha thought, her mind racing with determination. "Concrete evidence before I can act."

In her heart, she knew that justice must prevail, no matter the cost. But for now, she would have to walk a tightrope between her duty and her love, praying that she wouldn't lose herself in the process.

Samantha's fingers trembled as she dialed Detective Daniel Thompson's number, the weight of her suspicions threatening to suffocate her. She took a deep breath, steadying herself before he picked up.

"Thompson speaking," the detective answered, his voice crisp and professional.

"Daniel, it's Samantha," she whispered, glancing around to ensure that Edward was still out of earshot. "I need your help."

"Of course, Chief. What can I do for you?" Daniel replied, his tone shifting to one of genuine concern.

"Meet me at the Blue Moon Café in an hour. This...this can't be discussed over the phone," she said, her voice cracking with the strain of keeping her emotions in check.

"Understood. I'll be there," Daniel responded, sensing the urgency in her voice.

Samantha hung up, her heart pounding in her chest. As much as she hated involving someone else in her nightmare, she knew she couldn't navigate this treacherous path alone.

Samantha sat in a dimly lit corner booth of the café, anxiously sipping her coffee as she waited for Daniel. The tension in her body was palpable, every nerve on high alert.

"Sam?" Daniel approached; his brow furrowed with worry as he took in her haggard appearance. He slid into the seat across from her. "You look like hell. What's going on?"

"Promise me, whatever I say here doesn't leave this table," Samantha began, her eyes pleading for understanding.

"Of course," Daniel assured her, his expression serious.

With a heavy sigh, Samantha relayed her suspicions about Edward's potential involvement in the unsolved murders, watching Daniel's face contort with disbelief and horror. When she finished, they sat in silence for a moment, both grappling with the implications of what she'd just revealed.

"Sam, I..." Daniel stammered, struggling to find the right words. "I can't even imagine what you're going through right now."

"Neither can I," Samantha admitted, her eyes glistening with unshed tears. "But I need your help, Daniel. If my suspicions are right, we need to stop him before he hurts anyone else."

"Alright," Daniel agreed, his resolve hardening. "What do you need me to do?"

"Help me gather evidence. I want to set up surveillance on the rental properties, see if we can catch him in the act or find anything incriminating," Samantha proposed, her voice laced with determination.

"Consider it done," Daniel assured her, his hand reaching across the table to give her a reassuring squeeze. "We'll get to the bottom of this, Sam. Together."

"Thank you," she whispered, her heart heavy but bolstered by Daniel's unwavering support. As they began to devise their plan, Samantha couldn't help but fear the truth that lay waiting for them, lurking in the shadows like a malevolent specter.

The dim light of the police station cast eerie shadows on the walls as Samantha stared at the evidence board, her uneasiness intensifying with each passing second. The web of connections she'd uncovered weighed heavily upon her, and the reality of the situation seeped into every fiber of her being like a malevolent poison.

"Sam." Daniel's voice broke through her thoughts, his eyes filled with concern. "We've got everything set up for surveillance. We'll start monitoring the properties tonight."

"Thank you, Daniel," she replied, her voice barely above a whisper. She knew that without his unwavering support, she would be completely lost in this terrifying endeavor.

"Are you sure you're okay with all of this?" he asked, his hand resting briefly on her shoulder before retreating. "I know it's a lot to process."

"I don't have a choice," Samantha said, her jaw set with determination. "If Edward is responsible for these murders, then I owe it to the victims and their families to see this through. I swore an oath to protect and serve, and I won't let personal feelings get in the way of justice."

Daniel nodded solemnly. "Alright. Just remember, I'm here for you, Sam—every step of the way."

Samantha mustered a small smile, grateful for Daniel's presence in this dark hour. As they exited her office and made their way down the deserted hallway, she couldn't help but let her thoughts drift back to Edward, the man she had known and loved for so many years. Was it possible that beneath his affectionate facade lurked a monster capable of such heinous acts?

Her heart clenched as she pondered the possibility, her pulse quickening with each horrifying thought. The memories of their life together felt tainted now, marred by the specter of doubt and betrayal. No matter the outcome, Samantha knew that their lives would never be the same again.

"Daniel," she said, her voice cracking slightly as they reached the door leading to the parking lot. "I'm scared."

"Me too, Sam," he admitted, his eyes mirroring the fear and

uncertainty she felt within herself. "But we're in this together. And no matter what happens, I'll have your back."

"Thank you." The words were small and fragile, but they held a world of gratitude.

As they stepped out into the cold night, Samantha steeled herself for the dangerous path she was about to embark on. Fueled by her unwavering commitment to justice and haunted by the ghosts of the victims, she vowed to uncover the truth, no matter how dark or twisted it may be. There would be no turning back now—the hunt for answers had begun.

CHAPTER 11

Love's Deception

The flickering fluorescent light cast an eerie glow over the room, casting long shadows that seemed to dance on the walls. Samantha Kingsley sat at her desk in the dimly lit police station, her brow furrowed in determination as she poured over the files of unsolved murders that littered her workspace. Her short brown hair framed her face, a mask of steely focus as she searched for any clue that might lead her closer to the killer terrorizing her city.

"Chief Kingsley, any progress on the case?" asked Detective Andrews, his voice tinged with concern. He stood in the doorway, observing her intense concentration.

Samantha looked up briefly, her eyes meeting his. "Not yet, but I won't rest until we find this monster."

"Good luck, Chief," he said with a nod, before disappearing back into the bustling station.

Returning her attention to the files, she flipped through pages of crime scene photos and witness statements, seeking anything that might connect the victims. As she sifted through the documents, she noticed a familiar name - Edward Kingsley, her husband - listed as the owner of several rental properties in the city. She knew Edward's business was successful, but the extent of his property holdings was surprising.

"Edward…" she whispered under her breath, a cold shiver running down her spine. The coincidence was chilling, and her instincts as a seasoned investigator told her there was more to this than met the eye. But how could her loving husband, the man she had built a life with, be involved in something so sinister?

She shook her head, trying to dispel the dark thoughts creeping into her mind. Samantha couldn't afford to let her personal feelings cloud her judgment; she had a duty to uphold the law and protect her city from further harm. Gingerly, she traced the edges of the photographs, her mind racing as she sought to unravel this twisted puzzle.

"Chief, you've been working non-stop," said Officer Ramirez, a young woman with bright eyes and an eager expression. "Do you need anything? Coffee, maybe?"

"Thanks, Ramirez, but I'm fine. I need to stay focused on this case," Samantha replied tersely, her voice betraying her growing frustration.

"Understood. Let us know if you need anything," said Ramirez, understanding the gravity of the situation.

As she left the room, Samantha's gaze returned to the files in front of her, the name 'Edward Kingsley' seeming to mock her from the pages.

Her thoughts were consumed by the implications of this discovery, each new piece of information adding weight to the burden she carried.

"Edward, what have you done?" she murmured, her heart heavy with dread. There was no turning back now; she would follow the evidence wherever it led, even if it meant confronting the darkest corners of her world.

Samantha's heart hammered in her chest, the rhythmic pounding echoing through the narrow corridors of her mind. Edward's name, scrawled across the files before her, bore down on her like a haunting specter. As she stared at the inked letters, memories of his recent strange behavior flooded her consciousness – late nights spent away from home, hushed phone calls that seized the moment she entered the room.

"Sam?" Officer Daniels' voice cut through the fog in her mind. "You, okay? You look a bit shaken."

"Fine," she managed to choke out, her jaw clenched tight. "I just... I'm not sure what to make of all this."

"Hey, we're going to figure this out." Daniels' words were meant to be reassuring, but they felt hollow to Samantha's ears. He couldn't know the truth lurking beneath the surface, the darkness threatening to consume them both.

She forced herself to focus, pushing aside thoughts of Edward and their life together. She had to dig deeper and examine every facet of his background for any connections to the victims or suspicious activities. As chief of police, it was her duty to uncover the truth, no matter how painful it might be.

"Right," she said, taking a deep breath. "Daniels, I want you to pull up everything you can find on Edward Kingsley. Business records, financial statements, anything that might show a connection to these properties or the victims."

"Edward Kingsley?" Daniels frowned; concern etched into his features. "That's... your husband, right?"

"Listen to me." Samantha leveled her gaze at him, steeling herself against the storm of emotions raging within. "I need to know if there's something more going on here. It's my job to protect this city, and I can't let personal feelings stand in the way of that."

"Understood, Chief." Daniels nodded; his expression resolute. "I'll get on it right away."

"Thank you," Samantha whispered, the words heavy with unspoken regret.

As Daniels began his search, Samantha turned back to the files before her, her mind swirling with a maelstrom of fear and uncertainty. The man she loved, the one she'd built a life with – could he truly be capable of such monstrous acts? She had to know, and yet part of her recoiled at the very thought, fearing what terrible truths might lie hidden beneath the veneer of their seemingly idyllic existence.

"Stay focused," she muttered to herself, clenching her fists until her knuckles turned white. "You're a damn good cop, Samantha Kingsley. You can handle this."

But as she delved deeper into Edward's background, she couldn't shake the growing sense of dread that gripped her heart, squeezing it tight like the icy fingers of death itself.

Samantha's eyes darted around the dimly lit room, ensuring no one was near as she settled at her workstation. Her heart pounded in her chest, each beat echoing with a fierce urgency – a siren's call that demanded answers. She couldn't shake the gnawing suspicion that had taken root in her mind; she needed to know if Edward was involved in the unsolved murders plaguing their city.

"Damn it, Ed," she whispered under her breath, her fingers trembling as they danced over the keyboard. "Please let me be wrong about this."

She accessed the police database, her movements swift and precise. Time was of the essence; the fewer eyes on her, the better. Samantha entered Edward's name into the search bar and then navigated to his property records. She knew his success as a rental property owner in Florida had granted them a luxurious life, but now she needed to determine if it was tainted by something far more sinister.

"Come on, come on," she urged herself, scanning the digital files for any irregularities. As her eyes flitted across the screen, she stumbled upon an anomaly – a hidden compartment masked within the depths of the records.

"Gotcha," she breathed, her pulse quickening as she clicked on the concealed link.

The contents of the hidden compartment appeared on her monitor, and Samantha's breath hitched in her throat. There, displayed before her, were photographs of the victims – faces twisted in pain and terror, their lifeless eyes staring back at her, accusingly. The images were accompanied by detailed notes on the victims' lives, scribbled in Edward's familiar handwriting.

"God, no," Samantha choked out, the weight of her discovery pressing down upon her like a crushing vice. A cold sweat broke out on her brow, and her heart slammed against her ribcage, threatening to shatter her from the inside out.

"Chief?" a voice called out from behind her, causing Samantha to jump in fright. She quickly minimized the screen, composing herself as she turned to face Officer Daniels.

"Is everything all right?" he asked cautiously, his brow furrowed with concern.

"Everything's fine, Daniels," she replied, forcing a smile that felt like a betrayal of the turmoil churning within her. "Just following up on a lead."

"Let me know if you need any assistance," he offered, nodding respectfully before returning to his work.

"Thank you, Daniels," Samantha murmured, barely able to keep the tremor from her voice.

With a deep breath, she reopened the hidden compartment, her mind racing as she struggled to process the horrifying implications of her discovery. Samantha knew she had to tread carefully, for the man she loved now held the power to destroy not just himself, but her and the very city she had sworn to protect.

The dimly lit office cast eerie shadows around Samantha as she stared at the screen, her hands trembling with the weight of her revelation. A chilling silence enveloped her, broken only by the hum of the computer and the distant echoes of footsteps in the hallways.

"Edward," she whispered, disbelief lacing her voice. "How could you?"

Her thoughts flickered like a faulty light bulb between the man she loved and the monster he had become. The sound of his laughter filled her memories, contrasting sharply with the gruesome images on the screen. She wondered how she could have laid beside him every night, never suspecting the darkness that festered within.

"Chief Kingsley?" Officer Daniels called out from behind her once more, knocking on the doorframe before entering the room. "Sorry to bother you again, but we've got an update on the Jane Doe from last week."

"Go ahead, Daniels," Samantha managed, her voice barely audible, still locked in a battle between her heart and her duty.

"Turns out she wasn't a tourist after all," he said, handing over a sheet of paper with the victim's information. "Lived right here in town. We found her address in the system."

"Thank you, Daniels," Samantha replied, forcing herself to focus on the task at hand. As she scanned the report, her mind raced with a thousand questions, each one clawing at her sanity like a desperate animal.

"Something doesn't add up," she thought, her eyes narrowing in determination. "I need to dig deeper, find out what Edward's been hiding."

"Is there anything else we should look into, Chief?" Daniels asked, sensing her unease.

"Keep following this lead," she instructed her voice steady and authoritative despite the whirlwind of emotions raging within her. "And keep me updated on any new developments."

"Understood," Daniels nodded, leaving the room with a sense of urgency.

Alone once more, Samantha's thoughts spiraled out of control. Her love for Edward warred with her commitment to her duty and the safety of the citizens she had sworn to protect.

"Can I arrest my husband?" she wondered, a tear sliding down her cheek. The question hung in the air like a heavy fog, suffocating her with its cruel reality.

"Damn it!" she hissed, slamming her fist on the desk. "I have no choice. He's a killer. I must uphold the law."

Gathering her resolve, Samantha wiped away the tears that threatened to betray her, steeling herself for the unimaginable task ahead. As she prepared to confront the man she loved, she knew that her life would never be the same.

"Edward," she whispered once more, her voice a mixture of sorrow and determination, "I will find the truth, and I will stop you."

A single tear slipped down Samantha's cheek as she stared at the incriminating evidence laid out before her. Memories of laughter and love played like a cruel movie in her mind, taunting her with the stark contrast between who she believed Edward to be and the monster that lurked beneath his charming facade.

"Remember our honeymoon in Paris?" she whispered to herself, voice breaking. "The way you held me under the Eiffel Tower, promising me the world... How could I have been so blind?"

"Chief, are you alright?" Officer Daniels asked hesitantly from the doorway, concern evident in his tone.

"Fine," she replied quickly, wiping away her tears and forcing herself back into her authoritative role. "Just going through some difficult memories."

"Understood," Daniels nodded sympathetically, giving her a moment to regain her composure before he continued. "Is there anything else we should look into, Chief?"

"I've got it from here, Daniels," Samantha assured him, her voice betraying the turmoil within her. "You've done enough for now."

"Alright, Chief. Let me know if you need anything," Daniels said, exiting the room and leaving Samantha alone with her thoughts once more.

"More evidence," she muttered, her heart heavy with dread. "I need more evidence before I can confront him."

Samantha's hands shook as she reached for the photographs, her fingers tracing the faces of the victims Edward had so meticulously documented. She forced herself to focus on the task at hand, fighting back fresh waves of nausea and anger.

"Damn you, Edward," she thought as she fed the photographs into the copier, the machine wordlessly duplicating the shocking images. "How many lives have you destroyed? How many people have you betrayed?"

As the final image emerged from the copier, Samantha slowly gathered the stack of copies, careful not to leave any trace of her actions behind.

"Every step I take, every piece of evidence I uncover, brings me closer to the truth," she told herself, determination flaring within her. "I will see you brought to justice, Edward, no matter what it takes."

With a heavy heart, Samantha tucked the copies into a secure folder, her mind consumed by the weight of her discovery and the difficult choices she would soon have to make. The air in the room felt thick, suffocating, as she steeled herself for the harrowing journey that lay ahead.

"Edward," she whispered, her voice barely audible, "I loved you. But now... now I must stop you."

Samantha's heart pounded relentlessly in her chest as she surveyed the evidence before her. The cold steel of the safe loomed ominously, a constant reminder of the treacherous path that lay ahead. Each photograph and note felt like a leaden weight in her hands, dragging her further into the abyss.

"Get a grip, Samantha," she muttered, her voice barely audible.

"You're the chief of police, for God's sake. You can handle this."

She inhaled deeply, forcing herself to focus as she carefully arranged the copied documents within the safe. The smooth metal felt icy against her fingertips, sending shivers down her spine.

"Edward must never know what I've found," she whispered, her breath fogging up the combination lock. "Not until I'm ready to confront him. Not until I have everything I need."

Closing the safe with a decisive click, Samantha pressed her forehead against its cold surface, the gravity of her discovery sinking in.

"God help me," she murmured, her thoughts a swirling storm of fear and doubt. "What have I gotten myself into?"

As she stood there, images of Edward flickered through her mind – his charming smile, the warmth of his embrace, the sound of his laughter filling their home. How could such darkness lurk beneath that loving facade?

"Was it all just an act?" she wondered, her throat tightening with emotion. "Or is there still some shred of the man I thought I knew?"

Her heart raced as she considered the implications of her discovery. Edward was not only a danger to others but also to her own life and career. If word got out that she had been married to a serial killer for years without realizing it, her reputation would be forever tarnished.

"I can't let that happen," she resolved, determination hardening within her. "I won't let Edward destroy any more lives, including my own."

"Chief Kingsley?" came a voice from the door, snapping Samantha back to reality. It was Officer Daniels, his face etched with concern.

"Is everything alright?" he asked cautiously, eyeing the safe, but unable to see its contents.

"Everything's under control, Daniels," Samantha replied, her voice steady despite the turmoil within her. "I'm just working on something... personal."

"Understood, Chief," Daniels nodded, sensing her need for privacy. "If you need anything, just let me know."

"Thank you, Daniels," she said, offering him a tight-lipped smile. As the door closed behind him, Samantha exhaled slowly, her thoughts returning to the difficult road that lay ahead.

"Edward," she whispered, her eyes narrowing with resolve, "your reign of terror ends here. And I will be the one to stop you."

The flickering fluorescent lights overhead cast a harsh glow on the battered desk, papers strewn about like leaves in an autumn storm. Samantha's hands trembled as she clenched them into fists, her knuckles whitening under the strain. The air was thick with the oppressive weight of her decision, the room silent save for the hum of the lights and the ragged sound of her breathing.

"Edward," she whispered, her voice cracking with the gravity of her choice. "I can't let you do this anymore."

Her chest heaved with each deep breath as if the mere act of drawing air was a battle. "No matter what it costs me," she thought, "I must bring him to justice." She could feel the crushing responsibility bearing down upon her shoulders, the weight of lives lost, and futures destroyed.

"Chief Kingsley," came a voice from the doorway, breaking through the haze of her thoughts. It was Officer Daniels, his brow furrowed with concern. "Are you sure everything's alright?"

Samantha looked up, her face a mask of determination. "Yes, Daniels. I'm fine. Please, close the door behind you."

"Understood, Chief," he replied hesitantly, stepping back and allowing the door to swing shut.

As the latch clicked softly into place, Samantha turned her attention back to the file on her desk. The photographs of the victims stared back at her, their eyes pleading for justice even in death. "You won't be forgotten," she vowed silently, anger and sorrow mingling in her heart.

"Edward, my love," she thought, her mind filled with memories of happier times – laughter shared, secrets whispered, passion ignited. "How could you hide such darkness within you? How did I not see it sooner?"

But there was no time for regret or recrimination now. She had a duty to the people she had sworn to protect, a responsibility to see that no more innocent lives were shattered by her husband's twisted desires.

"May God have mercy on your soul, Edward," she murmured, closing the file with a decisive snap. "For I must do what must be done."

Her resolve solidified, Samantha rose from her chair, feeling the weight of her decision settle heavily upon her. There was no turning back now, no room for doubt or uncertainty. She would confront her husband and put an end to his reign of terror, whatever the cost may be.

"Justice will be served," she promised the silent room, her voice firm and unwavering. "I will make sure of it."

Rain pelted the city streets, the droplets reflecting in the amber glow of streetlights as they streaked down the windows of the police station. Samantha stood at the exit, her hand gripping the door handle tightly. She glanced back over her shoulder, scanning the room to ensure no one was watching her departure.

"Chief Kingsley," called Officer Reynolds from his desk. "Heading home?"

"Uh, yes," Samantha replied, her voice betraying a hint of unease. "It's been a long day."

"Be careful out there, Chief," he said with genuine concern. "The storm isn't letting up anytime soon."

"Thank you, Officer." Samantha mustered a tight-lipped smile before stepping out into the torrential rain, the door closing behind her with a definitive thud.

As she walked towards her car, her heels splashing in the growing puddles, Samantha's mind raced with thoughts of Edward. How could the man she had loved for so many years be capable of such atrocities? The icy rain seeped through the fabric of her coat, chilling her to the bone, but it did little to quell the fire that raged within her. She had vowed to protect and serve this city, and now that very vow demanded she bring her husband to justice.

"God damn you, Edward" she whispered, her voice barely audible beneath the relentless drumming of raindrops. "Why did you become this monster?"

Her fingers clenched around the keys in her pocket, cold and slick like the rain-drenched metal of her car door. As she slid behind the wheel, the car's interior light casting an eerie glow on her anguished face, Samantha grappled with the task that lay ahead.

"Justice first," she muttered, her hands gripping the steering wheel tightly. "I cannot let my feelings cloud my judgment."

With a determined nod, Samantha started the engine and pulled away from the curb. The city streets stretched out before her like a dark labyrinth, a twisted path that would lead her to confront the man she had once believed to be her soulmate. There was no turning back now.

"May you find redemption, Edward," she whispered into the night, her voice laced with sorrow and resolve. "But first, you must face your sins."

CHAPTER 12

Dive in the Dark

The sound of shattering glass echoed through the dimly lit hallway, violently pulling Edward back into his past. He was seven years old again, standing at the foot of the stairs, trembling with fear. His tiny hands clutched the railing, knuckles white, as the chaos unfolded before him.

"William, you bastard!" his mother screamed, her voice shrill and desperate. She hurled a vase at his father's head, narrowly missing him.

"Shut up, woman!" William snarled, lunging toward her as she cowered against the wall. Her eyes were wide with terror, mirroring those of young Edward.

"Please, don't hurt me!" she begged, her voice barely audible. The sickening sound of flesh meeting flesh reverberated throughout the house, and Edward could feel his heart drop as he saw his mother crumple to the floor.

"Mommy!" he cried out, tears streaming down his cheeks. But his voice fell on deaf ears, drowned out by the cacophony of his father's rage.

"Get away from her!" Edward yelled, his voice cracking. He stepped forward impulsively, fists clenched, only to be knocked aside by his father's brutal shove. As he lay sprawled on the floor, the bitter taste of blood filled his mouth, and he knew that something inside him had changed forever.

Edward leaned against the lockers, watching with detached interest as his classmates chattered excitedly about their weekend plans. At sixteen, he had long since learned to keep others at arm's length, finding solace in the shadows where he could nurse his dark thoughts and fantasies.

"Hey man, wanna hang out this weekend?" a familiar voice asked, breaking through Edward's reverie. He looked up to see Mark, a fellow student who had taken a liking to Edward despite his standoffish demeanor.

"Uh, I don't know," Edward replied, his eyes darting away. "I've got a lot of, um, homework to catch up on."

"Come on, dude," Mark persisted, flashing an easy grin. "It'll be fun."

"Thanks, but I'm good," Edward said, his voice flat and emotionless. He watched as disappointment flickered across Mark's face before he shrugged it off, moving on to make plans with someone else.

Edward's gaze returned to the bustling crowd of students, each one blissfully unaware of the darkness that lurked within him. He couldn't help but feel like an outsider, adrift in a sea of normalcy that he could never truly be a part of.

As the bell rang, signaling the end of another torturous day at school, Edward retreated further into the recesses of his mind, where the twisted desires that had haunted him since childhood continued to fester and grow.

The sun dipped below the horizon as Edward walked home from school, casting long shadows across the desolate streets. The usual din of laughter and conversation was absent, leaving him alone with the echoes of his footsteps and the relentless march of his thoughts. As he approached an alleyway, a sudden flash of movement caught his eye, followed by the sharp sound of breaking glass.

"Give me your money!" a gruff voice demanded, punctuating the tense silence. Edward hesitated, curiosity overcoming his instinct to flee. He slowly peered around the corner, witnessing a scene that would forever be seared into his memory.

A man held a knife to the throat of a terrified woman, her eyes wide with fear as she fumbled with her purse. The assailant's face twisted into a malevolent grin, his grip tightening on the weapon as he reveled in the power he held over his victim.

Edward's heart pounded in his chest, yet he found himself unable to look away. A dark thrill coursed through his veins, feeding the twisted desires that had been lurking within him for years. It was as if he could feel the rush of power surging through the attacker, intoxicating him with its seductive allure.

He knew he should have called for help, or at least tried to intervene. Instead, he remained hidden, his breath caught in his throat as he watched the events unfold before him. The woman eventually handed over her wallet, and the man released her with a shove. She stumbled away, sobbing, while the thief disappeared into the night.

In the days that followed, Edward couldn't shake the lingering sense of exhilaration that had seized him in that alley. His mind became consumed with fantasies of violence, each one more depraved than the last. He began to experiment, testing the limits of his newfound fascination.

"Hey, Edward," Mark greeted him one day after school, oblivious to the darkness that had taken root in his friend's soul. "You seem different lately. Everything okay?"

"Everything's fine," Edward replied, forcing a smile. Inside, however, he was anything but.

Unable to resist the siren call of his desires any longer, Edward sought out an opportunity to act on them. He found it in a stray cat that crossed his path one evening, its trusting eyes meeting his as it approached for affection. As he knelt and stroked its fur, he felt an irresistible urge to exert control over the vulnerable creature.

Edward tightened his grip around the cat's neck, feeling its sharp claws dig into his skin as it struggled against him. A perverse sense of satisfaction filled him as he watched its eyes bulge with terror, its breaths growing shallower by the second.

"Please, stop!" a voice screamed in his head - a last desperate plea from the part of him that still clung to humanity. But it was too late. The line had been crossed, and there was no turning back.

As life finally drained from the cat's body, Edward released his hold, staring down at the limp form with a twisted mixture of guilt and pleasure. He knew he should have felt remorse, but all he could think about was the power he had wielded, the intoxicating thrill of taking another being's life.

In that moment, Edward Kingsley had irrevocably given himself over to the darkness, setting forth on a path that would lead to unspeakable horrors.

The cold steel of the scalpel glinted under the dim light as Edward meticulously dissected the lifeless body before him. The once-white sheets that covered the table were now stained with dark red, an eerie testament to his growing obsession with death and the human body.

"Such a fascinating machine, don't you think?" murmured the figure standing beside him. Dr. Gideon Blackwood – a man renowned for his expertise in anatomy, but also whispered about in hushed tones for his other, darker interests.

Edward's fingers trembled slightly as he peeled back another layer of flesh, revealing the intricate network of muscle and sinew beneath. "It's…incredible," he replied, his voice barely audible over the sound of his own pounding heart.

"Indeed," agreed Dr. Blackwood, his eyes gleaming with a fervor that mirrored Edward's. "And just imagine the power one could wield if they understood how to manipulate this delicate system to their will."

As the days turned into weeks, Edward found himself consumed by an insatiable curiosity. He filled his room with morbid objects – antique surgical tools, skulls, and preserved organs – each one a testament to his growing fascination with mortality and the macabre. Late at night, he would pore over medical textbooks and anatomical atlases, studying the intricate illustrations with a hunger that gnawed at his very soul.

"Control, my boy," Dr. Blackwood would often say, his voice low and hypnotic as he guided Edward through their secret lessons. "That is what it all comes down to. To truly understand the human body is to possess the ultimate power – the ability to give life or take it away."

Edward listened intently, his mind racing with possibilities as he stared at the cadaver on the table. He imagined the feeling of warm blood on his hands, the rush of adrenaline that came with holding another's life in his hands. It was an intoxicating thought, one that both terrified and thrilled him.

"Remember," Dr. Blackwood continued, his eyes fixed on Edward's as he spoke, "You must never let your emotions rule you. To wield this power, you must be cold and calculating, always in control."

Edward nodded, swallowing hard as he forced himself to push past the fear that threatened to choke him. He wanted this – needed it – more than anything else. And with Dr. Blackwood's guidance, he would become the master of his dark desires.

"Promise me, Edward," Dr. Blackwood said, placing a firm hand on his shoulder. "Promise me that you will use what I have taught you wisely, and never let your emotions cloud your judgment."

"I promise," Edward replied, his voice steady despite the turmoil that raged within him. As he watched Dr. Blackwood walk away, leaving him alone with his thoughts and the lifeless body on the table, Edward knew that he had crossed a threshold from which there would be no return.

In the shadows of that dimly lit room, a darkness took root in his soul – a darkness that would grow and fester until it consumed him completely.

The room was bathed in a sickly yellow light, casting unsettling shadows on the walls as Edward stood over the small, trembling form of a stray cat. His fingers twitched with anticipation as he felt the power coursing through his veins. Dr. Blackwood's words echoed in his mind, a mantra that fed his growing obsession with control.

"Remember, Edward," he whispered to himself, "You must be cold and calculating, always in control."

He reached out, gripping the frightened animal tightly. Its eyes widened in terror as it tried to claw its way free, but Edward's grip was unyielding, his determination unwavering. He felt an odd mix of guilt and exhilaration, knowing that he held the power of life and death in his hands. This was a test – a chance for him to prove that he had what it took to wield the darkness within him.

"Please," a voice from the doorway interrupted his thoughts, and Edward turned to see a young woman standing there, her eyes wide with horror. "What are you doing?"

"Leave me alone," Edward growled, his rage boiling to the surface. He tightened his grip on the cat, feeling its bones creak beneath his fingers as it let out a pitiful mewl of pain.

"Stop it!" the woman cried, rushing forward to try to pry the animal from his grasp. But Edward was stronger, fueled by the adrenaline of his twisted desires. With one final, violent twist, he snapped the cat's neck, its limp body falling to the floor.

"Look what you made me do," he seethed, turning his fury on the woman who had dared to interfere. His heart pounded in his chest as he stalked towards her, the thrill of his actions leaving him feeling invincible. "You should've stayed away."

"Please, don't hurt me," she begged, backing away from him, but Edward's mind was consumed by his dark desires. He had crossed a moral boundary – committed an act of cruelty that could never be undone – and the guilt and exhilaration he felt only strengthened his resolve.

"Remember, Edward," he repeated Dr. Blackwood's words as he closed in on the frightened woman. "You must be cold and calculating, always in control."

As he raised his hand to strike her, Edward felt a sense of detachment from reality, like he was floating above it all, watching the scene unfold from a distance. He had become a god-like figure, capable of manipulating and destroying lives with a single touch.

The following days found Edward more entrenched in his dark desires than ever before. The incident with the young woman and the cat had opened a door within him – one that he was eager to explore further. Each time he exerted his power over another living being, he felt that intoxicating mix of guilt and exhilaration, driving him deeper into the abyss.

He began to view himself as a puppet master, pulling the strings of those around him with expert precision. His growing obsession with power and control consumed him, leaving little room for anything else. Friends, family, even the occasional passerby – all were mere pawns in his twisted game.

"Remember, Edward," he would tell himself as he continued down this dark path. "You must be cold and calculating, always in control."

As the world around him descended into chaos, Edward Kingsley reveled in the darkness that now resided within him, setting the stage for the horrors that would unfold in the rest of his story.

Edward's reflection stared back at him in the bathroom mirror, his eyes hollow and lifeless. The once-charming man now bore the weight of his secret sins, etched into the lines on his face. He splashed cold water onto his cheeks, attempting to drown out the whispers of guilt that clawed at the edges of his mind.

"Edward," a voice called from the other side of the door. It was his wife, Patricia. "Breakfast is ready."

"Coming," he replied, forcing a smile that never quite reached his eyes.

As Edward sat down at the table opposite his wife, he couldn't help but feel like an imposter - a wolf in sheep's clothing. He longed for the simplicity of normalcy, but the darkness within him demanded a different kind of sustenance.

"Are you alright, love? You seem distant," Patricia asked, concern furrowing her brow.

Edward forced a laugh. "Just tired, I suppose. Work has been exhausting lately." He hated lying to his wife, but what choice did he have? To reveal the truth would be to destroy everything he'd built.

"Maybe you should take a break, go on a vacation," she suggested. Edward nodded absentmindedly, his thoughts already miles away, caught up in the twisted fantasies he could no longer resist.

That night, as Patricia slept soundly beside him, Edward lay awake, his mind racing with dark thoughts. His insatiable craving for violence and control had driven him to the brink, and he knew it was only a matter of time before he crossed the point of no return.

The following week, while on a business trip to a small coastal town, Edward seized the opportunity to indulge his darkest desires. He had identified his prey – a young woman who worked at the local diner – and now stalked her through the shadows, his heart pounding with equal parts excitement and dread.

As he watched her walk alone towards her car, Edward felt a thrill like never before. This was the moment that would define him – the pivotal point where he would fully embrace the monster within.

With a surge of adrenaline, he lunged forward, catching the woman off guard. He stifled her screams as he dragged her into the darkness, relishing the cold fear that radiated from her trembling body.

"Please," she begged, tears streaming down her face. "Please, I don't want to die."

"Shh," Edward whispered, his voice dripping with malice. "This is what I was born to do." And as he committed the heinous act, his heart swelled with exhilaration and satisfaction, knowing that he had finally acted on his darkest fantasies.

In that moment, Edward Kingsley became something else entirely - a predator concealed by charm and intelligence, a man who would stop at nothing to exert his control over others. The guilt and shame that once plagued him were drowned out by the intoxicating power he now wielded, and he knew there was no turning back.

"Remember, Edward," he reminded himself as he left the lifeless body behind. "You must be cold and calculating, always in control."

And with that, he stepped into the night, ready to unleash a reign of terror unlike anything the world had ever seen.

Edward stared at the lifeless body sprawled out before him, her dark hair splayed like a halo around her head. Her eyes were wide open in terror, and her lips were parted as if she had been about to scream. He felt both repulsed and invigorated by the sight – it was a testament to his newfound power, the very manifestation of his darkest fantasies come to life.

"God," he muttered under his breath, wiping the blood from his hands with a grimace. "What have I done?"

As the reality of his actions began to set in, Edward knew that he needed to act quickly to cover up his crime. He glanced around the dimly lit alleyway, assessing his surroundings for any potential witnesses. To his relief, the night was eerily quiet; the only sound was the distant hum of traffic from the main road.

"Alright, let's get this over with," he told himself, steeling his nerves as he crouched down beside the body. He methodically stripped the woman of her clothing and jewelry, removing any identifiers that could link her back to her previous life. With each piece he discarded, he felt a thrill of excitement – it was as if he was erasing her very existence, asserting his control over her even in death.

Once he was satisfied that the body was unrecognizable, Edward dragged it deeper into the shadows, leaving a trail of crimson smears in his wake. He concealed the corpse beneath a pile of garbage and debris, the stench of decay mingling with the metallic tang of blood.

"Goodbye," he whispered, giving the lifeless form one last look before stepping away. As he walked back toward the mouth of the alley, he couldn't help but feel a sense of triumph. No one would ever know what he had done, and that knowledge sent a shiver of delight down his spine.

As Edward left the scene of his first kill, he couldn't help but reflect on the path that had led him to this point. The violent altercation between his parents in his childhood, the isolation and alienation he experienced during his adolescence, and the disturbing events that fueled his twisted desires – all these moments shaped him into the man he is today.

"Is this who I truly am?" he wondered; his thoughts were consumed by darkness. "Or is this simply the product of my past?"

Regardless of the answer, one thing was certain: Edward Kingsley was no longer an ordinary man. He was a predator, a monster driven by his insatiable craving for violence and control. As he walked away from his first kill, he knew that he had only just begun to embrace the darkness within.

"Let the world beware," he thought, a sinister smile gracing his lips. "For I am now free to unleash my true nature upon all who cross my path."

And with that chilling thought, Edward vanished into the night, leaving behind a trail of blood and terror that would soon become his twisted legacy.

CHAPTER 13

Deadly Descent

Samantha Kingsley stared at the crime scene photos spread across her desk, her brow furrowed in deep concentration. The familiar scent of stale coffee and paperwork hung in the air as she pieced together the evidence before her.

"Another one," she muttered, her fingers tracing the outline of a bloody handprint on the photo. "This time it's too close to home."

A shiver crawled down her spine as she realized that the handprint bore an uncanny resemblance to Edward's – a similarity she couldn't ignore any longer. But it was her husband; she couldn't accept the possibility without solid evidence.

"Chief, we've got a new tenant for one of Mr. Kingsley's properties," Officer Daniels announced, walking into her office with a file in his hands.

"Let me see," Samantha said, taking the file from him and opening it to reveal the details of one Carla Martinez. Carla's warm smile radiated from her photograph, and Samantha felt a pang of sympathy for the woman, who appeared to be a loving single mother excited to give her son a memorable vacation.

"Great. Keep an eye on her," Samantha ordered, making a mental note to ensure Carla's safety. "I don't want anything happening to her or her son."

"Understood, Chief," Daniels nodded, leaving the office with a sense of urgency.

As Samantha returned her gaze to the photos, her thoughts swirled with confusion and doubt. Could Edward be capable of such brutality? She thought back to their marriage vows, the promise to love and protect each other. Was it all a facade?

"Edward, what have you done?" she whispered, her voice strained by the weight of her suspicions.

Later that day, she decided to visit Carla, hoping to learn more about the woman and her connection to Edward. Arriving at the property, Samantha found Carla unpacking her car, her young son playing nearby.

"Carla Martinez?" Samantha asked, extending her hand. "I'm Chief Kingsley, Edward's wife. I wanted to welcome you to the neighborhood."

"Thank you," Carla replied, shaking Samantha's hand. "It's such a beautiful place, and my son is already having the time of his life."

Samantha looked at the boy, his laughter echoing through the air as he chased after a butterfly. She couldn't help but feel protective of the innocent child, determined to keep him safe from whatever darkness was lurking in the shadows.

"Edward mentioned your rental," Samantha said, forcing a smile. "If you need anything, don't hesitate to reach out."

"Much appreciated, Chief Kingsley," Carla responded warmly.

As Samantha left the property, she knew that she had to uncover the truth about Edward – for the sake of Carla, her son, and all the other potential victims. She couldn't shake the feeling that time was running out. And with each passing moment, the line between the man she loved, and a monster blurred beyond recognition.

The sun dipped below the horizon, casting an eerie glow over the lavish rental property where Carla and her son would be staying. The expansive house stood proudly amongst lush palm trees, their leaves rustling in the gentle breeze. A sparkling pool shimmered in the fading light, inviting relaxation and leisure.

Edward's breath hitched as he peered through the window, watching Carla move about the kitchen. His usually calculated demeanor was slipping away, replaced by a growing desperation. The urge to exert control, to feel the intoxicating thrill of taking another life, had become an insatiable hunger gnawing at him. This time, however, he knew he was taking a risk - his wife's suspicions were mounting, and the proximity to home could prove disastrous. But he couldn't resist any longer; he needed it, craved it.

"Carla," Edward said coolly, knocking on the door. "It's Edward, just wanted to check in and see how you're settling into the property."

"Hi, Edward!" Carla greeted her warmly, opening the door. "Come on in. We love it here. It's like a dream come true for us."

"Fantastic, I'm glad to hear that." He forced a smile, his stomach twisting with anticipation as he scanned the surroundings, mentally noting potential tools, hiding places, and escape routes.

"Your wife stopped by earlier," Carla mentioned as she poured them both a glass of iced tea. "She's so kind and welcoming."

"Ah, yes, Samantha," he replied, hoping to keep his voice steady. "She's always looking out for our guests."

As they sat down at the patio table, Edward's mind raced, his thoughts consumed by the darkness within him. He listened to Carla talk about her life and her dreams for her son, all the while contemplating the execution of his sinister plan. The contrast between the tranquil beauty of the property and the turmoil brewing inside him could not have been starker.

"Edward, are you okay?" Carla asked, noticing his distant expression. "You seem a little off."

"Apologies," he lied smoothly, his pulse quickening. "It's just been a long day. I appreciate your concern."

"Of course," she said, taking a sip of her tea. "I can't imagine how busy you must be with all these properties."

"Indeed," Edward replied, his gaze lingering on the sharp edge of a nearby gardening tool. "But it's all worth it to provide unforgettable experiences for our guests."

As Carla continued to share her stories, Edward's desperation only intensified. He knew he was playing a dangerous game, but the addiction to power and control had become all-consuming. And while this scene unfolded in the picturesque rental property, Samantha continued her relentless search for the truth – a truth that would bring their lives crashing down around them.

The sun dipped below the horizon, casting long shadows across the pristine lawn of Edward's rental property. He stood at the window, gazing out as Carla and her son played by the poolside, their laughter filling the air like a sweet melody. But beneath the surface of this idyllic scene, a storm was brewing – one that only Edward knew was coming.

"Such a shame," he muttered under his breath, observing Carla with a predatory glint in his eyes. "But it must be done."

He retreated to his study, where he had meticulously planned Carla's demise. Maps, blueprints, and timetables covered the walls – a testament to his twisted desires and the pleasure he derived from taking a life. His pulse quickened as he traced the route he would take to enter her home, picturing every step of the process in vivid detail.

"Edward?" Carla called from outside, her voice innocent and trusting. "Would you like to join us for a swim?"

"Perhaps later," he replied smoothly, forcing a smile onto his face. "I have some work to finish up first."

"Alright," she said, disappointment evident in her tone. "Just let us know if you change your mind."

As Carla returned to her son, her vulnerability and innocence were on full display. She had no idea of the danger lurking in the shadows, just waiting to strike. Throughout the day, she went about her daily activities – cooking dinner, helping her son with his homework, and tending to the flowers that bloomed around the property. All the while, Edward watched her from afar, growing more eager by the minute.

"Soon," he whispered to himself, clutching a knife tightly in his hand. "Very soon."

In the privacy of his study, Edward's thoughts raced, each one darker than the last. The anticipation of taking another life fueled him, pushing him toward the brink of madness. He knew he had to act soon, lest his desperation drives him to even greater acts of recklessness.

"Edward!" Carla shouted from outside, her voice strained with panic. "My son's cut himself on some glass! Can you help?"

"Of course," he said, the knife slipping from his grip as he rushed out the door. The opportunity was presenting itself sooner than he had anticipated, but he couldn't afford to pass it up.

"Stay calm, Carla," he commanded, his veneer of charm and control returning in an instant. "I'll take care of everything."

As Edward approached the scene, his heart pounding in his chest, he couldn't help but revel in the twisted satisfaction that came with knowing her fate. Little did she know that her trust in him would be the very thing that sealed her doom.

"Everything will be alright," he reassured her, his voice laced with false concern. "You have my word."

The sun dipped below the horizon, casting eerie shadows across the pristine white sands. Edward watched Carla from a distance, his eyes tracking her every move as she walked along the beach. The evening breeze whispered through the palm trees, carrying with it the faint scent of salt and seaweed. The scene was serene and picturesque, but beneath the surface, a malevolent darkness lurked.

"Such a perfect night for a walk," Edward mused, his voice low and menacing. "Don't you agree, my dear?"

Carla, unable to hear him, continued her path, her feet sinking into the soft sand. She paused occasionally to pick up shells, holding them up to the moonlight to examine their delicate patterns. Edward's gaze never wavered from her, relishing the power he held over her life. He could almost taste the fear that would soon engulf her.

"Your time is near, Carla," he thought while maintaining a safe distance behind her. "You have no idea what awaits you."

As they neared a secluded cove, Edward's heart raced with anticipation. This was the ideal location to execute his twisted plan. His practiced hands checked the items hidden within his coat pocket: a sharp knife, a roll of duct tape, and a length of rope. Everything was in place.

"Enjoy your final moments, my dear," he whispered under his breath, feeling a perverse thrill at the thought of what was about to happen.

"Beautiful night, isn't it?" Carla called out suddenly, turning to face

Edward with a warm smile. She was completely unaware of the danger that stood before her.

"Indeed, it is," Edward replied, his voice betraying none of his sinister intentions. "The stars are particularly bright tonight."

"Would you like to join me?" she asked innocently, gesturing towards the water's edge.

"Of course," he responded, his heart pounding with a mix of excitement and anxiety. This was the moment he had been waiting for.

As they walked side by side, Edward's mind raced with thoughts of how he would carry out his plan. He imagined the look of terror on Carla's face as he subdued her, the satisfaction he would feel as her life slipped away in his hands. The thought sent shivers down his spine, fueling his twisted desires.

"Such a shame it has to end this way," he mused, his eyes locked onto her vulnerable form.

The sound of crashing waves filled the air as they reached the water's edge. Carla laughed, kicking at the frothy surf that lapped at her feet.

"Isn't it amazing how something so simple can bring such joy?" she asked, looking up at Edward with genuine happiness.

"Indeed," he replied, tightening his grip on the knife hidden within his coat. "A fleeting moment of bliss before the darkness consumes everything."

Edward moved quickly, catching Carla off guard as he tackled her to the ground. Panic flashed across her face as she struggled beneath him, but it was too late – the element of surprise was on his side.

"Shh, my dear," he whispered into her ear, pressing the cold steel of the knife against her throat. "It's time for you to join the others."

As he carried out the grisly task with practiced precision, Edward reveled in the power he held over her life. With each labored breath, she grew weaker, closer to the oblivion he craved. And as the last flicker of light left her eyes, a twisted sense of satisfaction washed over him.

"Another life taken," he thought, standing over her lifeless body. "And with it, another piece of my soul lost to the darkness."

Edward stood in the shadows; his eyes locked on Carla as she played with her son on the beach. The golden sunlight bathed them, making the water sparkle like a thousand diamonds. His heart raced at the sight of their laughter, knowing it would soon be silenced forever.

"Mom, watch this!" the boy called out, excitedly building an elaborate sandcastle. Carla clapped encouragingly, and Edward couldn't help but feel a pang of regret. She was a devoted mother, and her son's happiness was her world. He pushed that thought aside, focusing on the task at hand.

"Good job, sweetie!" Carla praised her son, hugging him tightly. "You're so talented. I'm so proud of you."

"Thanks, Mom," he beamed, basking in her love. "I wish we could stay here forever."

"Me too," Carla agreed, her smile tinged with sadness. "But we'll always have these memories, no matter where life takes us."

As Edward watched from afar, he knew Samantha was closing in on him. Their last conversation had been tense, her probing questions unnerving him. But he refused to give in to fear - he'd worked too hard, become too skilled at this dark art.

"Edward," Samantha's voice cut through the silence like a razor, her words dripping with disappointment and betrayal. "How could you?"

He turned to face his wife, her eyes filled with tears and anger. "Samantha, I don't know what you're talking about."

"Cut the crap, Edward," she spat, holding up the damning evidence she'd collected. "I found this in your study - photos of all the victims, newspaper clippings... You think I'm stupid?"

"Sam, listen to me," he pleaded, his voice cracking with desperation. "There's a reasonable explanation for all of this."

"Is there, Edward?" she challenged, her eyes narrowing. "Because all I see is a monster hiding in plain sight."

As the confrontation unfolded, Carla and her son continued their blissful day at the beach, unaware of the sinister plot unfolding nearby. The boy splashed in the surf, giggling as Carla chased him through the water.

"Mom, you can't catch me!" he taunted playfully, darting away from her outstretched arms.

"We'll see about that!" Carla laughed, feeling the weight of her worries slip away for a moment in time.

But as the sun dipped below the horizon, casting eerie shadows on the sand, the terrible truth of their situation threatened to consume them all. Samantha faced her husband, the man she'd once loved and trusted, knowing he was capable of unspeakable horrors. And Edward, his world collapsing around him, prepared to take one more life in pursuit of his twisted desires.

Sweat trickled down Edward's temple as he stood in the dimly lit living room, his hands clenching and unclenching at his sides. Samantha's piercing gaze bore into him, her eyes filled with a mixture of disbelief and anger. He swallowed hard, forcing a smile onto his face.

"Sam, I know this looks bad, but I promise you, there's more to it than you think," Edward said smoothly, trying to regain control of the situation. "I've been researching the victims, trying to find patterns and help you solve these cases."

"Really?" Samantha scoffed, her brow furrowing in suspicion. "And when were you planning on telling me about this little side project of yours?"

Edward hesitated, his mind racing for an answer. "I wanted to be sure I had something concrete before bringing it to your attention. I didn't want to waste your time or resources."

"Or maybe you just wanted to cover your tracks," she shot back, taking a step closer. "You think I wouldn't notice the similarities between the victims? All beautiful, single mothers. All renting one of your properties."

"Coincidences, Sam," Edward insisted. His pulse pounded in his ears, adrenaline coursing through his veins as he struggled to maintain his composure. "I can't control who decides to rent my properties."

"Of course not," Samantha snarled. "But you could control what happens to them once they're here, couldn't you?"

"Sam, I love you," he implored, reaching out to touch her arm, only for her to recoil from his touch. "You have to believe me. I would never do anything to hurt you or our family."

"Then explain this!" she demanded, shoving the incriminating evidence into his chest. "If you're innocent, then tell me why you've been hoarding these photos and clippings like some kind of sick trophy?"

"Because I'm trying to protect us!" Edward exploded, his frustration bubbling over. "Don't you see? Whoever is doing this is trying to frame me, to tear our family apart!"

Samantha stared at him for a long moment, her expression unreadable. Edward could feel the tension in the room mounting, the air thick with unspoken accusations and doubt. He knew he had to convince her or risk losing everything.

"Please, Sam," he whispered, his voice raw with emotion. "You know me better than anyone. You know I couldn't do something like this."

She blinked back tears, shaking her head slowly. "I thought I did, Edward. But now... I'm not so sure."

The silence that followed was deafening, a chasm opening between them as they stood on opposite sides of a terrible truth.

A bead of sweat trickled down Edward's forehead as he clenched his fists, desperation gnawing at the edges of his sanity. Samantha's eyes, once filled with love and admiration, now bore into him like icy daggers.

"Edward, I want to believe you," she said, her voice cracking. "But how can I trust what you're saying when there's so much evidence against you?"

"Sam, please," Edward pleaded, feeling the walls closing in on him. "There has to be some other explanation for all this."

"Like what?" Samantha demanded, her voice rising. "That someone else just happened to commit these murders, and you're being framed? It doesn't add up."

"Look at me!" Edward shouted, grabbing her by the shoulders. "I am not a killer!"

"Let go of me!" Samantha yelled, shoving him away with a force that sent him stumbling backward.

"Fine!" Edward spat; his face contorted with anger. "You want the truth? Do you think I'm capable of killing those people? Then search the house! Go through every inch of it! You won't find anything connecting me to those crimes because I didn't do it!"

Samantha hesitated, her resolve wavering for a moment. Could she truly bring herself to tear apart their home in search of proof that her husband was a monster?

"Alright," she said finally, her voice cold and detached. "I will."

As she turned to leave, Edward's mind raced, searching for a way out of this nightmare. He couldn't let her find his trophies – the pieces of his victims that he'd kept as souvenirs. Desperation clawed at him, urging him to act.

"Wait," he said, his voice barely more than a whisper. "There's something I need to show you."

"What is it?" Samantha asked warily, her hand instinctively reaching for the gun at her hip.

"Follow me," he said, leading her toward the basement door. "But you have to promise not to freak out."

"Edward," she warned, her eyes narrowing. "If you're trying to pull something—"

"Trust me," he interrupted, his voice filled with a false calm he didn't feel. "I'll explain everything once we're downstairs."

As they descended into the darkness, Samantha's heart pounded in her chest, dread coiling like a serpent in her stomach. What could Edward possibly have to show her that would exonerate him?

Edward flicked on the light, revealing a scene that made Samantha's blood run cold: a hidden room filled with chilling mementos from each of his victims, their faces staring back at her from the shadows.

"Dear God..." she whispered, her hand flying to her mouth in horror.

"Sam, I can explain—" Edward began, but his words were cut off by the sharp report of a gunshot, echoing through the dimly lit chamber.

The bullet tore through the air between them, embedding itself in the wall just inches from Edward's head.

"Stay back!" Samantha screamed; her eyes wild with terror as she aimed the gun directly at her husband's heart. "I won't hesitate to shoot!"

"Sam, please—" Edward choked out, but she was already gone, racing up the stairs and slamming the door behind her, leaving him trapped in the darkness with only the ghosts of his past for company.

"Sam!" he called, pounding on the door. "Let me out! You don't understand!"

But there was no answer, save for the distant sound of sirens drawing ever closer.

CHAPTER 14

Bloody Truths

A single tear rolled down Samantha's cheek as she stared at the man, she thought she knew, her husband Edward. The dim living room light cast eerie shadows across their faces, revealing the lines etched into each of them by years of love and now, betrayal. "Edward," she whispered, her voice trembling with anger, sadness, and determination, "I need you to tell me the truth."

Edward looked up from his leather armchair, his eyes wide and feigning shock. "Sam, I don't know what you're talking about," he replied, attempting to maintain his innocent facade. He rose from the chair, slowly approaching Samantha with an air of confusion.

"Stop it, Edward. You know exactly what I'm talking about," Samantha choked out, her fists clenched at her sides. She had spent years defending the citizens of this city against criminals, but nothing could prepare her for facing the monster in her own home.

"Darling, you're scaring me," he lied, hoping to manipulate Samantha's trust in him. His brow furrowed with worry as he reached out a hand to touch her shoulder, only for her to shrug it off in disgust.

"Scaring you?" Samantha scoffed, her heart pounding in her chest. "You're the one who's been terrorizing this community, Edward. The murders, the lies... I can't believe I didn't see it before."

"Sam, please," Edward pleaded, desperation creeping into his voice as he tried to deny any involvement in the murders. "I don't know anything about those horrible crimes. I would never hurt anyone."

Samantha shook her head, her resolve unwavering. "No, Edward. Your lies won't work on me anymore. I've seen the evidence." As she spoke, her mind raced over the photos, documents, and witness statements that pointed directly to him. She knew that the truth was too damning to ignore, even if it shattered her world.

"Whatever you think you've found, it's not what it seems," Edward insisted, his voice cracking under the weight of his guilt. "I can explain everything, just give me a chance."

"Save your explanations for the police, Edward," Samantha replied, her voice cold and steady. She refused to allow her husband's charm and cunning to sway her any longer. The time for manipulation was over, and there would be no escape from the consequences of his actions.

The room seemed to shrink around Edward as Samantha walked over to the coffee table, her hand gripping a thick manila folder. With deliberate movements, she opened it and began to lay out its contents before him – photographs of mutilated bodies, documents detailing suspicious financial transactions, and witness statements that sent chills down his spine.

"Explain this," Samantha demanded, her voice cold as steel. She pointed at one of the photos, where a young woman's lifeless eyes stared back at them, her throat slashed open. "And this," she continued, her finger moving to a bank statement showing a large sum transferred to an offshore account just days before the murder.

Edward's chest tightened, his breath coming in short gasps as he tried to maintain his composure. He could feel the walls closing in around him, the weight of his secrets threatening to crush him.

"Sam, I-I don't know what you're talking about," he stammered, his eyes darting between the incriminating evidence and his wife's steely gaze. He knew he had been meticulous in covering his tracks, but somehow, Samantha had found the truth. "I swear to you, I have nothing to do with any of this."

Samantha shook her head, her expression unyielding. "You can't talk your way out of this, Edward. You can't charm me into believing your lies anymore. The evidence is right here, and it all points to you." Her voice wavered for a moment, the hurt and betrayal she felt evident in her words.

Desperation clawed at Edward's insides as he wracked his brain for explanations that would satisfy Samantha. "Maybe it's a setup," he suggested, his voice rising in pitch as panic set in. "Someone's trying to frame me, Sam. They must be jealous of our success, or they have a grudge against me. But I didn't do this, I would never hurt anyone like that!"

"Edward," Samantha said quietly, her voice cracking with a mix of anger and sorrow. "I want to believe you, but the evidence is overwhelming. I can't ignore it any longer." She stared at him, her eyes searching for any hint of the man she once knew – the man she loved.

As Edward looked into Samantha's eyes, he felt his carefully constructed facade begin to crumble. He had always been able to charm and manipulate others with ease, but now, faced with the undeniable truth of his actions, his confidence waned. He knew he couldn't outrun his sins forever, and the day of reckoning had finally arrived.

Edward's heart hammered in his chest, the sound of it deafening as he stared into Samantha's eyes, her fury reflected in their depths like a storm brewing on the horizon. He tried to maintain his composure, but the weight of his misdeeds bore down upon him, threatening to crush him beneath its inexorable pressure.

"Edward," Samantha seethed, her voice sharp and cutting as she finally found the words to express her anger. "You've betrayed me, our marriage, and the trust of this entire community. You've disgraced us, upon our family name."

"Sam, please," Edward pleaded, desperation lacing his every word. "You have to understand... I never wanted—"

"Save your lies!" she spat, her hands clenched into fists at her sides. "I refuse to let you manipulate me any longer!"

Edward could see the resolve in her eyes, the unwavering determination that had made her such an effective chief of police. He knew that if he didn't escape now, she would ensure he faced justice for his crimes. A cold sweat broke out across his brow as he searched the room for an exit, his eyes darting from one potential route to another.

"Where are you going to go, Edward?" Samantha demanded, her voice low and dangerous. "There's no escaping this. No running from what you've done."

"Nothing is set in stone yet, Sam," he said, trying to buy himself some time as his mind raced through countless scenarios, each more desperate than the last. "There might still be a way to salvage our lives, our reputations..."

"Your reputation, maybe," she scoffed, her eyes narrowing with disgust. "But not mine. Not after what I've learned about you."

Edward couldn't bear the contempt in her voice, the disappointment etched into her features. He felt as though he was being torn apart from the inside, his body a battleground between the man he had once been and the monster he had become. And as Samantha's anger continued to boil over, he knew that the odds were stacked against him.

"Sam, I—" he began, but she cut him off with a dismissive wave of her hand.

"Enough!" she shouted, her voice echoing through the room like thunder. "I won't be swayed by your pathetic excuses or empty promises. It's time you faced the consequences of your actions."

Edward's pulse raced as the walls seemed to close in around him, the air thick with tension and fear. He glanced around the room one last time, his eyes settling on an open window that offered a glimmer of hope – a chance at freedom.

"Sam," he said softly, trying to keep her attention focused on him as he inched closer to his escape route. "Please..."

"Edward, stop," she warned, her expression hardening as she took a step towards him. "You're only making this worse for yourself."

But it was too late. Edward's desperation had reached a boiling point, and there was no turning back now. As the last vestiges of his self-control slipped away, he made a split-second decision that would change their lives forever.

Edward's heart pounded in his chest, the beat echoing through the tense silence of the living room. Samantha's eyes bore into him, a fierce determination radiating from her as she blocked the doorway, her arms crossed and stance wide. There would be no easy escape.

"Edward," she said, her voice cold and resolute, "you're not leaving this house until the police arrive. You will face justice for what you've done."

His mind raced, searching feverishly for any plan that could save him from the consequences of his actions. The walls seemed to crawl closer, suffocating him as he stared into the unwavering gaze of his wife. A chill crept down his spine at the thought of being hunted by someone who knew him so intimately.

"Sam," he pleaded, grappling for a hint of sympathy, "you don't understand—"

"Save it," she snapped, cutting him off. "I won't let you manipulate me anymore. Your lies won't work this time."

A desperate energy pulsed through Edward's veins as he scanned the room, his breaths shallow and rapid. And then, like a beacon in the darkness, he spotted an open window just beyond Samantha's line of sight. It was risky, but it was his only chance.

"Fine," he muttered, feigning defeat and lowering his gaze to the floor. "I'll wait for the police."

Samantha narrowed her eyes, suspicion flickering across her features as she studied Edward's sudden change in demeanor. He couldn't afford to hesitate now – every second brought him closer to a fate he couldn't accept.

As if propelled by some unseen force, Edward lunged towards the window, adrenaline surging through his body. Samantha's instincts kicked in, her hand reaching out to grasp at him, but he was already a step ahead, anticipating her movements.

"Edward, stop!" she shouted, her voice laced with both fury and fear. But he was committed now, the consequences of his actions driving him forward like a wild animal backed into a corner.

In a single, fluid motion, Edward dove through the open window, the cool night air whipping past his face as he tumbled into the darkness beyond. The sounds of Samantha's shouts followed him, but they were nothing more than echoes in the wind – a reminder of a life that had already slipped through his fingers.

The room seemed to vibrate with the intensity of their emotions, a storm brewing between them. Edward could feel his heart thundering in his chest as Samantha's hand shot out, her fingers digging into his arm like talons. He gritted his teeth against the pain but refused to let her see that she'd hurt him.

"Let go of me!" he snarled, pulling away from her with all his might. The force of his resistance slammed their bodies together, a brief, chaotic dance of desperation and determination.

"You're not going anywhere, Edward," Samantha growled, tightening her grip on his arm. Her eyes burned into his, a challenge he couldn't ignore. "I won't let you."

"Damn it, Samantha," Edward spat, struggling to keep his composure as panic bubbled beneath the surface. "You don't understand. You can't-"

"Can't what? Believe the evidence that's right in front of me?" She shook her head, disappointment etched into her features. "No more lies, Edward. No more manipulation. We both know the truth now."

As Samantha's words cut through the tension, Edward realized that there was only one way out of this nightmare. With a surge of strength born from pure necessity, he thrust his shoulder forward, using the momentum to break free from her grasp.

"Edward!" Samantha cried out, her voice laced with betrayal and shock. For a moment, she stood frozen in place, unable to comprehend what had just happened.

But Edward wasted no time – he sprinted towards the open window, each step bringing him closer to freedom. He knew that he would never be truly free of the darkness that consumed him, but if he could just escape this room, there might be a chance to salvage what remained of his life.

"Stop!" Samantha screamed, her voice echoing through the house. But Edward didn't – couldn't – listen. The open window beckoned him, a siren call to the only path left to his survival.

With one last desperate leap, Edward soared through the open window, leaving behind the shattered remains of his once-perfect life.

The doorframe shook as Samantha slammed her hand against it, the noise jolting her back to life. Her heart thundered in her ears as she sprinted after Edward, their once-peaceful home now resonating with the echoes of betrayal and desperation.

"Edward!" she bellowed, each stride fueled by a mixture of rage and determination. She couldn't let him escape – not after everything he had done. It was her duty to protect this community, and she would be damned if she let her husband slip through her fingers.

As Edward reached the window, he hesitated for a fraction of a second, glancing back at Samantha with wild eyes. The fear that radiated from his gaze struck her like a physical blow, a haunting reminder of the man she had married – and the monster he had become.

"Please," he whispered, his voice barely audible over the sound of their labored breathing. "Don't do this, Sam."

"Justice isn't negotiable," Samantha spat, her words laced with venom.

"You know that better than anyone."

With a final, desperate effort, Edward hurled himself through the window, the glass shattering around him like a storm of razor-sharp raindrops. The crash echoed throughout the house, a cacophony of chaos and destruction that mirrored the turmoil within Samantha's soul.

As she watched Edward land on the grass outside, her mind raced with thoughts of capture and retribution. This wasn't the man she had vowed to love and cherish; he was a shadow, a twisted reflection of the person she thought she knew. And she would chase that shadow to the ends of the earth if it meant protecting the innocent lives he had threatened.

"Damn you, Edward," she muttered under her breath, steeling herself for the pursuit. "Damn you for making me do this."

And with that, Samantha launched herself through the shattered window, shards of glass biting into her skin as she followed Edward into the darkness. The night enveloped them both, swallowing their fractured lives and leaving only the pounding of their footsteps and the relentless rhythm of Samantha's resolve.

The shards of glass crunched beneath Samantha's boots as she landed, her heart hammering against her ribs like a caged animal. She fumbled for the radio clipped to her belt, her fingers slick with sweat and determination.

"Dispatch, this is Chief Kingsley," she barked into the device, her voice rough from exertion. "I need backup at my location immediately.

The suspect is Edward Kingsley, Caucasian male, middle-aged, approximately six feet tall, brown hair, wearing a dark suit."

Edward's fleeing figure darted between the shadows cast by moonlit trees, his rapid footfalls betraying his panic. The night seemed to close in around Samantha, suffocating her like a shroud as she sprinted after him.

"Direction of travel is west through the woods behind our house," she continued, struggling to maintain both her breath and her composure. "He's dangerous and knows police tactics. Approach with caution."

"Copy that, Chief," crackled the voice on the other end of the line. "Units are en route to your location. Stay safe."

"Thanks," Samantha muttered, the word barely audible as she fought to keep her focus on the chase.

"Edward!" she shouted, her voice echoing through the darkness like a harbinger of doom. "Stop running! You can't escape!"

But Edward only quickened his pace, his desperation lending him a speed that belied his age. He was a man possessed, a creature born of fear and self-preservation, and Samantha knew that he would do whatever it took to evade capture.

"Damn him," she thought, her legs burning with exhaustion as she pushed herself harder. "Why did it have to come to this?"

"Edward, please!" she called out again, her tone laced with equal parts anger and anguish. "Don't make me use force!"

But her words fell on deaf ears, swallowed by the darkness as Edward disappeared into the night. The man she once loved was now a specter of his former self, consumed by the very shadows he sought refuge in.

"Backup will be here soon," Samantha told herself, her resolve unwavering. "I won't let him win. I won't let him hurt anyone else."

With renewed vigor, she plunged deeper into the woods, the moonlit branches casting eerie patterns on the ground like skeletal fingers reaching for her soul. She refused to give up, even as her breath came in ragged gasps and her limbs threatened to betray her.

"Justice," she whispered, her voice barely audible above the howling wind that seemed to carry Edward's taunting laughter through the trees. "Justice will prevail."

The moon bathed the dense forest in a cold, silvery light as Samantha stood rooted to the spot, her eyes following Edward's rapidly fading figure. The darkness swallowed him whole, leaving her with nothing but the echo of his footfalls and the bitter taste of betrayal.

"Edward!" she screamed into the night, her voice strained and pleading. Her heart hammered in her chest, a relentless drumbeat that amplified her sense of urgency. She clenched her fists, the radio in her hand creaking under the pressure.

"Damn you, Edward," she muttered under her breath, her mind racing with a torrent of emotions. "You won't slip away this easily."

She darted forward, her legs pumping furiously as she tore through the underbrush, branches snapping like brittle bones in her wake. As she sprinted, her mind was ablaze with questions, doubts, and fears.

"Was our entire marriage a lie?" she wondered, her thoughts laced with pain and resentment. "How could I have not seen the monster lurking beneath the surface?"

"Chief Kingsley, do you have a visual on the suspect?" crackled a voice from her radio, jolting her back to the present.

"Negative, he's disappeared into the woods," she replied, her voice taut with tension. "I'm in pursuit."

"Understood, we're closing in on your location now," the voice responded.

Samantha let out a ragged breath, forcing herself to focus on the task at hand. She knew that capturing Edward would be an uphill battle fraught with danger and uncertainty, but her resolve remained steadfast.

"Justice will be served," she vowed, her determination flaring like a beacon in the darkness. "And I will be the one to bring it."

As she plunged deeper into the inky shadows of the forest, she couldn't help but feel as though she was being watched, as if a malevolent presence was stalking her every move. The hairs on the back of her neck stood on end, and a shiver coursed through her body.

"Get a grip, Samantha," she scolded herself, shaking off the sensation. "You're a cop, you've faced worse than this."

"Edward!" she shouted once more, her voice echoing through the trees like a ghostly lament. "Give yourself up! You can't run forever!"

But there was no response, only the sinister whispers of the wind as it rustled through the leaves above her head. And yet, she refused to relent in her pursuit, driven by an unyielding hunger for justice that would not be denied.

"Your twisted reign ends tonight," she promised, her eyes narrowing with steely determination. "I won't rest until you're behind bars...or worse."

CHAPTER 15

—————————————————

Dark Night of the Soul

The light from the fireplace flickered across Samantha's pale and tear-streaked face as she sat alone in the darkening living room. She clutched a framed photo of her and Edward on their wedding day, now the joyous smiles they wore a cruel mockery of the life they once had. Her heart ached with betrayal, and her mind raced with memories and questions.

"Edward," she whispered, choking back a sob. "How could you?"

She replayed the events of the past few days in her mind, searching for any signs that she may have missed, any indication that her husband was capable of such heinous acts. The gruesome crime scenes, the lifeless bodies of innocent victims... all the work of her husband, a man she thought she knew inside out.

"Was it always there?" Samantha mused aloud. "Did I not see it? Or did I just not want to see it?"

Her grip on the photo tightened as she continued to sift through the details. The dinner parties with friends where Edward would charm everyone with his wit and charisma; the quiet nights spent curled up on the couch together, talking about their day. Such normalcy, such happiness. And yet, lurking beneath it all, a monster.

"Was it your power over them that drove you?" she asked, her voice shaking. "Or was it just the thrill of the hunt?"

As the chief of police, Samantha had faced countless criminals in her career, but never had she been so personally affected by a case. The idea that she had shared her bed with a killer sent shivers down her spine. What was worse, she couldn't escape the gnawing feeling that she had somehow failed in her duty to protect the community.

"I should have seen it," she muttered, tears streaming down her face. "I should have known."

In her desperate search for answers, Samantha began to dissect every interaction she had ever had with Edward. Every smile, every touch, every whispered word of love – was it all just an act? A carefully constructed facade to hide the darkness within?

"Tell me, Edward," she pleaded with the photo in her hands. "Give me something to understand. Please."

But there were no answers, only silence and shadows that seemed to close in on her, suffocating her with their weight. The truth was a bitter pill to swallow: her husband, the man she had loved and trusted, was a monster. And as she sat there, drowning in her sorrow and fear, Samantha realized that there was only one thing left to do.

"Edward Kingsley," she said, her voice resolute. "I will bring you to justice. No matter what it takes."

The whiskey bottle glistened beneath the dim light, its amber liquid promising a brief escape from the nightmare that had become Samantha's reality. With trembling hands, she reached for the glass, her knuckles white as she gripped it tightly. The scent of the aged whiskey filled her nostrils, but it did little to calm the storm raging within her.

"Damn you, Edward!" she spat, venom dripping from every word. "How could you do this? How could you betray me so completely?"

As the liquid fire burned down her throat, memories of their life together played like a cruel slideshow in her mind. She saw the laughter in his eyes as they danced at their wedding, the way he held her close on cold winter nights and the tender smile that graced his lips when he looked at her – all now tainted by the dark truth she had uncovered.

"Did any of it mean anything to you?" she whispered, despair tinging her voice. "Or was I just another pawn in your sick game?"

Samantha slammed the glass down, the sound echoing through the empty room. Her breath came in ragged gasps as she fought to contain the tidal wave of emotion threatening to overwhelm her. All those years of love and trust were shattered in an instant by the gruesome revelation of Edward's true nature.

"I thought I knew you," she confessed, her voice barely audible. "I thought we were a team, partners in everything."

But the man she had loved was gone, replaced by the specter of a monster wearing his face. It was a bitter pill to swallow, one that left an acrid taste in her mouth and a deep ache in her chest.

"Chief Kingsley?" The sudden crackle of her police radio startled her out of her reverie.

"Go ahead," she managed to choke out, her voice raw with emotion.

"Ma'am, we've got a lead on Edward's whereabouts," the voice on the other end reported, the urgency clear in his tone.

"Good," Samantha replied, her jaw set with determination. "I'm on my way."

As she turned to leave, she caught sight of the framed photo still clutched tightly in her hand. The smiling faces of her and Edward stared back at her from a happier time, a cruel reminder of what she had lost – and what she would now have to do.

"Edward Kingsley," she murmured, the words heavy with both sorrow and resolve. "I will bring you to justice. No matter what it takes."

The whiskey burned its way down Samantha's throat as she paced the empty living room, her fingers tingling with an unsettling mix of adrenaline and alcohol. The dim light cast eerie shadows on the walls, flickering like the storm of emotions raging inside her. Her footsteps echoed through the house; their persistent rhythm was punctuated by the pounding of her heart.

"Damn it, Edward," she muttered between gritted teeth, pausing for a moment to stare at the floor. "Why? How could you do this?"

Samantha clenched her fists, the knuckles turning white as her mind raced with questions that seemed to have no answers. The implications of her husband's actions weighed heavy on her shoulders, threatening to crush her beneath their terrible burden. Her career, her reputation, her very life – all were now inextricably linked to the monstrous deeds of the man she had loved.

"Think, Samantha, think," she urged herself, desperate to find some sense in the chaos that had become her world.

As she resumed her pacing, her gaze fell upon a stack of files piled haphazardly on her desk. The evidence of the investigation she had been leading into the gruesome murders seemed to mock her from across the room. She shook her head in disbelief.

"Was I so blind?" she asked herself, her voice laced with doubt and self-recrimination. "How did I not see the connection to Edward?"

Samantha crossed the room in long strides, her eyes fixed on the dossiers that now held the key to her husband's dark secrets. She picked up the top file, running her fingers over the worn edges and stains that marked its pages.

"Clues," she murmured, her thoughts shifting gears as she focused on the task at hand. "There must be something here that I missed. Some hint of what he was capable of."

She began to leaf through the papers, her eyes scanning each line of text with relentless determination. The victims' faces stared back at her from the crime scene photos, their lifeless eyes an unspoken accusation.

"Edward's brutality was right under my nose," Samantha whispered, feeling the cold grip of guilt tighten around her heart. "I failed them."

But as she searched for answers among the countless reports and interviews, a small flicker of hope began to emerge. Perhaps there was still something she could do to make things right.

"Edward," she said quietly, her voice infused with a new resolve. "You will not win this game. I will find the truth, and I will bring you down."

A single tear dripped onto the cold, unyielding surface of the desk as Samantha leaned over the stack of files. The room seemed to close in around her, suffocating her with the weight of her failures.

"Damn it," Samantha muttered under her breath, her fingers gripping the edges of the files. "All those years of training, and I couldn't even see the monster sleeping beside me."

The silence in the room was oppressive, punctuating every creak on the floorboards and tick of the clock on the wall. Her thoughts swirled like a tempest within her mind, threatening to consume her completely.

"Have you become so blind, Samantha?" she asked herself bitterly. "Or did you simply choose not to see?"

As the enormity of her husband's betrayal bore down upon her, the fierce determination that had driven her throughout her career began to falter, replaced by an all-consuming self-doubt.

"Was there ever a moment when I could have stopped him?" she wondered, her voice barely audible. "A chance to save them?"

Her eyes drifted back to the gruesome photographs, images of lost lives that would haunt her dreams for years to come. And as she stared into the void left behind by their senseless deaths, a steely resolve began to take root deep within her heart.

"Edward will pay for what he's done," she vowed, her voice low and dangerous. "I may have failed these victims, but I will not fail the ones who come next."

With newfound purpose, Samantha gathered the files and strode towards the door, her shoulders squared against the challenges that lay ahead. For though darkness surrounded her, she would no longer be its pawn, but its conqueror.

The moon cast a ghostly pallor upon the living room as Samantha traced her finger along the cold glass of the framed photograph. She could feel the anguish of each victim, their final moments clawing at the edges of her consciousness.

"Edward," she whispered, her voice barely audible. "How could you do this?"

Her hands trembled as she set the photo down, a churning storm of emotion threatening to overwhelm her. The faces of the victims filled her thoughts, each one a brutal testament to Edward's dark desires. Samantha felt the weight of her responsibility, and it crushed her like an iron vice.

"Damn it!" Her fist slammed into the coffee table, the force sending ripples through the whiskey she had poured earlier. "I should have seen the signs. I should have stopped him."

As she paced the room, the shadows seemed to whisper their agreement, their voices insidious and taunting. The floorboards groaned beneath her, echoing her despair and anger.

"Chief Kingsley?" The sudden sound of her deputy's voice from the other side of the door caused her to jump. "Is everything alright in there?"

"Fine, just... thinking," she replied, her voice strained with the effort to maintain control.

"Alright, if you need anything, I'll be right outside."

"Thank you." The door clicked shut, leaving Samantha alone once more with her thoughts.

"Edward, why did you have to become a monster?" she asked the empty room, her mind reeling with memories of happier times before the darkness took hold.

"Those people didn't deserve to die," she continued, her voice choked with sorrow. "They had families, dreams, futures..."

Samantha clenched her fists, nails digging into her palms as her heart raced with a blend of fury and guilt. She allowed herself one final moment to grieve for the lives lost, then drew a deep breath, steeling herself for what must come next.

"Edward will pay for his crimes," she vowed, the words echoing with conviction. "And I will be the one to bring him to justice."

The room seemed to close in on Samantha, shadows creeping along the walls like tendrils of darkness reaching out to grasp her. She stumbled over to the couch, her legs suddenly weak beneath her, and collapsed onto the worn cushions. Burying her face in her hands, she let the tears flow freely, no longer able to contain the storm of emotions raging inside her.

"Edward... How could you?" she whispered between sobs, her voice barely audible even to herself. "How could I not see it?"

As despair threatened to consume her, Samantha recalled memories of their life together – laughter-filled dinners, warm embraces, shared dreams. But those moments now felt tainted, overshadowed by the horrifying truth of her husband's actions.

"Chief Kingsley," came her deputy's voice through the door, strained with concern. "Are you alright?"

"Y-Yes..." Samantha choked out, attempting to regain some semblance of composure. "Just... give me a moment."

"Of course, ma'am," the deputy replied, retreating down the hallway.

Samantha's thoughts raced, torn between her duty as a police officer and her love for Edward. The man she had known for years, had married, and had built a life with was now revealed to be a monster. And yet, her heart ached at the thought of bringing him to justice, shattering the last remnants of the life they had shared.

"Can I truly bring him down?" she questioned, her mind reeling with doubt and trepidation. "But how can I not? He took innocent lives... and I am responsible for upholding the law."

Tears continued to stream down her cheeks, each droplet a testament to her inner turmoil. In that darkened room, she grappled with the weight of her responsibilities, her love for Edward, and her obligation to the victims whose lives he had cruelly cut short.

"Edward... I loved you," Samantha whispered, grief and anger lacing her words. "But I cannot let your actions go unpunished."

Slowly, with a resolve born of heartache and determination, she lifted her tear-streaked face and stared into the encroaching darkness. The shadows seemed to recede ever so slightly as if sensing the steel in her gaze. With newfound strength, Samantha Kingsley, Chief of Police, rose from the couch, ready to face the horror her life had become – and to bring justice to those who had suffered at the hands of her husband.

The cold steel of Samantha's police badge brushed against her fingertips, its familiar touch providing a sudden jolt of clarity. Splayed out before her on the coffee table lay the various pieces of her life: the badge that represented her commitment to justice, the framed photo of her wedding day – now tainted by the atrocities Edward had committed – and the glass of whiskey that seemed to offer little solace.

"Damn you, Edward," she muttered through clenched teeth, her voice barely audible amidst the oppressive silence in the room.

Samantha reached for her phone, her trembling fingers hovering above the screen. She knew what she had to do, but her heart pounded with uncertainty as she considered the ramifications of her actions. As the chief of police, she had an obligation to bring criminals to justice, no matter who they were. But Edward was her husband – could she truly be the one to take him down?

"Edward," she whispered, seeking answers from his image in the wedding photo, "did you even love me at all?"

The silence that followed felt like a knife twisting into her heart. She gripped her badge tightly, feeling its solid weight anchoring her resolve.

"Enough," she said firmly, her voice steady despite the storm of emotions raging inside her. "I am Chief of Police Samantha Kingsley, and I will not let this monster go unpunished."

She contemplated her next move, each option fraught with difficulties and uncertainties. In the end, it was her duty to the victims that steeled her resolve.

"Justice will be served, no matter the cost," she vowed, her voice echoing throughout the empty house.

The shadows that clung to the corners of the room seemed to recoil from the fire that burned in her eyes. With a newfound determination, Samantha rose from the couch and approached the desk where the files from the investigation lay stacked in disarray.

"Edward," she murmured, her voice now steady and resolute, "I will confront you. I will expose your evil deeds, and I will make sure you pay for the lives you've stolen."

As she leafed through the files, her fingers brushing against the gruesome photos of Edward's victims, Samantha felt a growing sense of responsibility – not only as a police officer but also as a woman who had been deceived by a man she loved.

"Those innocent souls deserve justice," she thought, her heart heavy with the weight of it all. "And I am the one who must deliver it to them."

Samantha knew that the path ahead would be treacherous, filled with pain and self-doubt. But she refused to let fear dictate her actions any longer. She would confront Edward, and she would bring him to justice – for the sake of the victims, for her healing, and for the hope of a future unmarked by the darkness that had consumed her life.

The echo of footsteps resounded through the empty room, a haunting reminder of Samantha's isolation. Her face, once strong and determined, was now a canvas of raw emotion – pain, anger, and disbelief etched into every line and curve. The room seemed to close in on her, suffocating in its silence.

"Enough," Samantha whispered to herself, steeling her resolve. She wiped away the tears that streaked her cheeks, leaving behind trails of silent determination. Standing tall, she squared her shoulders and strode towards her office with purposeful strides, each step an act of defiance against the darkness that threatened to consume her.

"Chief Kingsley?" A voice called out from the shadows, causing Samantha to halt mid-step. "I heard you were back at the office... I wanted to check in on you."

"Detective Harris," Samantha acknowledged, her tone professional yet tinged with a hint of vulnerability. "Thank you for your concern, but I'm fine. I have work to do."

"Of course, Chief," Detective Harris replied, concern evident in his eyes. "But remember, we're all here to support you through this."

Samantha looked at him, her gaze steady. "I appreciate that, but I must face this alone. Edward is my responsibility."

"Understood, Chief," he said with a nod, backing away to give her space.

Entering her office, Samantha could feel the oppressive weight of the task ahead, but she refused to falter. It was time to confront the monster who had lurked within her own home – the man she had loved, trusted, and shared a life with.

As she sat down at her desk, the cold metal of her gun pressing against her hip brought an odd comfort. It was a reminder of her duty and the power she held to bring an end to the nightmare that had gripped their city. Her fingers drummed rhythmically on the desk, a steady beat that seemed to match the pounding of her heart.

"Edward," she whispered, her voice barely audible yet filled with determination. "I will find you, and I will bring you to justice."

Her mind raced, thoughts swirling like a maelstrom – snippets of memories, fragments of evidence, and the faces of the victims, all haunting her every waking moment. But within that chaos, a spark of clarity began to emerge. A plan began to form, one that would lead her down the path to redemption and closure.

"Justice will be served," Samantha vowed, her words echoing through the empty office. "For them… and myself."

She took a deep breath, steeling herself for the challenges ahead. And as the door closed behind her, sealing her away from the world outside, she knew that the time had come to confront the darkness head-on– and emerge victorious on the other side.

CHAPTER 16

Eternal Terror

The sun dipped below the horizon, casting dark shadows that slithered through the damp streets like sinister serpents. Edward Kingsley stood in the alleyway beside Mia's rental home, his heart pumping with adrenaline as he watched her approach. His neatly combed hair and well-tailored suit did little to betray the twisted desires festering inside him.

"Hey!" he called out as Mia passed by the opening of the alleyway, feigning surprise at seeing her. "Fancy meeting you here."

"Edward?" Mia asked, her voice quivering with uncertainty. She looked around, sensing something was off but unable to pinpoint what it was. Her soft brown eyes met his icy gaze, searching for reassurance that never came.

"Let me help you with your bags," he offered, stepping forward and grabbing her arm with a vice-like grip.

"Ouch! Edward, you're hurting me," she cried out, trying to twist away from his grasp.

"Sorry, my dear," he said, his voice dripping with insincerity. "I didn't mean to startle you." And with that, he pulled her into the darkness of the alleyway, muffling her screams with his other hand.

"Please, don't do this," Mia whimpered, her words muffled against his palm. But her pleas fell on deaf ears as Edward expertly bound her hands together behind her back, using a silk tie he had been carrying in his pocket. He then secured her ankles with another one, taking pleasure in the way she squirmed beneath his touch.

"Comfortable?" he asked, chuckling darkly as he hoisted her over his shoulder. "I'd hate for you to be uncomfortable during our little...adventure."

"Edward, I don't understand," Mia sobbed, her fear palpable. "Why are you doing this?"

"Ah, now that would be telling," he replied, his voice a low, menacing growl. "But let's just say it's in my nature to seek...control."

As he carried her back towards the rental home, Mia struggled against her restraints, desperate for any chance of escape. But Edward had tied her too well – a testament to his meticulous nature and craving for power over those he deemed weaker than himself.

"Please," Mia whispered, her voice barely audible through her tears. "Please let me go."

"Sorry, sweetheart," Edward replied, a cruel smile playing on his lips as he prepared for the next stage of his twisted plan. "That's not an option."

Edward's icy gaze bore into Mia's tear-filled eyes, his grip on her wrists unyielding as he held her captive in the dimly lit room. Her pulse raced beneath his fingertips, a reminder of her fragile humanity that only fueled his insatiable desire for control.

"Please," Mia choked out between sobs, "I won't tell anyone about this. Just let me go."

Her desperate plea did nothing to soften Edward's cold countenance. Instead, he regarded her with a predatory gleam in his eyes that sent shivers down her spine.

"Your silence means nothing to me," he replied, his voice dripping with malice. "However, your fear does have its uses. You see, Mia, you are my ticket to freedom."

Mia's breath hitched at the revelation, her mind racing to make sense of his words. "Wh-what do you mean?" she stammered, her voice barely audible over the pounding of her heart in her ears.

"Ah, I thought that might pique your interest." A sinister smile curved Edward's lips as he continued. "You'll soon be receiving a visitor who will stop at nothing to find you. And when she does, well..." His grip tightened around her wrists, causing Mia to wince in pain. "Let's just say we'll both get what we want."

As the implications of his plan began to sink in, Mia's body trembled with a mixture of fear and dread. The realization that Edward intended to use her as bait for someone else filled her with a visceral terror that threatened to consume her.

"Who...who is coming?" she whispered, dreading the answer.

"Ah, now that would spoil the surprise," Edward teased, his voice a chilling contrast to the terror coursing through Mia's veins. "But rest assured, your role in this little game is essential."

"Please, Edward," Mia implored, her voice shaking with emotion. "There has to be another way."

"Unfortunately for you, my dear," he responded, his tone devoid of any warmth or compassion, "there isn't."

As the weight of her situation settled upon her, Mia's thoughts raced in a futile attempt to find a way out, all the while feeling the chilling presence of Edward Kingsley as an unrelenting force, determined to bend her to his will.

The wind howled through the trees, whipping up leaves and debris as Samantha Kingsley pulled her car to a screeching halt outside Mia's rental home. The ominous clouds above cast a foreboding shadow over the property, setting her nerves on edge. Dread gnawed at her insides as she stepped out of the car, her breath visible in the chill air.

"Damn it, Edward," she muttered under her breath, slamming the car door shut. She had received a frantic call from one of Edward's employees, claiming that Mia hadn't been seen or heard from since the previous day. The pit in her stomach deepened as she approached the front door, noting the scratches and splintered wood around the lock.

"Please let her be okay," Samantha whispered to herself, drawing her gun and cautiously pushing the door open. The eerie creak echoed through the silent house, sending shivers down her spine. Inside, the scene was devastating – furniture toppled, items broken, and disarray throughout the living room. It was clear that a struggle had taken place, and Mia was nowhere to be found.

"Shit," Samantha hissed, quickly scanning the room for any signs of her husband's involvement. Her heart raced, pounding painfully against her chest as she fought the urge to succumb to her rising panic. She couldn't let her emotions get in the way of her duty – not when Mia's life was potentially hanging in the balance.

"Focus, Sam," she told herself, taking a deep breath. "You're a damn good cop. You can find them."

With renewed determination, Samantha began combing the area for clues that might lead her to Edward and Mia. The disheveled state of the house made her task more difficult, but she refused to give up. As she searched, she grappled with the unsettling knowledge that her husband was capable of such violence and cruelty.

"Edward, why are you doing this?" she wondered, frustration and pain lacing her thoughts. "What the hell happened to you?"

She forced herself back to the task at hand, searching for any trace of their whereabouts. Her heart caught in her throat as she stumbled upon a small, torn piece of fabric on the floor, stained with drops of blood. It was a match to the shirt Mia had been wearing in one of her sketches Samantha had seen earlier.

"Damn it," she whispered, pocketing the evidence. "Hang on, Mia. I'm coming for you."

As the wind continued to howl outside, Samantha's resolve hardened into an unbreakable determination. She would find Mia and bring Edward to justice, no matter what personal cost it required. The shadows cast by the storm clouds above mirrored the darkness that had descended upon her life, but Samantha refused to let it consume her. She would face the monster that her husband had become and do whatever was necessary to save an innocent life.

The storm outside raged on, the raindrops drumming a sinister melody against the windows as Samantha stood alone in the dimly lit rental home. With every passing minute, her anxiety heightened, knowing that Mia's life hung in the balance. The thunderous growl outside seemed to mirror her internal turmoil. Her phone buzzed in her pocket, startling her. The room suddenly felt colder as she read the message from an unknown number. It was Edward.

"Hello, my love," the text read. "I have dear Mia with me. She's safe... for now. But if you want her to stay that way, I need your help."

Samantha's blood ran cold, and a wave of nausea washed over her. she replied, trying to keep her tone calm, and controlled. "What do you want, Edward?"

"Safe passage. I know you can make that happen. Just one call to the right people, and we can all go our separate ways. No more pain, no more fear. You know I never wanted it to come to this."

Samantha clenched her fists, her knuckles turning white as she fought to maintain her composure. As much as she wanted to bring him to justice immediately, she couldn't risk Mia's life. She weighed her options, considering the best course of action for buying some time.

"Edward," she said through gritted teeth, "if I help you, how can I be sure you'll release Mia unharmed?"

"Ah, Samantha, always the skeptic," he responded. "You don't have much choice, do you? You know what I'm capable of. Help me and Mia walk free. Refuse and... well, I think you can imagine."

A flash of lightning illuminated the room, casting jagged shadows across the walls. Samantha realized that she had to play along, at least for now. She needed time to formulate a plan, to save Mia and bring Edward down.

"Alright," she texted back, her heart pounding in her chest. "I'll do it. But I need proof that you won't hurt Mia."

"Very well," he replied. "I'll send you a picture of her, safe and sound. And don't even think about trying anything clever, my love. You know me better than that. One wrong move and things will get very ugly for our sweet little artist."

Samantha's mind raced as she tried to stay one step ahead of Edward, knowing that any misstep could cost Mia her life. As she waited for his response, she contemplated the man she had married – the man who had become a monster. How could she have been so blind to the darkness lurking within him?

As much as Samantha wanted justice, she couldn't help but feel a pang of sorrow for the man she had once loved. But she pushed those thoughts aside, focusing on the task at hand. Mia's life depended on it.

And if there was breath in her body, Samantha Kingsley would not abandon an innocent soul to the clutches of evil.

Samantha's heart thundered within her chest as she stared into Edward's cold, calculating eyes. She had to choose her words carefully, lest she trigger his wrath and endanger Mia further.

"Edward," she began, her voice steady despite the fear coursing through her veins. "I know you're smarter than this. You've always been a master of strategy, able to see the long game. Letting Mia go now can only benefit you."

Edward regarded her with icy indifference, his grip on Mia's arm tightening like a vice. The young artist whimpered in pain, but her eyes never left Samantha, pleading for help.

"Your escape won't work if you hurt her," Samantha continued, fighting to maintain her composure. "You know I'll do everything in my power to bring you down if you harm an innocent woman."

"Your loyalty to your job is touching, really," Edward sneered, his voice dripping with condescension. "But I'm afraid I need more than your words, Samantha. I need something concrete."

"Fine," Samantha gritted her teeth, struggling to contain her anger. "What do you want?"

"An assurance that I'll be allowed to leave this city unharmed and without pursuit," he replied, his tone menacingly calm. "Otherwise, our dear Mia here will suffer the consequences."

As Edward's attention momentarily shifted back to Samantha, Mia seized the opportunity to make eye contact with her captor's wife. Her gaze was filled with terror, yet also determination, as if urging Samantha to save her from this nightmare.

"Alright," Samantha conceded, steeling herself for the difficult road ahead. "I'll arrange it. But you have to promise me that you'll release Mia once you're safe."

"Of course, my love," Edward purred, a sickening smile spreading across his face. "I knew you'd see the reason eventually. Just remember, one false move, and our sweet little artist will pay the price."

Samantha nodded, suppressing the bile that threatened to rise in her throat. She could only hope that her plan would work and that she would be able to outmaneuver Edward before it was too late for Mia.

"Fine," she spat, glaring at him with a mixture of hatred and determination. "You'll get what you want, but only if you keep your end of the bargain."

"Deal," Edward replied, his lips curling into a sinister grin. "I look forward to seeing how this all plays out."

As Samantha backed away, her eyes locked on Mia's desperate face, she vowed to herself that she would do whatever it took to save the young woman and bring Edward to justice. She just prayed that she hadn't made a deal with the devil from which there would be no escape.

Samantha observed Edward's fingers drumming anxiously on the armrest of his chair, a growing storm brewing behind his eyes. She knew that her next move could be the difference between life and death for Mia.

"Edward," Samantha began, her tone measured but not patronizing, "I know you're feeling cornered right now, but I have an idea that might just work for both of us."

"Really?" he sneered, his gaze flicking between Samantha and the bound figure of Mia, who struggled to suppress her whimpers. "And what would that be?"

"Listen carefully," Samantha said, her heart pounding in her chest as she devised the plan on the spot. "You need to get away, and we want Mia safe. So, let's stage an escape for you – something that'll throw off the other officers while I help you slip out undetected."

Edward's eyes narrowed; his agitation momentarily silenced as he considered her proposal. Samantha pressed on, knowing she had to keep him engaged.

"Once you're safely away, you release Mia, and everybody gets what they want," she continued, forcing herself to maintain eye contact with him despite the revulsion churning in her gut. "Think about it, Edward. This is your best shot at getting out of this mess without any more bloodshed."

"Very clever, Samantha," Edward mused, leaning back in his chair. He stared at her, his eyes cold and calculating. "But how can I trust that you'll keep your word?"

"You know me, Edward," she replied, swallowing the lump in her throat. "When have I ever lied to you? Besides, my priority is saving Mia. If making sure you escape is what it takes, then that's what I'll do."

Edward's gaze lingered on her for a few tense moments before he finally nodded. "Alright," he agreed, though his voice held an edge of suspicion. "We'll try it your way – but remember, if you betray me, Mia will suffer the consequences."

"Understood," Samantha said, her resolve hardening. As she looked at Mia's tear-streaked face, she vowed to herself that she would do whatever it took to save her and bring Edward to justice, even if it meant walking the razor's edge between trust and betrayal.

Edward's eyes narrowed, scrutinizing Samantha as he contemplated her proposal. His fingers drummed rhythmically on the table, the sound echoing through the dimly lit room. In the corner, Mia trembled, bound and frightened, her wide eyes silently pleading with Samantha for help.

"Alright, Samantha," Edward said, his voice low and measured. "Assuming I entertain this idea of a staged escape, what guarantee do I have that you won't stab me in the back? That you won't take advantage of the situation to bring me down?"

"Edward, our years together have been filled with both love and loyalty," Samantha replied, her voice steady despite the pounding of her heart. She knew she had to tread carefully, using her intimate knowledge of Edward's mind to manipulate him without arousing suspicion. "You know I've always respected your ambition and intelligence. It's one of the things that drew us together in the first place."

She paused, watching as his expression softened ever so slightly. It was a small victory, but one that gave her hope. Samantha continued, careful to sprinkle her words with just enough flattery to appeal to his ego.

"Besides, if I wanted to bring you down, I could have done so at any moment during these past few weeks," she pointed out. "But I didn't, because I still believe in the man I married. The man who built a successful business from nothing. The man who achieved what others couldn't even dream of."

Edward's eyes flicked toward Mia, then back to Samantha. The uncertainty in his gaze betrayed his inner turmoil. Samantha pressed on, her voice taking on a more urgent tone.

"Edward, we both know that what you've done is… unspeakable," she admitted, swallowing hard. "But there's still a chance for redemption. For forgiveness. If you let Mia go and disappear quietly, you can start over – create a new life, far away from the darkness that has consumed you here."

As she spoke, she watched Edward's face closely for any sign of resistance, any hint that he might lash out. But to her surprise, she saw something else in his eyes – a flicker of hope, quickly masked by a veil of suspicion.

"Is that what you truly want, Samantha?" he asked, his voice barely above a whisper. "For me to disappear and never return?"

She hesitated for a moment, torn between her sense of duty and her love for the man she had once known. Finally, she forced herself to nod.

"Yes," she said softly, her heart aching with the weight of her decision. "It's the only way to save both Mia and you."

Edward leaned back in his chair, a slow, thoughtful smile spreading across his face. He seemed to be weighing her words, considering the implications of her proposal. Samantha held her breath, praying that her gamble would pay off.

"Very well, Samantha," Edward said, at last, his voice cold and resolute. "We'll do it your way. But remember – if you betray me, there will be no mercy for either of you."

The dim light from a single candle flickered, casting eerie shadows on the walls of the cramped room. Edward's eyes locked onto Samantha's; his expression unreadable as he mulled over her proposal. The air was thick with tension, each breath they took feeling heavier than the last.

"Alright," Edward said finally, his voice low and measured. "I'll go along with your plan – but only if you swear to protect me, to guarantee my freedom."

Samantha hesitated, her mind racing as she weighed the consequences of her actions. She knew that agreeing to Edward's demands would mean betraying her duty as a police officer, yet she couldn't help but feel an overwhelming sense of responsibility for the situation at hand.

If she didn't act, Mia's life would be at risk, and so would countless others who might fall victim to Edward's twisted desires.

"Edward, you have my word," Samantha replied solemnly, locking eyes with him. "I will do everything in my power to ensure your escape. But once you're free, you must promise never to harm anyone again."

"Agreed," he responded, a hint of reluctance in his tone. "Now tell me, what's the next step in this little charade of yours?"

As Samantha detailed the plan, she couldn't help but notice the way Edward's fingers twitched, betraying his tightly controlled exterior. At that moment, she realized that beneath his calm, calculating facade, he was just as afraid as she was. He had placed his trust in her – a trust she intended to exploit to save Mia and herself from the danger that loomed over them.

"Once you release Mia, I'll arrange for a car to be waiting nearby," she continued, her voice steady despite the turmoil brewing inside her. "It will take you to a safe house where you can lay low until we find a more permanent solution."

"And you're certain that no one will suspect your involvement?" Edward asked, his eyes narrowing with suspicion.

"Trust me, Edward," Samantha replied, her voice laced with determination. "I know how to cover my tracks and keep you safe. But you must remember – any deviation from the plan could jeopardize everything."

He nodded slowly, the gravity of their agreement settling upon him like a heavy shroud. It was clear that neither of them relished the thought of what they were about to do, but they both understood that it was the only way forward.

"Very well, Samantha," he said, extending his hand towards her. "I'll hold you to your word."

As their hands met in a firm clasp, Samantha felt a cold shiver run down her spine. The die had been cast, and there would be no turning back. With every ounce of her being, she vowed to outwit Edward and protect Mia, whatever the cost.

The chill of the midnight air hung heavy as a shroud, the darkness seemingly whispering of the sinister deeds that were about to unfold. Edward's face was barely visible in the dim light of the streetlamp, his eyes flickering with a mixture of doubt and determination.

"Let's go over the details one more time," Samantha said, her voice betraying no hint of her growing apprehensions. Edward nodded, casting furtive glances around them to ensure they remained unobserved.

"Tomorrow night, at precisely eleven o'clock, I'll release Mia near the old warehouse on 5th Street," he began, his words clipped with a cold, calculating precision. "You'll have officers stationed nearby, but not too close – we don't want to spook her or arouse suspicion."

"Right," Samantha agreed, forcing herself to maintain her composure. She couldn't afford to let her feelings interfere with the task at hand. "My team will be positioned several blocks away, ready to move in only when I give the signal."

"Good," Edward replied, his gaze locked onto hers as if trying to read her thoughts. "Once you've secured Mia, I'll make my way to the waterfront where a boat will be waiting for me."

Samantha felt her heart constrict as she forced herself to continue outlining their treacherous plan. "I'll arrange for a trusted contact to be there with the boat. He won't ask any questions, and he knows how to avoid attracting attention."

"Perfect," Edward murmured, almost to himself. There was an eerie calmness to his demeanor that sent shivers down Samantha's spine.

"Remember," she warned, steeling herself for what lay ahead, "if you harm Mia in any way or deviate from our agreement, I won't hesitate to bring you down myself."

Edward's lips curled into a twisted smile, the darkness in his eyes momentarily giving way to a flicker of admiration. "I have no doubt about that, my dear."

As they parted ways, Samantha's mind raced with the enormity of the situation. She knew she was walking a razor's edge, her duty as a police officer and her love for Edward tugging her in opposite directions. And yet, she couldn't allow Mia to become another victim of his twisted desires.

The night seemed to close in around her as she prepared herself for the dangerous game she was about to play. Every step that brought her closer to the moment of truth echoed with the weight of her choices. The success of her plan hinged on her ability to outwit Edward – there could be no room for error.

"Only one more day," she whispered into the darkness, her voice caught between fear and determination. "Mia, I promise I'll save you...no matter what it takes."

CHAPTER 17

Haunted Vows

The phone vibrated violently on Samantha's desk, its shrill ring echoing in the dimly lit room. Her heart raced as she picked it up, noting the unknown number on the screen.

"Chief Kingsley speaking."

"Listen carefully," a gravelly voice whispered on the other end, "Mia Evans is being held captive in an abandoned warehouse on the outskirts of town. You don't have much time."

"Who is this?" Samantha demanded, but the line went dead. A chill ran down her spine, and the weight of responsibility settled on her shoulders like a leaden cloak. She had to act, and fast.

"Commander Davis, Sergeant Thompson, meet me in the conference room immediately," she barked into her radio, her voice betraying no hint of her inner turmoil. The two officers arrived seconds later, their expressions serious and focused. Samantha didn't hesitate as she laid out the situation before them.

"An anonymous tip just informed me that Mia Evans is being held at an abandoned warehouse outside of town. We need to move now. Gather your most trusted men and meet me in the parking garage in five minutes."

"Understood, Chief," Commander Davis nodded, his deep-set eyes filled with determination. He and Sergeant Thompson hurried out of the room, leaving Samantha alone with her thoughts.

As the team assembled in the parking garage, Samantha couldn't help but think of Edward. What had driven him to this dark path? She shook her head, pushing aside her personal feelings. Now was not the time for questions – now was the time for action.

"Alright, everyone," she began, addressing the dozen officers who stood before her, "Our mission is simple: we find Mia, we apprehend Edward, and we bring them both back safely. I want this operation to be swift and efficient. No mistakes."

"Chief," Sergeant Thompson interjected, his brow furrowed in concern, "are you sure you want to lead this personally? I mean, with Edward-"

"Edward is a criminal," Samantha cut him off, her voice cold and steely. "He's dangerous, and he needs to be stopped. That's all that matters right now."

The officers exchanged uneasy glances, but none questioned her resolve further. They knew their Chief was strong and dedicated to her duty; if anyone could bring Edward to justice, it was her.

As they climbed into their vehicles and sped towards the warehouse, Samantha steeled herself for the confrontation ahead. The darkness outside seemed to mirror the darkness within Edward, and she couldn't help but wonder how far he would go to maintain his twisted grip on power. But one thing was certain: she would not back down. Not when Mia's life was at stake.

"Let's put an end to this," she whispered, her knuckles white as she gripped the steering wheel. The night air filled with the sound of sirens, cutting through the eerie silence like a knife.

The moon hung heavily in the sky, casting an eerie glow over the dilapidated warehouse. Its once-red bricks were now stained by years of neglect, and the rusted metal doors groaned in protest against the wind. Samantha stared at the foreboding structure, her heart pounding in her chest as she tried to reconcile the man she had loved with the monster he had become.

"Chief, we're ready when you are," Officer Daniels said, his voice tense but steady. The rest of the team stood poised behind him, their weapons drawn and faces grim.

"Alright," Samantha replied, swallowing hard as she forced herself to focus on the task at hand. "Remember the plan—two teams, one enters through the front, the other through the back. We sweep every inch of this place until we find Mia and Edward."

"Copy that," Daniels nodded and signaled for the team to split up. As they moved into position, Samantha couldn't help but feel a pang of guilt for not seeing the darkness within Edward sooner. How could she have been so blind?

"Focus, Samantha," she muttered under her breath, shaking off the doubt that threatened to cloud her judgment. She couldn't afford to let her emotions dictate her actions, not when there were lives on the line.

"Team One, moving in," Sergeant Thompson's voice crackled over the radio, breaking Samantha from her reverie. She took a deep breath, mentally preparing herself for the horrors that might await her inside the warehouse.

"Team Two, in position," she responded, her voice void of the turmoil raging inside her. With a final nod to her officers, she kicked open the rusted door, sending a shower of debris across the floor.

As they entered the gloomy interior, the air seemed to grow heavier, suffused with a palpable sense of dread. The only light came from the flashlights mounted on their guns, casting long shadows along the walls and floor.

"Edward!" Samantha called out, her voice echoing through the vast emptiness. "We know you're in here! Give yourself up and release Mia!"

The silence that followed was deafening as if the very walls of the warehouse were holding their breath.

"Stay sharp," Samantha whispered to her team, her eyes scanning the dark corners for any sign of movement. They moved cautiously through the open space, their footsteps muffled by the layer of dust that coated everything in sight.

"Chief, we've found something," Officer Daniels' voice suddenly broke through the radio, urgency lacing his words.

"What is it?" Samantha demanded, her heart rate spiking at the thought of what horrors they might have discovered.

"A locked door," Daniels replied. "It's the only one we've come across so far. We think Mia might be behind it."

"Stand by; I'm on my way," Samantha said, her pulse quickening with anticipation. As she raced towards the location, a thousand thoughts raced through her mind—fears for Mia's safety, anger towards Edward, and a deep ache for the love that had once been so pure between them.

"Let him go, Samantha," she silently urged herself, knowing that she couldn't allow her feelings for Edward to interfere with her duty. "He's not the man you loved anymore."

As she arrived at the door, her team stood ready for her order. With a resolute nod, Samantha signaled for them to break down the barrier that separated them from both Mia and the monster who had torn their lives apart. As the door splintered beneath their force, Samantha steeled herself for the confrontation that would change everything forever.

Moonlight cast ghostly shadows over the abandoned warehouse as Samantha stood at its entrance. She gripped her gun tightly, feeling the weight of responsibility and her conflicting emotions. The smell of damp decay filled her nostrils as she signaled to her team.

"Check every corner," she ordered, her voice a hushed whisper. "Stay alert and keep in touch through the radios."

The officers nodded, their faces set with determination. As they moved into the cavernous building, the darkness seemed to swallow them whole, leaving only the faint echo of their footsteps as evidence of their presence.

Samantha advanced cautiously, her eyes darting from side to side as she tried to make out any shapes or movements in the gloom. Each creak and groan of the ancient structure sent shivers down her spine, intensifying the mounting dread that clawed at her chest.

"Where are you, Edward?" she thought bitterly, her love for him now tainted by the monstrous reality of his actions. "How could you do this?"

"Chief, I've found something," Officer Daniels' voice crackled through the radio, jolting Samantha from her thoughts.

"Report," she replied, her heart pounding against her ribs.

"Traces of blood near the back of the warehouse," he answered, his voice tense. "We might be close."

"Stay on your guard," Samantha commanded, her pulse quickening. "I don't want any surprises."

"Roger that," Daniels confirmed, and the line went silent.

As Samantha continued her search, her mind raced with questions. How could she have been so blind to Edward's true nature? Was there anything left of the man she had loved? And, most importantly, would they find Mia before it was too late?

"Damn it," Samantha muttered under her breath as she stepped around a pile of rotting debris. The suffocating darkness seemed to close in around her, the oppressive silence only broken by the distant murmur of her team's movements.

"Keep it together, Samantha," she told herself, trying to stave off the creeping panic that threatened to overwhelm her. "You've faced worse than this."

As she rounded a corner, her flashlight caught on something metallic glinting in the darkness. She approached cautiously, her heart hammering with anticipation. A door loomed before her, its padlock gleaming in the cold light.

"Could this be it?" she wondered, her stomach twisting into knots. She reached for her radio, ready to call for backup and confront whatever lay behind that door. But first, she had to steady her resolve and prepare for the battle ahead - the battle against her own heart and the man who had once been her everything.

Samantha's flashlight beam cut through the darkness like a scalpel, revealing the gnarled and twisted shadows that lurked in every corner. The air was thick with decay and neglect as if even time itself had abandoned this forsaken place.

"Chief," Officer Daniels whispered urgently, snapping Samantha's attention back to the present. "We've got something."

He gestured toward an ominous-looking door at the end of the corridor, its hinges rusted and groaning with the weight of years. Samantha's pulse quickened, her instincts screaming that they were on the right track. She approached the door, her boots crunching on the debris-strewn floor, and reached out to test the handle. It was locked.

"Guys, get ready," she murmured into her radio, her voice barely more than a breath. "I think we've found them."

Her team tensed, weapons drawn and eyes narrowed, as they prepared for what lay ahead. Samantha could feel their collective heartbeats pounding like war drums, the adrenaline coursing through their veins like wildfire.

"Okay," she said, steeling herself for the confrontation. "On my signal."

The world seemed to slow down as she lifted her hand, her fingers trembling ever so slightly, poised to give the order. Every nerve in her body hummed with anticipation, the undeniable weight of responsibility settling heavily on her shoulders.

"Three... two... one... breach!"

The door exploded inward in a shower of splinters and dust, the abrupt violence of the act shattering the fragile silence like glass. As the dust cleared, Samantha's worst fears were confirmed: there stood Edward, a wild gleam in his eyes, holding Mia captive with a knife pressed against her throat.

"Drop it, Edward!" Samantha barked, her gun trained on her own husband's heart. "Let her go!"

Edward's face contorted into a twisted grin, his grip on Mia only tightening. "You think you can stop me, Sam?" he taunted, the darkness in his voice sending a shiver down her spine. "You don't have it in you."

"Edward, please," Samantha pleaded, her resolve wavering for just a moment, her love for him fighting against her duty as a police officer. "This isn't you."

"Isn't it?" Edward sneered, his eyes glittering with malice. "Maybe this is who I've always been, and you were just too blind to see it."

Samantha's heart clenched at his words, but she forced herself to push aside her doubts and focus on the task at hand. She had to save Mia, even if it meant facing the man she once loved.

"Let her go, Edward," Samantha repeated, her voice firm. "Or I swear, I will put you down."

The sharp glint of the knife's edge caught a stray beam of moonlight filtering through the broken warehouse windows, slicing through the darkness and casting eerie shadows on Edward's taunting grin. Samantha's heart pounded in her chest as she stared into the eyes of the man she had once loved, now twisted by rage and desperation.

"Edward," Samantha's voice was ice-cold, every word a dagger aimed at his heart, "release Mia immediately and surrender yourself. There's still a chance for you if you do this peacefully."

"Is there?" Edward barked out a laugh, the sound echoing unnervingly throughout the warehouse. "Is there really, Sam? Look at us - surrounded by your little army, guns pointed at me... It seems we're past the point of peaceful resolutions, don't you think?"

As he spoke, Samantha scanned the room, noting the positions of her team members - each one tense, ready to act at the slightest signal. She gripped her gun tighter, knuckles white with the strain. Her mind raced, devising strategies, calculating risks, and weighing the consequences of every possible move.

"Please," she whispered, unwilling to let him see her inner turmoil, "I don't want to hurt you, Edward. But I can't let you hurt Mia either. This ends now."

Edward's gaze never wavered from Samantha's, his eyes burning holes into her very soul. "You always did have a soft spot for the helpless ones, didn't you, Sam?"

"Enough!" Samantha snapped, cutting through his mockery. "You have one last chance, Edward. Release her, and we'll talk about what happens next. Refuse, and I promise you, there will be no mercy for you."

A flicker of fear passed across Edward's face, betraying the conviction in his voice as he spat, "You don't have the guts, Samantha. Do you think you can take me down? Go ahead and try. I'll take her with me."

"Is that your final answer?" Samantha's finger hovered over the trigger, a heartbeat away from making a decision that would change all their lives forever.

"Always so dramatic," Edward sneered, but his grip on Mia tightened ever so slightly, betraying the fear he tried so desperately to hide. "Go on then, Sam. Do your worst."

Samantha stared into Edward's eyes, searching for any trace of the man she had loved and married - the man who had sworn to protect her, to stand by her side through thick and thin. But all she saw was darkness, and she knew what she had to do.

The dim light from the moon cast eerie shadows in the desolate warehouse, as drops of sweat trickled down Samantha's forehead. Her heart pounded like a war drum, drowning out all other sounds.

"Pathetic," Edward hissed, his eyes locked onto hers with an intensity that sent shivers down her spine. "You think you can save her? You're nothing but a puppet, dancing to someone else's tune."

Samantha's grip tightened on her gun, knuckles turning white as she struggled to keep her emotions in check. Her mind raced, thoughts tumbling over one another as she forced herself to focus. She needed to protect Mia and bring her husband to justice, no matter the personal cost.

"Let her go, Edward," Samantha demanded through gritted teeth, taking a calculated step forward. "This ends now."

"Or what?" Edward sneered, yanking Mia closer to him, her whimper of pain echoing off the walls. "You'll shoot me? Go ahead, Samantha. Pull the trigger."

"Edward, I don't want to hurt you," she said, her voice wavering with uncertainty. But she couldn't let fear dictate her actions, not when Mia's life hung in the balance. "But I will do whatever it takes to save her."

"Save her?" Edward laughed, a cold, cruel sound that made her blood run cold. "Just like you were supposed to save all those other people you failed to protect?"

Samantha swallowed hard, memories of past cases flooding her mind – the faces of victims who had slipped through her fingers. But she couldn't dwell on those failures now. This was her chance at redemption.

"Enough!" she roared, her voice echoing throughout the warehouse. "Release Mia, and face the consequences of your actions!"

"Never!" Edward spat, defiance written across his twisted features. "You'll have to kill me first!"

"Then so be it," Samantha whispered, knowing deep down that there was no other option. She took another step forward, her finger tightening on the trigger as she stared down the barrel of her gun, straight into the eyes of the man she had once loved.

As she prepared to make the most difficult decision of her life, the weight of responsibility pressed down on her shoulders, threatening to crush her. But she couldn't falter now. The lives of Mia and countless others hung in the balance, and it was up to her to tip the scales in their favor.

The oppressive darkness of the warehouse seemed to close in on Samantha, her heartbeat pounding in her ears as she held her gun steady, aimed at Edward. Sweat trickled down her temple as her thoughts raced faster than the thrum of her pulse.

"Go ahead," Edward sneered, his voice dripping with malice. "Pull the trigger, Sam. You think you have what it takes to end this?"

Her finger twitched on the trigger, but Samantha fought the urge to fire. She couldn't let him get under her skin – not when Mia's life was on the line. Her eyes darted to the frightened girl, bound and gagged in a corner, and she felt a surge of protectiveness course through her veins.

"Last chance, Edward," Samantha warned, trying to keep her voice steady despite the turmoil raging inside her. "Let her go, or I swear to God, I won't hesitate."

Edward's laughter echoed through the space, sending shivers down Samantha's spine. His eyes glittered with cold amusement, devoid of any remorse or humanity. The man she had once loved was long gone, consumed by his twisted desires.

"Prove it," he taunted, his gaze locked onto hers with unyielding intensity. "Show me just how far you're willing to go for your precious duty."

Time seemed to slow as Samantha stared into the abyss of Edward's merciless eyes. Questions and doubts swirled within her, threatening to cloud her resolve. But she couldn't afford hesitation now. Not when every second counted when the lives of others hung in the balance.

In that moment of infinite tension, Samantha made her choice. With a sharp intake of breath, she squeezed the trigger, sending a bullet whizzing past Edward's ear. The shot rang out like thunder in the enclosed space, its echo reverberating through the air.

Edward's face contorted with shock and anger, but Samantha's expression remained resolute. Her heart hammered in her chest as she stared him down, the adrenaline coursing through her system making her feel more alive than ever.

"Next time, I won't miss," she warned, her voice hard and steady as iron. "Now release Mia, and end this madness."

Edward's eyes narrowed, his jaw clenched as he weighed his options. Samantha held her breath, praying that her demonstration of determination had been enough to tip the scales.

The sound of the bullet ricocheting off the cold metal wall reverberated through the warehouse, a chilling reminder of Samantha's unwavering resolve. The standoff hung in the balance, a precarious dance on the edge of order and chaos.

"Is that what you want, Edward?" Samantha asked, her voice laden with the weight of their shared history. "To be hunted down like the monster you've become?"

Edward's lips curled into a sneer, his eyes darkening with fury. But beneath that anger, a flicker of fear betrayed his confidence. He glanced at Mia, trembling in his grip, and then back to Samantha. It was a battle between his twisted desires and the very real threat of consequence.

"Alright, you win," he spat, the words bitter on his tongue. He released Mia, shoving her towards Samantha, who caught her before she stumbled to the ground. She held her tightly, relief mingling with the lingering tension in the air.

"Hands up, Edward," Samantha ordered, not allowing herself to relax until he complied. His hands rose slowly, shaking with rage and frustration.

"Are you happy now, Sam?" he growled, the name he used to call her with affection now dripping with disdain. "Is this what you wanted? To bring me down?"

Samantha's mind raced, grappling with the remnants of love she once felt for him. But she knew her duty came first, and the man before her was no longer the person she had married. Through gritted teeth, she responded, "No, Edward. I wanted justice."

"Justice?" he scoffed, his laugh hollow and bitter. "You think this is justice? You don't know the meaning of the word."

"Maybe not," Samantha admitted, her heart heavy with regret. "But I know I can't let you hurt anyone else, and I'll do whatever it takes to stop you."

"Even if it means losing me?" Edward challenged the last vestiges of their shared past hanging in the air between them.

"Especially then," Samantha whispered, her voice barely audible over the sound of her heart breaking. She knew she had made the right choice, but the pain of that decision was a wound that would never truly heal.

"Take him away," she ordered the officers behind her, her voice strong despite the storm of emotions within. They moved forward, handcuffing Edward and leading him out of the warehouse as he shot her one last, venomous glare.

Samantha held Mia close, a silent promise to protect her from the darkness that had nearly consumed them all. As they stepped out into the night, the cool air a balm on her frayed nerves, Samantha knew that her mission had been accomplished. But the scars left behind would serve as a constant reminder of the price they had paid for justice.

CHAPTER 18

Captive Confrontation

The pale moonlight cast an eerie glow on the luxurious property, its shadows stretching like twisted limbs across the manicured lawn. Samantha's heart pounded in her chest as she approached, fear and determination warring within her. Though her role as police chief had prepared her for countless dangerous situations, this was personal – this was her husband.

"Edward," she whispered under her breath, her eyes scanning the surroundings with a practiced gaze. She searched for any signs of Mia, the young woman who had unwittingly become ensnared in Edward's dark web.

"Looking for someone?" a voice called out mockingly.

Samantha's head snapped to the side, spotting movement in the corner of her eye. There stood Edward near the entrance of the property, his sinister smile sending chills down her spine. As their eyes locked, anger and resolve surged through her, fueling her determination to see this through.

"Edward, where is she?" Samantha demanded, her voice steady despite the chaos brewing inside her.

"Ah, our dear little artist," he drawled, his cold eyes gleaming with malicious amusement. "You think you can save her?"

"Damn right I do," Samantha replied, her grip tightening on her gun. "Now tell me where Mia is."

"Or what? You'll shoot me?" Edward taunted, stepping closer. "You wouldn't dare."

Samantha's thoughts raced as she tried to predict Edward's next move. Knowing him as well as she did, she knew that he would not relinquish control easily. But she also knew that beneath his suave, charming exterior lay the mind of a predator, one who had gone too far this time.

"Edward, don't make this any worse than it already is," she warned, desperately hoping that some shred of humanity remained within him. "This isn't you."

"Isn't it?" he challenged, his smile widening. "I've been this way for years, Samantha. You just never saw it."

"Edward, please," she pleaded, her voice cracking. "I can help you. We can get through this together."

"Help me?" Edward scoffed, his rage bubbling to the surface. "You want to 'help' me? You're the one who put me in this position, Samantha. Your pathetic sense of duty and justice. Well, guess what?

There's no saving either of us now."

With that, he turned and disappeared into the shadows, leaving Samantha standing alone in the cold, desolate night. Her breath caught in her throat as she realized the gravity of the situation – she had to find Mia, and she had to do it now. Determination surged through her veins as she stepped forward, ready to face whatever horrors lay ahead.

As Samantha entered the property, her senses heightened and her heart was pounding with a mix of fear and determination, she couldn't shake the feeling that she was walking straight into the lion's den. But there was no turning back now – she had made her decision, and she would see it through to the end, no matter the cost.

The moon cast distorted shadows across the neglected lawn, taunting Samantha with their menacing dance. She clenched her fists, the fear and determination within her fueling her resolve. Taking a step forward, she stared directly into Edward's eyes, her voice steady and commanding.

"Release Mia. Now," she demanded, her tone leaving no room for negotiation. "If you don't cooperate, I promise you, the consequences will be more than you can bear."

Edward's smile only widened, his eyes gleaming with a wicked amusement that sent a chill down Samantha's spine. He crossed his arms, leaning casually against the doorframe as if they were discussing something trivial, like the weather.

"Ah, Samantha," he drawled, the mockery in his voice evident.

"Always so sure of yourself. But tell me, do you truly believe you have what it takes to stop me?" He let out a sinister chuckle, sending a shiver through her. "My dear wife, you've always been so...weak."

Samantha ground her teeth, her blood boiling at Edward's taunts. Still, she refused to show him any sign of weakness. She focused on her breathing, inhaling deeply before responding. "Your arrogance will be your downfall, Edward. Let Mia go, or face the consequences."

Edward laughed again, a harsh sound that echoed through the night air. He cocked his head, his gaze never leaving Samantha's. "You won't win this time, my love," he whispered, the words dripping with venom. "I've grown tired of playing your games."

A bead of sweat rolled down Samantha's temple as she tightened her grip on the gun, her finger hovering over the trigger. The moonlight casting eerie shadows around them seemed to amplify the tension that hung in the air. She could feel the weight of Edward's taunts but refused to let him see her falter. Her mind raced, calculating the moves and weighing the consequences.

"Edward," she said, her voice cold and resolute, "You've left behind too much evidence this time. There's no escaping it. Give yourself up now, and maybe you'll have a chance for leniency."

His eyes narrowed, his once amused expression transforming into one of cold rage. The air around them seemed to grow colder as if the very atmosphere was responding to the shift in his demeanor. Samantha braced herself, her instincts telling her that the situation was about to escalate.

"Leniency?" Edward spat out the word, disgust lacing his tone. "For me? You think I need your pathetic offer of leniency?" He took a menacing step towards her, his hands clenching into fists at his sides.

Samantha's heart pounded in her chest, but she didn't allow herself to back down. "The evidence against you is solid, Edward. You can't outrun the truth forever. It's over."

"Is it?" he snarled, his face contorted with anger. "I don't think so."

In an instant, Edward lunged towards Samantha, his body fueled by rage and desperation. He moved with surprising speed, attempting to overpower her and seize control of the situation. But Samantha had anticipated his move, her years of police training kicking in as she prepared to counter his attack.

As Edward reached for her, Samantha's thoughts were filled with determination. She couldn't let him win – not this time. Too many lives had been lost, too much pain inflicted. She steeled herself for the confrontation, vowing to bring Edward to justice and protect the innocent from his twisted desires.

The chilling grip of the night air hung heavy around Samantha as she eyed Edward, her instincts sharpening in response to his sudden aggression. She could feel the danger pulsating throughout the scene, a primal force that threatened to consume them both.

"Edward, don't do this," Samantha warned, her voice steady despite the chaos swelling within her. But it was too late – he had already committed to his attack.

With lightning-fast reflexes, Samantha sidestepped Edward's lunge and used her years of training to disarm him. Her movements were fluid, a well-rehearsed dance of self-defense honed by countless hours spent in the police gym. She swept his legs out from under him, sending him crashing to the ground with a thud that echoed through the desolate property. The gun he had been reaching for skittered across the gravel, disappearing into the shadows.

"Ugh!" Edward grunted, pain etching itself into his once-charming features. Samantha didn't hesitate, pinning him down with her knee pressing firmly against his chest. The pressure made it difficult for him to breathe, each gasp a desperate struggle for air.

"Where is Mia?" Samantha demanded, her eyes boring into Edward's as she sought to extract the truth from him. He spat in response, defiance still burning brightly in his dark gaze.

"Go to hell," he hissed, but Samantha's resolve remained unbroken. She couldn't afford to waste any more time on him, not when Mia's life hung in the balance. With a swift motion, she handcuffed Edward's wrists together, ensuring he wouldn't pose a threat while she searched the property.

"Backup's on the way," she said, her tone cold and unforgiving. "Stay put."

As she turned her attention away from her husband, Samantha's mind raced with worry for Mia. The young woman represented everything Edward sought to destroy – innocence, vulnerability, a future untarnished by his twisted desires. Samantha couldn't – wouldn't – allow him to claim another victim.

"Keep it together, Samantha," she whispered to herself, the weight of her responsibility bearing down on her shoulders. "You can do this."

With Edward subdued Samantha's focus shifted entirely to finding Mia. She listened intently for any signs of distress, her senses heightened as she scoured the property. Every rustle in the underbrush, every creak of a door hinge set her nerves on edge, but she refused to let fear paralyze her.

"Please, be okay," she prayed silently, her heart pounding with each step she took.

As she approached an isolated outbuilding, a faint whimper reached her ears. It was barely perceptible over the cacophony of the night, but it was enough to spur Samantha into action. She kicked open the door, gun at the ready, and prayed that she wasn't too late.

"Stay back! I'll get you out of here," she called out, her voice echoing through the small space. The sight of Mia, her face streaked with tears and her body trembling with fear, only fueled Samantha's determination to bring Edward to justice – whatever it took.

Samantha's flashlight beam cut through the darkness, illuminating a padlocked door at the far end of the dimly lit corridor. Her heart sank, and she knew, with chilling certainty, that she had found where Mia was imprisoned.

"Stay calm, Mia," Samantha called out softly, her voice steady as she approached the door. "I'm here to get you out."

"R-really?" Mia's voice trembled from within the room, hope and fear mingling in her tone. "You'll keep me safe?"

"Absolutely," Samantha replied, her resolve unshakable. She holstered her gun and reached for the lock, determined to free Mia as quickly as possible. "Edward will never hurt you again. I promise."

As Samantha struggled with the padlock, Edward's eyes flashed open, his fury igniting like wildfire. He'd been waiting for this moment, biding his time until Samantha's attention was elsewhere. And now, finally, he saw his opportunity to escape.

"Chief Kingsley," he hissed, his voice dripping with venom, "you think you can stop me?"

Edward lunged towards Samantha, using every ounce of strength to break free from her hold. His hands clawed at her wrist, desperate to regain control and reclaim the power he'd lost.

"Let go!" Samantha shouted, her grip on the padlock slipping as Edward's sudden assault took her by surprise. She fought to maintain her composure, knowing that if she failed, Mia would be left at Edward's mercy once more.

"Never," Edward snarled, his face contorted with rage. The two of them grappled, their bodies locked in a deadly dance as each sought to overpower the other.

"Get... off... me!" Samantha gritted her teeth, her muscles straining with the effort as she tried to repel Edward's assault. She couldn't afford to lose this fight – Mia's life, and her future, were at stake.

"Please... help," Mia's voice was barely audible above the sound of their struggle, but it was enough for Samantha. Her resolve hardened, and with a surge of adrenaline, she managed to shove Edward away from her.

"Stay back, Mia," she warned, her voice wavering slightly as she tried to catch her breath. She knew that she couldn't let her guard down, not for a second, as long as Edward was still capable of fighting back.

"Are you sure you can protect her?" Edward taunted, his smile twisted and cruel. "You won't be able to watch over her every moment, Chief Kingsley. I'll always be there, lurking in the shadows, just waiting for my chance."

"Shut up!" Samantha snapped, her eyes blazing with fury. She knew that Edward was trying to get under her skin, to exploit her fears and doubts, but she refused to let him succeed. She would do whatever it took to ensure Mia's safety and bring Edward to justice – even if it meant facing her demons along the way.

Samantha's heart raced as she fought to maintain her grip on Edward, his strength surprising her despite their shared history. The dimly lit room cast eerie shadows on the walls, making the scene appear even more sinister than it already was. Her voice strained with desperation, and Samantha pleaded with him.

"Edward, please, just give up. If you continue this, there will be no way out for you. Do you want to throw everything away?"

His eyes were wild, almost animalistic in their intensity, and he sneered at her words. "You don't know me, Sam. You never did. I won't let you take me down."

The ensuing struggle was a blur of movement, sweat, and raw emotion. Samantha dug deep within herself, tapping into reserves of strength and determination she didn't even know she possessed. As each second passed, the danger of losing control grew stronger.

Edward grappled with Samantha, trying to overpower her. She felt her muscles straining to keep him at bay, knowing that if she faltered, Mia's life would be in jeopardy once more.

"Is this the legacy you want to leave behind, Edward?" Samantha's thoughts raced, searching for something, anything that might break through to her husband. "Do you want to be remembered as a monster? Is this who you truly are?"

Edward snarled, his face contorted with rage, but there was a flicker of uncertainty in his eyes. Samantha knew she had struck a nerve, but it wasn't enough to halt his relentless assault.

Just as it seemed that Edward might succeed in overpowering Samantha, the sound of footsteps echoed through the hallway outside the room. The backup had arrived. Officers burst into the room, weapons drawn and aimed at Edward, their faces set in grim determination.

"Drop to the ground, now!" one of the officers commanded, his voice steady and authoritative.

Edward hesitated, the reality of his situation finally sinking in. He was surrounded, outmanned, and outgunned. Glancing at Samantha one last time, a mixture of anger and despair etched into his features, he released her and slowly dropped to his knees.

Samantha exhaled sharply, relief washing over her as she realized the nightmare was finally ending. But the horror of what had transpired lingered, reminding her that the darkness within Edward would forever cast a shadow over both their lives. The road ahead would be long and difficult, but she knew she had to face it head-on – for Mia, for herself, and for the community she had sworn to protect.

The air hung heavy with tension as Mia, trembling but unharmed, was gently led from the confines of the small room by one of the officers. Samantha's chest tightened a mixture of relief and anger coursing through her veins. She watched as Edward, his once-charming face twisted and marred by rage, was handcuffed and pulled to his feet.

"Is this what you wanted, Samantha?" Edward spat, his voice dripping with venom. "To see your husband brought low like this?"

Samantha's gaze remained steady, her jaw set in a firm line. She couldn't allow herself to falter now, not when she had come so close to bringing him to justice. "You brought this on yourself, Edward," she replied, her voice cold and unwavering. "I swore to protect this community, and that means stopping monsters like you."

"Monsters?" Edward scoffed, his eyes narrowing into slits. "You have no idea what real monsters are."

"Neither do you," Samantha shot back, her hand gripping the handle of her gun unconsciously. "You preyed on innocent people, Edward. You let your twisted desires control you. But it's over now."

As the officers began to lead Edward away, he chuckled darkly, the sound sending chills down Samantha's spine. "We'll see about that, my dear," he whispered, his gaze never leaving hers.

With Edward gone, Samantha allowed herself a moment to collect her thoughts. The adrenaline-fueled chaos of the past few hours gave way to a sobering realization: she had faced unimaginable danger and put her life on the line to save Mia and others like her. Despite the personal cost, she knew that there could be no other choice – she had made a vow to serve and protect, and she would honor that commitment, no matter the consequences.

She closed her eyes for a moment, allowing herself to process the wave of emotions that threatened to overwhelm her. Fear, anger, sadness – they all mingled together, creating a storm within her that she knew would take time to dissipate. But through it all, one feeling stood out above the rest: determination.

This ordeal had tested her resolve, forcing her to confront the darkness that lurked beneath the surface of her seemingly perfect life. But Samantha refused to let it consume her. Instead, she would use this experience as a catalyst for change, vowing to redouble her efforts in the fight against evil and injustice. For Mia, for herself, and for the community she had sworn to protect, she would remain vigilant, a guardian against the monsters that walked among them.

"Chief," a voice called out, pulling her from her reverie. "We need you to sign off on some paperwork."

Samantha nodded, steeling herself for the task ahead. There would be time later to reflect on what had happened, to come to terms with the enormity of it all. But for now, her duty called.

"Coming," she replied, her voice steady and strong. She took one last look at the room where Mia had been held captive, etching it into her memory as a reminder of the battle she waged against the darkness. And with that, she turned away, ready to face whatever challenges lay ahead.

The scent of fear still lingered in the air, a palpable reminder of the horrors that had unfolded within these walls. The once opulent property now felt tainted, a chilling monument to Edward Kingsley's twisted desires. Samantha stood amidst the chaos, her eyes scanning the room as she mentally cataloged each piece of evidence that would help to seal her husband's fate.

"Chief," Officer Davis called out, holding up a notebook filled with scribbled notes. "I think you should take a look at this."

Samantha strode over, taking the notebook from him and flipping through the pages. Her brow furrowed as she read the meticulous details of Edward's plans – the sickening extent of his obsession laid bare for all to see. She felt a cold shiver run down her spine, the weight of her husband's betrayal settling heavily upon her shoulders.

"Good find, Davis. Bag it and make sure it's properly logged." Her voice was firm, betraying none of the turmoil that churned inside her.

"Chief," he replied, carefully placing the notebook into an evidence bag.

As Samantha continued to oversee the collection of evidence, her thoughts raced, grappling with the reality of what her husband had become. How could she have been so blind to the darkness lurking beneath his charming exterior? She shook her head, banishing the doubts that threatened to consume her. There would be time for self-recriminations later; right now, her focus needed to be on ensuring that justice was served.

"Chief, there's something else you should see," another officer called out, gesturing toward a locked cabinet in the corner of the room.

Samantha approached, her heart pounding in her chest as she prepared herself for whatever new horror awaited her. The officer carefully unlocked the cabinet, revealing a collection of photographs – haunting images of young women who had fallen prey to Edward's twisted desires.

"Dear God," Samantha whispered, her hand clenching into a fist at her side as a wave of nausea washed over her. She forced herself to maintain her composure, knowing that she needed to stay strong for the sake of those who had suffered at Edward's hands.

"Make sure these are cataloged and cross-referenced with any missing person reports," she ordered, her voice tight with barely restrained anger. "We need to identify these victims and notify their families."

"Understood, Chief," the officer replied, his face pale as he began the painstaking process of documenting each photograph.

As the investigation continued, Samantha found herself grappling with a mix of emotions – fear, anger, betrayal, and grief all swirling together in a maelstrom that threatened to overwhelm her. But beneath it all, one thought remained clear: she would not let Edward's darkness define her. She would continue to fight, to protect, to serve. And in doing so, she would ensure that justice prevailed.

"Chief Kingsley, we've collected everything we can find," Officer

Davis reported, his expression solemn. "We're ready to wrap up here."

"Good work, everyone," Samantha commended, her gaze sweeping across the room one last time. "Let's get this evidence back to the station and start building our case. We need to make sure that monster never sees the light of day again."

CHAPTER 19

Crimson Vengeance

The room was a cacophony of shadows, and the air was thick with tension. Samantha's heart raced as she kicked open the door, gun drawn, her eyes scanning the dimly lit space. She could feel the weight of her duty pressing down on her shoulders, threatening to crush her. But she wouldn't let it. Not now.

"Edward!" she barked, her voice echoing through the room like a gunshot. "Let her go!"

There, in the far corner, stood her husband. Edward held Mia captive, his arm wrapped tightly around her slender neck, fingers digging into her delicate skin. The juxtaposition of this man she had loved for so long, now twisted by his dark desires, sent shivers down her spine.

"Sammy," Edward said with a chilling smile, his voice dripping with false affection. "You shouldn't have come."

"Drop it, Edward. You're not getting away with this," Samantha growled, her finger resting on the trigger, muscles tense and ready to fire.

"Am I not?" he replied, his grin never faltering. Mia whimpered under his grip, her wide brown eyes pleading for help.

As Edward's eyes flickered between Samantha and the gun, she could see the moment his desperation overrode his cunning nature. His gaze hardened, and he released Mia, lunging at his wife with a guttural roar. Samantha braced herself for the impact, her mind racing.

He mustn't get the gun, she thought. *If he does, it's all over.*

"Edward, please!" Mia cried out, backing away from the chaos unfolding before her, hands trembling.

Despite the dark thoughts that plagued his soul, Edward had once been a loving husband, supportive and compassionate. How could he have fallen so far? Gripped by an icy fear, Samantha steeled herself, determined not to let Edward's twisted desires destroy any more lives.

The sound of ragged breaths echoed in the room, punctuating the tense silence as Samantha sidestepped Edward's desperate lunge. Adrenaline coursed through her veins, each heartbeat a drumroll announcing the deadly dance unfolding before her eyes.

"Edward, don't make me do this," she warned, her voice betraying a tremor of emotion. She fired a warning shot into the ceiling, plaster raining down around them like snowflakes. "There's still a chance for you. Surrender now."

Edward's eyes narrowed dangerously, his chest heaving with exertion and fear. "You think I'll just give up? Just let you take everything away from me?" he spat, his voice dripping with venom.

Samantha's grip tightened on her gun, her knuckles white against the cold metal. *This isn't the man I fell in love with,* she thought, her heart aching with the weight of her duty. *But I can't let him hurt anyone else.*

"Edward, please," Mia whispered, huddled in a corner, her body trembling with terror.

"Shut up!" Edward screamed at her, his rage a palpable force in the air. He turned his attention back to Samantha, his gaze icy and calculating. "You always were stubborn, Sammy. But it won't save you this time."

With a guttural growl, Edward charged towards Samantha once more, his desperation lending strength to his limbs. She tried to brace herself for the impact, but it was too late. The force of his attack sent them both crashing to the ground, the gun skittering across the floor beneath them.

"Edward, stop!" Samantha gasped, struggling to free herself from his crushing weight. Her mind raced with strategies, grasping at any opportunity to regain control. *I need to get that gun. It's the only way to stop him,* she thought, her heart pounding in her chest.

"Give up, Samantha," Edward hissed, his breath hot against her face. "You can't save them all. You can't save yourself."

As their bodies strained against one another, a twisted dance of power and control, Samantha knew that she had to make a decision. There was no turning back; it was either her life or his. And she would not let Edward's darkness consume her.

"Never," she whispered, steeling herself for the battle ahead.

Samantha's vision blurred as her head collided with the cold, unforgiving floor. She could feel the blood rushing to her skull, a relentless pounding that threatened to overpower her senses. But she refused to give in. This was not how it would end.

"Is this all you've got, Samantha?" Edward taunted, his voice dripping with malice. "I expected more from my wife."

"Shut up and let Mia go," she gritted her teeth, using every ounce of strength she had left to push Edward off her.

"Or what? You'll shoot me?" he sneered, catching sight of the gun that lay just out of reach. "You don't have the guts."

As Samantha struggled beneath him, she recalled her years of police training. The countless hours spent learning to defend herself and others, honing her skills in a bid for justice. She couldn't let it all go to waste now. Not when lives were at stake.

With one swift motion, she drove her knee into Edward's side, forcing him to buckle and momentarily lose his grip. She seized the opportunity, rolling away from him and lunging towards the gun.

"Edward, I swear to God, if you don't stop now, I won't hesitate," she warned, aiming the weapon at him with a steady hand.

"Go ahead," Edward spat, his eyes wild with fury. "Shoot me. Just like you do all those criminals you claim to protect us from."

"Edward, please," Samantha pleaded, her voice cracking under the weight of her emotions. "This isn't you. We can get help. We can fix this."

"Too late, Sammy," he said, his voice heavy with resignation.

In an instant, Edward lunged again, managing to grab Samantha's gun hand as they both fell to the ground. They grappled over the weapon, a desperate tug-of-war with life and death hanging in the balance.

"Give it up, Samantha," Edward growled, his fingers digging into her wrist as he tried to wrestle the gun away from her. "You can't beat me."

"Watch me," Samantha hissed, her resolve hardening with every passing second. She knew she had to end this, one way or another. And she would do whatever it took to protect those she loved.

As their struggle continued, Samantha's thoughts raced, searching for any advantage that might tip the scales in her favor. *I need to disarm him,* she thought, her heart pounding in her chest. *I have no other choice.*

The room seemed to close in around them, the darkness pressing into their every breath. Samantha's pulse roared in her ears, drowning out even the struggle for control over the weapon.

"Edward, you don't have to do this," she said, her voice strained with effort and fear. The man she loved was slipping away before her eyes, consumed by the monster within.

"Shut up!" Edward snarled, his grip tightening on her wrist as they grappled on the floor. Sweat beaded on his brow, his handsome face twisted in a rictus of rage. "This is all your fault!"

Samantha felt a flash of anger cut through her fear, a fierce determination rising in its wake. She wouldn't let Edward destroy everything they had built together – not without a fight. With a practiced move honed by years of training, she swung her free hand, connecting with a sharp blow to Edward's jaw.

"Ugh!" he grunted, momentarily stunned by the unexpected counterattack. His grip faltered, giving Samantha the precious seconds she needed to regroup.

"Get off me!" she shouted, twisting her body and planting her feet firmly on the ground. As she surged upward, she drove her knee into Edward's chest, the force of the impact pushing him back and freeing her from his grasp.

Edward stumbled backward, his expression a mix of disbelief and fury. Heaving for breath, Samantha scrambled to her feet, her gun still clutched tightly in her hand. The room seemed to spin around her, the shadows pooling at the edges of her vision as adrenaline coursed through her veins.

"Stay down, Edward," she warned the weight of her authority lending strength to her voice. "I won't ask again."

"Damn you, Samantha," he spat, his eyes blazing with malice. And yet, beneath the surface, she could see the flicker of fear, the dawning realization that he might not escape this encounter unscathed.

"Please," she whispered, her heart aching with the knowledge that their lives had come to this. "Just give up."

"Never," Edward growled, defiance etched into every line of his face. "I'll take you down with me if I have to."

As Samantha stared into the abyss of her husband's soul, she knew that she had no choice but to stand her ground. For the sake of everything they had once shared – and for the innocent life still at stake – she would fight until the bitter end.

Edward's eyes narrowed, and in that split second, before he moved, Samantha knew his pride would not allow him to back down. With a guttural snarl, he sprang forward like a feral animal, his fingers extending into claws as they aimed for her face.

"Sam!" he roared, desperation laced with fury.

Samantha instinctively swung her head to the side, narrowly avoiding his swipe. The air stirred by Edward's fingers brushed against her cheek like a sinister caress. She could feel the cold malice radiating from him, but it only fueled her resolve.

"Enough!" she barked, gritting her teeth against the fear that threatened to claw its way up her throat.

"Never enough," Edward hissed, lunging again.

His hands closed around her arms, and she felt the cruel pressure of his fingers digging into her flesh. It was as though he sought to conquer her, to break her spirit even as he fought to maintain control over Mia and his crumbling world.

"Get off me!" Samantha growled, twisting her body to escape his grasp.

"Submit!" Edward snarled, his breath hot and fetid against her face. "You're mine!"

"Like hell I am," she thought, refusing to let his poisonous words take root in her mind. With every ounce of strength she possessed, Samantha managed to wrench one arm free from his grip.

"Give up, Edward!" she warned, fighting to keep the quaver from her voice. "You can't win."

"Watch me," he sneered, tightening his hold on her remaining arm.

"Is this what you've become?" she demanded, allowing herself a moment of pain-filled introspection as she stared into the dark abyss that had once been her husband's soul. "A deranged monster?"

"Better a monster than a fool!" he shot back, his voice shrill and manic.

"Then let me put an end to your madness," Samantha retorted, her defiance sparking a surge of adrenaline that coursed through her veins. She felt the energy building, coiling in the pit of her stomach like a tightly wound spring. And then, with a primal scream that echoed through the room, she wrenched her arm free from Edward's grasp and delivered a swift, devastating punch to his gut.

The blow sent him reeling, a look of shock and betrayal etched into his features. But Samantha knew there would be no turning back now — not for either of them.

The room seemed to pulsate with an eerie silence as Edward doubled over, clutching his stomach in pain. Samantha's heart pounded in her ears like a war drum, drowning out any lingering doubts. This was the moment that had been building for so long - the culmination of a horrifying path they both had walked.

"Edward," Samantha said, her voice firm yet tinged with fear, "you've lost. It's over."

She seized the opportunity to retrieve her gun from where it had fallen, its cold metal surface offering a semblance of comfort. Samantha leveled the weapon at her husband, her hands steady despite the whirlwind of emotions threatening to consume her. Memories of their life together flashed through her mind, but she forced them away, focusing on the man who now held Mia captive – the monster Edward had become.

"Let her go and surrender," Samantha warned him, her eyes locked on his. "You don't have to die today."

Edward slowly straightened, his eyes wild and desperate as he stared down the barrel of the gun aimed at him. His breath came in ragged gasps, and for a moment, Samantha thought she saw a flicker of remorse in his eyes. But then, the darkness returned, swallowing any hint of the man she had once loved.

"Is this how it ends, Samantha?" Edward spat, his voice dripping with venom. "You, my wife, ready to put a bullet in me?"

"Stop talking, Edward!" Samantha snapped, her patience wearing thin. "This is your last chance. Don't make me pull the trigger."

As she spoke, Samantha felt a strange sense of detachment, as if she were watching the scene unfold from afar. The weight of her responsibility as chief of police mingled with the bitter taste of betrayal and loss, and she fought to maintain her composure. Her duty was clear, but that didn't make it any less painful.

"Too late for that, my love," Edward sneered, a sadistic grin spreading across his face. "I'm already long gone."

"Then you leave me no choice," Samantha whispered, her voice cracking under the strain. She took a deep breath, bracing herself for the terrible deed she was about to commit. And as the room seemed to close in around her, she knew that no matter what happened next, nothing would ever be the same.

In the dimly lit room, shadows danced along the walls like sinister specters, heightening the palpable tension. Samantha's heart pounded in her chest as if trying to escape the horror of the situation, but she refused to back down.

"Edward!" she shouted, her voice filled with a mix of fear and determination. "This is your last chance! Surrender now or face the consequences!"

"Ha," Edward scoffed, his eyes narrowing into cold slits that bore into Samantha like daggers. "You don't have the guts."

Samantha's grip tightened on her gun, her knuckles turning white. Her mind raced with memories of their life together, of the man she had once trusted implicitly. But that man was gone, replaced by the monster before her.

"Enough games, Edward," Samantha growled through clenched teeth.

"I won't hesitate to do what needs to be done."

"Really?" he taunted, his voice dripping with malice. "Let's find out, shall we?"

With a sudden burst of speed, Edward lunged at Samantha, his fingers outstretched like talons. The world seemed to slow down around her as she realized there was no way out for either of them. This was it – the moment she had been dreading since she had first discovered her husband's dark secret.

In that split-second, Samantha grappled with the gravity of the decision she was about to make. Images of their happier times flashed through her mind, but she couldn't let sentiment cloud her judgment. She was the chief of police, sworn to protect and serve, and now she had to put duty above love.

"Forgive me," she whispered, as much to herself as to Edward.

Her finger tightened on the trigger, and a gunshot echoed through the room like the tolling of a death knell. Edward's body crumpled to the floor, his face contorted in a mixture of shock and pain.

"Edward…" Samantha breathed, her voice barely audible amidst the ringing in her ears. The weight of her actions bore down on her like an avalanche, threatening to crush her beneath its suffocating pressure.

But as she stood there, gun still trembling in her hand, she knew that she had done what was necessary. The nightmare was finally over, and now it was time to pick up the shattered pieces of her life and find a way to move forward – without Edward.

The metallic tang of blood filled the air as Edward's body hit the floor with a sickening thud. Samantha's chest heaved, her breaths coming in short gasps as she tried to steady herself. The room seemed to close in on her, the darkness pressing down like a suffocating shroud.

"Are you okay?" she called out to Mia, her voice wavering with the strain of what had just transpired.

"Y-yes," Mia stammered, her eyes wide and fearful as they locked onto Edward's lifeless form.

Samantha's gaze flickered from the body to the terrified woman bound to the chair, and she sprang into action. Her heart raced in her chest, adrenaline coursing through her veins as she fought to keep the encroaching panic at bay.

"Stay calm," she told herself, her thoughts racing as fast as her pulse. "You need to get her out of here."

As she reached Mia's side, she fumbled with the restraints that held her captive, her fingers numb and clumsy from the shock of what had just occurred.

"Thank God you came," Mia whimpered, tears streaming down her cheeks. "I don't know what he would've done if you hadn't stopped him."

"Neither do I," Samantha whispered, her hands shaking as she struggled to undo the knots. "But it's over now. He can't hurt anyone ever again."

"Is...is he dead?" Mia asked, her voice barely audible.

"Yes," Samantha confirmed, her gut-wrenching at the thought of her once-beloved husband lying cold and lifeless on the floor. "I had no choice."

"None of us did," Mia replied softly, her eyes dark with understanding.

Finally freeing Mia from her restraints, Samantha pulled her to her feet, wrapping a protective arm around her as they both stared down at Edward's lifeless form.

"Let's get out of here," Samantha urged, her voice cracking with emotion. "We need to call for backup and get you to safety."

"Thank you," Mia whispered, leaning into Samantha's embrace as they made their way towards the door, leaving behind the grisly scene and the remnants of a shattered life.

As they emerged from the darkness of the room, Samantha couldn't help but feel that they were stepping from one nightmare into another – a world forever changed by the revelation of Edward's twisted desires and the terrible price she had been forced to pay to stop him.

"Forgive me," she thought once more, the words echoing through her mind like the ghost of a past she could never escape. But deep down, she knew there was no absolution for what she had done – only the cold, stark truth of a future marred by loss and regret.

CHAPTER 20

Chains of Justice

The shrill ring of Samantha's phone cut through the silence of her office like a knife, shattering her concentration. She hesitated for a moment - 2

, her hand hovering over the receiver. She knew that this call could change everything.

"Chief Kingsley," she answered with an air of authority.

"Chief, it's Officer Reynolds. We've located Edward. We're preparing to make an arrest."

Samantha felt her heart constrict in her chest. The man they were referring to was not just any criminal – he was her husband. She had long suspected there was a dark side to him but never imagined it would come to this.

"Send me the coordinates," she ordered, her voice laced with determination. "I'm assembling a team and heading there immediately."

"Understood, Chief," Officer Reynolds replied before hanging up.

Samantha's mind raced as she quickly gathered her thoughts. She knew that she needed to put her personal feelings aside and treat this like any other case. The safety of the community depended on it.

"Johnson, Martinez, O'Reilly, you're with me," she barked at the officers standing nearby. "Gear up and meet me in the garage in five minutes."

She could see the concern etched on their faces, but no one dared to question her orders. Samantha led by example, and they respected her for it.

As they loaded into their vehicles, Samantha couldn't help but think about the life she had built with Edward. They had been together for over twenty years – the loving wife and the doting husband, both pillars of their community. And now it seemed that the foundation of their lives was crumbling beneath them.

"Chief, are you alright?" Officer Johnson asked cautiously from the driver's seat.

"Focus on the task at hand, Johnson," Samantha replied sharply, masking her emotions. "We need to be prepared for anything when we confront Edward."

"Understood, ma'am."

As they sped through the streets towards Edward's hideout, Samantha couldn't help but wonder how he had managed to keep his twisted desires hidden for so long. She was a skilled investigator, trained to spot deception and lies, yet he had eluded her detection.

"Remember," she said to her team as they approached the location, "we don't know what kind of resistance we might encounter. Stay alert, communicate, and watch each other's backs."

"Roger that, Chief," the officers responded in unison.

The sun was setting as they arrived at the hideout, casting eerie shadows over the dilapidated building. Samantha drew her weapon, steeling herself for the confrontation ahead. She knew that no matter what happened, there would be no turning back.

The moon hung heavy above the abandoned warehouse, its light casting distorted shadows that seemed to reach out and grasp at Samantha and her team. As they approached the hideout, the air grew thick with tension, the hairs on the back of Samantha's neck standing on end.

"Alright," Samantha whispered, her voice steady despite the pounding in her chest. "Surround the building and secure all exits. No one gets in or out without my say-so."

"Copy that, Chief," came a chorus of hushed replies. The officers moved with precision, dispersing into the darkness like ghosts.

Samantha drew her weapon, feeling its familiar weight in her hand as she steeled herself for what was to come. There was no room for hesitation; Edward had taken too many lives already. She couldn't afford to let him slip through her fingers.

"Johnson, you're with me," Samantha commanded, not taking her eyes off the building's entrance. "Keep your guard up. We have no idea what he's capable of when cornered."

"Understood, Chief," Johnson replied, his weapon drawn and ready.

The warehouse loomed before them like a tomb, an oppressive silence hanging over it. Samantha could feel the malevolence within, a palpable darkness that threatened to swallow her whole. But she wouldn't be deterred. This was justice, plain and simple.

"Edward!" she called out, her voice echoing off the walls. "This is Chief Samantha Kingsley! You are surrounded! Come out with your hands up!"

Silence followed her words, weighing heavily on her as she waited for a response. She could feel her pulse reverberating through her veins, the anticipation gnawing at her.

"Damn it," Samantha muttered under her breath. "We'll have to go in after him."

"Are you sure that's wise, Chief?" Johnson asked, his voice betraying a hint of fear.

"Edward's not getting away," Samantha said resolutely, her eyes fixed on the entrance. "Not this time."

With that, she took the lead, cautiously stepping into the hideout, weapon drawn and senses heightened. The darkness seemed to close around her like a shroud, swallowing her whole. But she refused to let it smother her resolve; Edward had nowhere left to run, and she would see him brought to justice.

The dim light from Samantha's flashlight cut through the oppressive darkness, revealing a small room concealed within the maze-like warehouse. The air was thick with tension, and her breaths felt shallow as she edged closer to the door. She could feel her heart pounding in her chest, a reminder of how much was at stake; not just for her, but for the grieving families of Edward's victims.

"Edward Kingsley," Samantha announced, her voice steady despite the turmoil raging within her. "You have nowhere left to run."

Peering into the room, she saw him: hunched over in a corner, his once immaculate appearance now marred by desperation. The sight of her husband – the man she had pledged her life to – in such a pathetic state sent a shiver down her spine. But she couldn't afford to let her emotions cloud her judgment; not when so many lives were on the line.

"Sam... please," Edward whispered, his voice trembling. "You don't understand."

"Understand?" Samantha snapped, her anger flaring. "I understand that you're responsible for the deaths of innocent people, Edward. That you've caused unfathomable pain and suffering."

She leveled her gun at him, her grip firm and unwavering. "Now stand up, put your hands on your head, and surrender."

"Sam, I never meant for any of this to happen," he pleaded, tears streaming down his face. "It was never supposed to go this far."

"Your intentions don't matter anymore," she said coldly, refusing to let his words sway her. She couldn't forget the images seared into her mind – the crime scenes, the blood, the broken bodies. All of it was a testament to the monster her husband had become.

"Please, Sam... I love you," Edward choked out, his voice barely audible.

"Love?" Samantha scoffed, her heart aching with the weight of betrayal. "You don't know the meaning of the word."

As Edward reluctantly rose to his feet, hands trembling above his head, Samantha couldn't help but feel a crushing mix of relief and despair. This was the man she had shared her life with, and now he stood before her as the embodiment of all she had sworn to fight against.

"Edward Kingsley," she said, her voice laced with finality, "you are under arrest for the murder of five innocent people. You have the right to remain silent..."

As she recited his rights, her thoughts drifted to those who had suffered at his hands. And though she knew this was only the beginning of a long and arduous journey towards justice, she vowed to see it through to the end – for them, and herself.

The dim light cast eerie shadows on the walls as Edward's once strong and confident posture crumbled, his shoulders slumping in defeat. He raised his hands slowly, shaking from fear or perhaps a realization that there was no way out of the corner he had painted himself into.

"Fine," he spat, his voice barely a whisper. "You've won, Sam. Are you happy now?"

Samantha kept her weapon trained on him, heart pounding in her chest as she carefully approached. She couldn't let her guard down for even a moment; Edward knew how to manipulate people, and she wouldn't put it past him to try something desperate.

"Put your hands behind your head," she ordered, doing her best to keep her voice steady despite the roiling emotions inside her. Edward complied, albeit with a resentful glare.

As Samantha moved closer, she could see the fear in his eyes, but also something else – a flicker of disbelief, as if he still couldn't comprehend that his wife had been the one to bring him down. It hurt her more than she cared to admit, but she steeled herself against the pain, knowing that she had a duty to fulfill.

"Edward," she said softly, almost a plea. "Why? Why did you do this?"

He hesitated, his gaze darting around the room as if searching for some kind of reprieve from the truth. But there was no escaping it, not anymore. "I... I don't know," he finally admitted, his voice cracking. "It started small, but it grew into something I couldn't control."

"Five lives, Edward," Samantha whispered, tears threatening to spill as the weight of their shared tragedy pressed down on her. "Five souls lost because of your actions."

"Sam, I'm sorry," he choked out, his eyes pleading for understanding that she simply couldn't give.

"Sorry doesn't bring them back," she said coldly, her resolve hardening. She expertly maneuvered him into a pair of handcuffs, ensuring they were tight enough to prevent any possibility of escape.

As Samantha secured Edward's arms behind his back, she couldn't help but think about the life they had once shared – the laughter, the love, the dreams they had built together. Now, it was all tainted by the darkness that had been lurking just beneath the surface, hidden even from her keen instincts.

"Sam," Edward whispered, trying one last time to break through her emotional armor. "Please, don't let this destroy you."

"Goodbye, Edward," she replied, her voice devoid of any warmth or affection. And as she led him away, she knew that the man she had once loved was gone forever, replaced by a monster she could never forgive.

The incessant ringing of her phone sliced through the eerie silence of the interrogation room. Samantha glanced down at the screen and recognized the number - it was the first of the victim's families she needed to contact. Taking a deep breath, she accepted the call.

"Mrs. Thompson? This is Chief Samantha Kingsley," she began, her voice steady and professional. "I wanted to inform you personally that we have arrested the man responsible for your daughter's murder. His name is Edward Kingsley."

A choked sob echoed on the other end, followed by a trembling voice. "Thank you, Chief Kingsley. You've given us some closure... I hope he pays for what he did to Lily and the others."

"Believe me," Samantha replied, her knuckles whitening as she gripped the phone, "he will face the full consequences of his actions."

As she hung up, Samantha allowed herself a brief moment of grief for the young lives cut short, their families forever scarred by tragedy. But there was still work to be done.

"Johnson, O'Malley, I need you to comb through Edward's properties for any evidence related to the murders," Samantha instructed, addressing two seasoned detectives. "Take your time; we need a watertight case."

"Understood, Chief," Detective Johnson nodded, determination flaring in his eyes.

"Connors, I need you to track down any financial records or communications that could tie Edward to the crimes," Samantha continued, turning to a tech-savvy officer. "Leave no stone unturned."

"Of course, Chief," Officer Connors affirmed with a steely resolve.

As her team sprang into action, Samantha couldn't help but feel the weight of her responsibility pressing down upon her. The horrifying reality of Edward's crimes gnawed at her conscience, threatening to consume her from within.

How could I not have seen it? How could I have been so blind? she berated herself internally. *But I can't let my emotions hinder our pursuit of justice.*

"Chief Kingsley," a hesitant voice interrupted her thoughts. It was Officer Diaz, a young and dedicated officer who had been with the force for only two years.

"Officer Diaz, what is it?" Samantha inquired, fighting to maintain her composure.

"I... I just wanted you to know that we're all here for you," Diaz offered sincerely. "And we'll do everything in our power to make sure Edward pays for his crimes."

"Thank you, Diaz," Samantha replied, her voice cracking ever so slightly. "I appreciate your support."

As Samantha continued her calls to the victims' families, offering words of solace and reassurance, she vowed to stay focused on the task at hand – ensuring that justice was served, no matter the personal cost.

A cold wind swept through the cemetery, rustling the leaves and bending the branches of the ancient oaks. Standing before a sea of mourners, Samantha Kingsley addressed the families of Edward's victims.

"Good evening," she began solemnly, her voice cracking slightly under the weight of her words. "In light of recent events, I've arranged for grief counselors to be available to each of you, to help navigate this difficult time."

"Thank you, Chief Kingsley," murmured a tearful woman, clutching a tissue tightly in her trembling hands. The others nodded in appreciation, their eyes brimming with a mixture of gratitude and despair.

"Edward's crimes have shaken our community to its very core," Samantha continued, forcing herself to meet the gaze of each family member present. "It's important that we support one another as we heal from this tragedy."

As she spoke, images of the crime scenes flashed through her mind – the lifeless bodies, the bloodstained walls, the lingering scent of terror. It was a living nightmare, one that had haunted her every waking moment since Edward's arrest.

"I want to assure you," she added firmly, "that justice will be served. Edward will pay for the pain he has caused."

"Chief Kingsley," a reporter called out, raising his hand to catch her attention. "Will there be a press conference addressing the public about Edward's arrest?"

"Tomorrow at 9 a.m., outside the police station," Samantha replied, her jaw clenched. "I'll be making a statement on behalf of the department, reassuring our citizens that they're safe once again."

"Thank you," the reporter nodded, scribbling notes onto his pad.

Later that night, Samantha stood alone in her dimly lit office, her thoughts racing like a frenzied storm. She stared blankly at the wall, her mind consumed by the memories of her life with Edward – the happy moments, the laughter, and the love, now tainted by the grisly truth.

How could he have done this? How could I not have known? she wondered, her heart aching with betrayal.

"Chief Kingsley," a voice interrupted her thoughts. It was Officer Connors, looking pale and somber.

"Officer Connors, what can I do for you?"

"Tomorrow's press conference… are you ready to face the questions? The public will want answers."

Samantha took a deep breath, steeling herself for the task ahead. "I'll do whatever it takes to set things right," she replied decisively. "The people deserve to know that they're safe and that justice has prevailed."

With a nod, Officer Connors left her office, closing the door quietly behind him.

As Samantha prepared for the press conference, she vowed to uphold her duty as the city's chief of police – even if it meant confronting the darkest parts of her soul.

The flickering glow of a computer screen cast eerie shadows on the walls of Samantha's office. Her eyes, bloodshot and weary, scanned through the thousands of files she had pulled from Edward's secret hard drive. The digital labyrinth was as twisted as his desires - cryptic messages, suspicious contacts, and disturbing images haunted her every click.

"Chief Kingsley," Detective Thompson spoke up, breaking the silence that hung heavy in the room, "I've been cross-referencing some of these names with our database. Some of them have criminal records, but they're mostly low-level offenses. It's unclear how deep their involvement may be."

"Keep digging," Samantha replied, her voice a mix of determination and exhaustion. "We need to find out if any of them were part of Edward's... activities. We can't let anyone else get away with this."

Detective Thompson nodded solemnly, returning to his search. Samantha leaned back in her chair, rubbing her temples as she tried to make sense of the nightmare that had unfolded before her. *How many lives were destroyed by this man I thought I knew?* she thought bitterly.

"Chief?" Officer Ramirez piped up, his voice hesitant. "What about our town? How do we repair the fear and mistrust that's been planted here?"

Samantha stared at him for a long moment, considering her words carefully. "We rebuild," she said softly. "Together. We have a responsibility to those who have suffered because of Edward. We owe it to them to make this place safe again, and to make sure nothing like this ever happens under our watch."

"Damn straight," Detective Thompson murmured, his eyes never leaving the screen.

"Get some rest, all of you," Samantha ordered, her voice firm but gentle. "We'll regroup in the morning and continue our investigation."

As her team filed out of her office, Samantha sat in the dark, the weight of her thoughts threatening to crush her. She had always believed that she could protect the people she loved - and now, in the face of unspeakable horror, that belief was shaken to its core.

But we caught him, she reminded herself, clinging to the glimmer of hope amidst the darkness. *We stopped Edward before he could hurt anyone else.*

With a heavy heart, Samantha turned off her computer and rose from her desk, the shadows swallowing her whole as she stepped out into the night. The road ahead was long and treacherous - but she knew that she had no choice but to face it head-on. For the sake of her community, for the victims, and herself, she would see this nightmare through to the end.

The full moon cast eerie shadows on the police station's brick walls, its chilling light reflecting off Samantha's badge as she stood outside the building. She couldn't shake the feeling of unease that gripped her, even after Edward's arrest.

"Chief Kingsley," a voice called out from behind her. It was Detective Thompson, his face showing a mixture of admiration and concern.

"Detective," Samantha acknowledged, her eyes never leaving the haunting moon above.

"Are you alright?" Thompson asked hesitantly.

"Am I alright?" Samantha echoed, her voice hollow. "How can any of us be alright after this? We've lost lives to a monster who hid in our midst." Her mind couldn't help but replay the horrors that Edward had inflicted upon innocent victims, and the realization that her husband had been capable of such atrocities shook her to the core.

"Edward's capture is a victory for us, Chief," Thompson reminded her gently. "You led us through this nightmare. You made sure justice was served."

"Justice..." Samantha murmured, her thoughts wandering to the families left shattered by Edward's actions. "I just wish we could have saved more lives. Prevented all of this somehow."

"None of us could have predicted what he would become," Thompson said softly. "But we can do something now. We can make sure nothing like this ever happens again."

"Exactly," Samantha agreed, her resolve hardening. The wind picked up, ruffling her short brown hair. "I vow to continue my work in protecting this community and preventing similar crimes from happening in the future. No one else will fall victim to the darkness lurking beneath our sunny Florida coast."

"Count me in, Chief," Thompson replied, his determination matching hers. "We're with you every step of the way."

"Thank you, Thompson," Samantha said, grateful for his support. She glanced back at the station, her fellow officers working tirelessly to restore order and safety to their community.

"Edward's arrest has shown us that evil can lurk anywhere," Samantha mused, her thoughts heavy but resolute. "But it has also shown us that we have the power to face it head-on and triumph. We will be vigilant, and we will be relentless in our pursuit of justice."

"Damn right, Chief," Thompson agreed, a fire igniting in his eyes. "We'll make this city a place where people can feel safe again."

As the shadows of the night danced around them, Samantha and Thompson stood united, vowing to protect their community from the darkness that had threatened to consume it. With unwavering determination, they prepared to forge a new path toward a safer future for all.

CHAPTER 21

Shadow of Guilt

The early morning fog clung to the police station like a shroud, its tendrils obscuring the red and blue lights that flickered in the distance. Samantha Kingsley gripped the steering wheel tightly as her car came to a stop, her knuckles turning white with the effort. She stared at the building before her, the place where she had devoted so many years of her life to upholding justice and maintaining order. Now, it felt as though the very foundations were crumbling beneath her feet.

"Get a grip, Sam," she muttered under her breath, forcing herself out of the car. The chilly air bit into her skin, but she welcomed the sting. It reminded her that she was still alive, still capable of weathering whatever storm lay ahead.

As she approached the entrance, Samantha took a deep breath and squared her shoulders, doing her best to project an image of confidence and authority. She knew that the revelations about her husband, Edward, would have sent shockwaves through the department, but she could not afford to let them see her falter. She was the chief of police, after all, and she had a duty to serve her city.

"Morning, Chief," greeted Officer Reynolds as he held the door open for her. His eyes flicked away from hers for a moment before returning, betraying his discomfort. Samantha nodded curtly in response, trying to shake off the uneasy feeling that crept up her spine as she walked through the station.

"Morning, Samantha," another officer chimed in, her voice wavering slightly. Samantha offered a tight-lipped smile, her gaze darting around the room as she continued down the hallway. She couldn't help but notice the whispers and sidelong glances that followed her every step, each one a painful reminder of the knowledge that now hung over her head like a dark cloud.

"You think she knew?" she heard someone whisper from behind a cubicle wall as she passed by.

"Does it matter?" another voice replied, low and harsh. "She's still gonna have to live with it."

Samantha's heart clenched in her chest, but she refused to let herself break down. She had dealt with difficult situations before – crime scenes that turned her stomach, grieving families who cried on her shoulder, suspects who spat venomous words in her face. This was no different. She would carry the weight of their judgment just as she carried the weight of her badge, knowing that it was part of the price she had to pay for the truth.

As she continued down the hall, Samantha steeled herself for the long day ahead. There would be no reprieve from the whispers and the stares, but she had no choice but to push forward. For the sake of her city, her colleagues, and the innocent women who had suffered at Edward's hands, she would not let the darkness consume her.

The door to Samantha's office clicked shut behind her, muffling the whispers and stares that seemed to echo through every crevice of the station. A soft glow from the desk lamp illuminated the tidy expanse of her workspace, casting shadows in the corners of the room like specters bearing witness to her turmoil.

Samantha forced her trembling hands onto the surface of her desk, willing them to be still as she sat down. Her eyes darted around the familiar space – the framed diplomas on the wall, the carefully arranged stack of case files, the photograph of her and Edward on their wedding day – all reminders of a life that felt increasingly foreign with each passing moment.

"Focus," she whispered to herself, summoning the strength that had carried her through countless difficult cases. "You can't let Edward's sins define you."

She took a deep breath, steeling herself for the task at hand when the shrill ring of her office phone pierced the silence like a dagger. She hesitated for only a moment before answering it, her voice steady despite the roiling emotions within her.

"Chief Kingsley speaking," she said, her tone authoritative and professional as she mentally pushed aside thoughts of Edward.

"Uh, hi, Chief," came the hesitant voice on the other end of the line. "I live by the park, and there's a group of teenagers causing a ruckus. I think they're drinking, maybe even doing drugs. Could you send an officer to check it out?"

"Of course," Samantha replied, scribbling down the details as she spoke. "Thank you for reporting this. We'll have someone there shortly."

"Thank you, Chief." The relief in the caller's voice was palpable.

As Samantha hung up the phone, she couldn't help but reflect on how mundane the call had been – a minor disturbance, the sort of thing she'd dealt with a thousand times before. And yet, in that moment, it felt like a lifeline – a tether to the world she knew and the responsibilities she still had to fulfill.

"Edward may be a monster," she thought, her jaw set with determination, "but I will not let his darkness consume me. I am still the chief of police, and I have a duty to this city."

With renewed resolve, Samantha turned her attention back to her work, ready to face whatever challenges lay ahead – both personal and professional. She refused to let the weight of Edward's sins crush her, for she was stronger than the ghosts that haunted her office.

The sharp contrast between the case files scattered across Samantha's desk and the dark bloodstains that marred her thoughts made it nearly impossible to concentrate. The gruesome images of her husband's unspeakable acts against innocent women haunted her, and she found herself gripping the edge of her desk in an attempt to anchor herself in the present moment.

"Focus," she whispered to herself, her eyes scanning the documents before her. But it was useless; the horrors crept back in, making her stomach churn with disgust and disbelief.

"Chief Kingsley?" A knock on her office door interrupted her thoughts. She looked up to see Detective Daniels standing in the doorway, concern etched on his face like a map of unspoken questions.

"Come in, Detective," Samantha said, her voice steady despite the storm raging inside her. The room seemed to shrink as he stepped inside, the air thickening with tension.

"Are you alright?" Detective Daniels asked, his brown eyes reflecting both genuine worry and the need for reassurance that their work would continue uninterrupted.

"Let's focus on the case," Samantha replied, forcing herself to meet his gaze. "What do we have so far?"

"Of course." He straightened, pulling out a notepad from his pocket. "We've uncovered more evidence tying Edward to the murders. We found fibers from the victims' clothing in his car, and DNA evidence under their fingernails matches his profile."

Samantha's heart sank, her mind teetering on the edge of despair. Yet, she couldn't afford to show weakness now. "Good work, Daniels," she managed to say, pushing aside the sickening feeling that threatened to overwhelm her. "Keep digging. We need to build an ironclad case against him."

"Understood, Chief," Detective Daniels nodded, his brow furrowed in determination.

"Thank you... for everything," Samantha said, the words catching in her throat. She was grateful for his unwavering support, but she couldn't help wondering if he, too, questioned her innocence in the matter.

"Of course, Chief," he replied, giving her a small, understanding smile before leaving her office.

As the door clicked shut, Samantha took a deep breath, steeling herself against the darkness that threatened to consume her. Despite the horrors her husband had inflicted, she had a duty to fulfill – and she would not be defeated. The ghosts of her past may have risen, but they would not define her future.

The dim light from the desk lamp cast long shadows across the room, creating an eerie atmosphere that reflected Samantha's troubled thoughts. She stared at the case files strewn across her desk, forcing herself to focus on the details as she discussed the progress of the investigation with Detective Daniels.

"Have we established a clear timeline for Edward's activities?" Samantha asked, her voice steady despite the turmoil raging inside her.

Detective Daniels nodded, flipping through his notes. "Yes, Chief. We've managed to piece together a pattern that coincides with his business trips. It seems he was using them as cover for his... extracurricular activities."

Samantha clenched her jaw, surprised by the wave of anger that washed over her. How could she have been so blind? "What about security footage? Anything that places him at the scenes?"

"Still working on it," Daniels replied, his tone apologetic. "But we're confident we'll find something soon."

"Good," Samantha said curtly, her mind warring between the desire for justice and the heartbreak of betrayal.

Just then, the phone on her desk rang, jolting her back to reality. Samantha picked it up, bracing herself for another concerned citizen or reporter hounding her for information. Instead, she found herself listening to the tearful voice of a woman – a mother who had lost her daughter to Edward's twisted desires.

"Chief Kingsley," the woman sobbed, "I just need to know... is there any progress? Are you going to catch him and make sure he never hurts anyone again?"

Samantha's heart ached for the woman and her unimaginable pain. She wished she could reach through the phone and offer some form of comfort, but all she could do was provide reassurance through her words. "Mrs. Thompson, I understand how difficult this must be for you," Samantha said, her voice gentle yet firm. "I promise you that we're doing everything in our power to bring your daughter's killer to justice. We've made significant progress in the investigation, and I won't rest until he's behind bars."

"Thank you, Chief Kingsley," Mrs. Thompson replied, her voice wavering. "I trust that you'll keep your promise."

Samantha felt a renewed sense of determination as she hung up the phone. The weight of her turmoil was still heavy on her shoulders, but she knew she couldn't let it interfere with her duty to protect her community and bring closure to families like the Thompsons.

"Detective Daniels," Samantha said, catching the attention of her colleague who had been patiently waiting at her side. "Let's go over the evidence one more time. We need to make sure we don't miss any detail, no matter how small."

"Of course, Chief," Daniels agreed, his eyes reflecting the same resolve that burned within Samantha.

Together, they pored over the case files and crime scene photos, working tirelessly to piece the puzzle that would put an end to Edward Kingsley's reign of terror. And even though Samantha's heart still ached with the knowledge of her husband's monstrous deeds, she refused to waver in her commitment to justice.

The conference room buzzed with the murmurs of law enforcement agents from various agencies as they settled into their seats. Samantha stood at the head of the table, her hands folded in front of her, a projector displaying the case details on the screen behind her. The storm raging within her was hidden beneath an unwavering facade of professionalism, her gaze fixed on each person as they took their places.

"Good morning, everyone," Samantha began, her voice steady and composed. "As you all know, we're here to discuss the progress of our investigation into the gruesome crimes committed by Edward Kingsley."

The room fell silent, attentive eyes focused on her as she continued.

"Over the past few weeks, our team has been working tirelessly to gather evidence and piece together the puzzle that will lead us to Kingsley's apprehension. We've uncovered several key pieces of information that have brought us closer to understanding his motives and methods."

"Chief Kingsley," a grizzled detective from the neighboring city interrupted, "What exactly are these key pieces of information?"

Samantha clicked through the slides on the projector, revealing maps and photographs of crime scenes. "We've determined that Edward specifically targeted women who frequented nightclubs in certain areas. He would abduct, torture, and ultimately kill them, leaving a trail of destruction in his wake."

"Have you found any connections between the victims?" another agent asked, leaning forward in his seat.

"From what we've gathered, there doesn't appear to be any personal connection between the victims," Samantha replied, her thoughts momentarily drifting to the dark secrets she had discovered about her husband. "Edward seems to have chosen them purely based on availability and opportunity."

The meeting continued, with Samantha fielding questions and providing updates as the other agents absorbed the information. Despite her inner turmoil, she remained poised and confident, determined to bring the monster responsible for these horrific acts to justice.

As the meeting broke for a short recess, Samantha stepped outside for a breath of fresh air. The crisp autumn breeze greeted her as she leaned against the building, her eyes fixed on the horizon. She found solace in the vastness of the world beyond her troubled thoughts - a world where evil could be conquered, and justice would prevail.

"Chief Kingsley," Detective Daniels approached her, his face etched with concern. "Are you holding up okay?"

Samantha nodded, her jaw set with determination. "I'm fine," she replied. "We have a job to do, and I won't let my emotions interfere with our mission."

"Good," Daniels said, patting her shoulder reassuringly. "We'll get through this together."

With renewed resolve, Samantha returned inside, ready to continue the fight against the darkness that threatened to consume her world.

The sun dipped low in the sky, casting long shadows through the blinds of Samantha's office as she returned, her heels clicking against the cold tiled floor. She sank into her chair with a heavy sigh and stared at the pile of case files that cluttered her desk. The faces of Edward's victims seemed to stare back at her from the pages, their lives cut short by the man she'd once loved. She steeled herself, determined to bring closure to their grieving families.

"Alright," she muttered under her breath, "let's do this." Samantha began poring over every detail of the files, meticulously examining crime scene photos, witness statements, and the evidence collected so far.

"Chief," Detective Daniels said, poking his head through the door. "Sergeant Wilson found the surveillance footage we were looking for."

"Thank you, Daniels," Samantha replied, her voice steady despite the tightness in her chest. "Bring it in, and let's go over it together."

As they watched the grainy footage, Samantha's stomach churned with disgust at the sight of Edward stalking his prey. How could she have been so blind to the monster he truly was?

"Damn him," Samantha whispered harshly, her knuckles white as she clenched her fists. "He won't get away with this. Not on my watch."

Daniels nodded solemnly. "We'll make sure of it, Chief."

Hours slipped away as they dissected the evidence before them, leaving no stone unturned. As twilight settled upon the city, Samantha leaned back in her chair, her eyes bloodshot and weary but her spirit undeterred.

"Look at us," she mused aloud, "fighting the good fight against the darkness. What a pair we make."

"Never underestimate the power of teamwork, Chief," Daniels replied with a small smile. "And never forget—you're not alone in this."

Samantha nodded, the weight of his words sinking in. She knew the journey ahead would be long and fraught with challenges, but she had found strength within herself that she never knew existed. And with allies like Daniels by her side, she felt a renewed sense of resolve.

"Thank you, Daniels," she said sincerely. "Now let's call it a day. Tomorrow, we will continue our pursuit of justice."

As darkness enveloped the city, Samantha Kingsley stood tall against the encroaching shadows, ready to face whatever lay ahead with unwavering determination. No matter how deep the evil ran, she would not rest until every last trace had been eradicated. For the sake of the victims, their families, and her own shattered heart, Samantha would see this nightmare through to its bitter end.

CHAPTER 22

Healing Hearts

Rain pattered against the car window as if even nature itself was weeping for the victims of Edward's heinous acts. Samantha gripped the steering wheel tightly, her knuckles white from the strain. How could she have been so blind to her husband's dark side? The weight of guilt pressed heavily on her shoulders, but she knew she couldn't afford to let it consume her. Families were suffering the consequences of Edward's twisted desires, and she had a duty to support them.

Pulling up to Reynolds' residence, Samantha took a deep breath before stepping out into the downpour. As she approached the front door, her heart pounded with trepidation. What could she say to provide any semblance of comfort to these grieving people?

"Mrs. Reynolds?" Samantha called softly, as the door creaked open to reveal a frail, middle-aged woman with tear-stained cheeks.

"Chief Kingsley," Mrs. Reynolds uttered, her voice quivering. "Please, come in."

"Thank you, ma'am." Samantha stepped inside, aware of the hollow eyes that bore into her soul. She could feel the raw pain emanating from every corner of the dimly lit living room. It was suffocating.

"Mrs. Reynolds, I can't even begin to express how truly sorry I am for your loss," Samantha began, her voice choked with emotion. "I promise you, I will do everything in my power to bring justice to Lara and the others who were taken too soon."

"Thank you, Chief," Mr. Reynolds replied, his voice barely audible. "But what good is justice when our daughter is never coming back?"

Samantha swallowed hard, struggling to maintain her composure. "You're right, sir. Nothing can ever bring Lara back. But we can honor her memory by making sure this never happens again."

The room fell silent, as the grief-stricken family absorbed her words. Samantha knew there was no easy way to mend their broken hearts, but she refused to let their pain go unanswered.

"Mrs. Reynolds, I'm organizing a community gathering to honor Lara and the other victims," Samantha finally said, breaking the heavy silence. "I hope that by coming together, we can find solace in each other's company and begin the healing process."

"Thank you, Chief Kingsley," Mrs. Reynolds whispered, wiping away fresh tears. "We'll be there."

The night of the gathering, Samantha stood on a makeshift stage beneath a canopy of stars, her heart aching for every soul gathered before her. She could see the pain etched into their faces, a haunting reminder of the atrocities committed by the man she had once loved.

"Tonight, we come together not only to mourn those who were taken from us but also to celebrate the lives they lived," Samantha began, her voice strong and steady despite the turmoil raging inside her. "In the face of this unimaginable tragedy, it's essential that we stand united, supporting one another through our shared grief."

She paused, allowing her words to resonate with the crowd. "To the families of the victims: know that you are not alone in your pain. We, as a community, will carry this burden alongside you. Together, we will find the strength to heal, to rebuild, and ultimately, to overcome this darkness."

As Samantha finished her speech, she looked out at the sea of tear-streaked faces, their eyes shining with determination and resilience. In that moment, she knew that despite the horrors they had endured, they would not be defeated. They would rise from the ashes, united by their love for those they had lost and their unwavering belief in justice.

The door to the grief counselor's office creaked open, casting a ghostly sliver of light across the otherwise darkened room. Samantha stepped over the threshold, her breath catching in her throat as she surveyed the dim space.

"Mrs. Kingsley, I've been expecting you," said a soft voice from the shadows, causing Samantha to jump. A tall figure emerged, his features obscured by the low light. "I'm Dr. Howard. Please, have a seat."

"Thank you, Dr. Howard," Samantha replied, settling into one of the plush chairs that faced the counselor's desk. Her mind raced with thoughts of the families that had been torn apart by her husband's heinous crimes, and she knew that providing them with professional support was crucial in helping them navigate their grief.

"First, let me say how sorry I am for what you and the community are going through," Dr. Howard began, his voice gentle yet firm. "I understand that you want to arrange counseling services for the families affected by these tragedies?"

"Yes, Doctor. They need all the help they can get," Samantha responded, her voice tinged with determination. "I'll do whatever it takes to ensure they have access to the support they need."

"Very well," Dr. Howard nodded solemnly, scribbling notes on his notepad. "We can set up group counseling sessions, as well as individual appointments for those who prefer one-on-one support. And, rest assured, we will maintain absolute confidentiality."

"Thank you, Dr. Howard," Samantha murmured, feeling a small weight lift from her shoulders. But there was still much work to be done.

Samantha stood before a gathering of local organizations and volunteers in the town hall, her eyes surveying the crowd with a fierce intensity. She took a deep breath and addressed the room. "Ladies and gentlemen, we cannot bring back those we have lost, but we can ensure that their memory lives on. That's why I am proposing the establishment of a memorial fund in honor of the victims."

A murmur rippled through the crowd, quickly replaced by hushed whispers and nods of agreement.

"We will need to raise funds and awareness," Samantha continued, her voice unwavering. "I'm asking for your help in organizing charity events, spreading the word about the fund, and providing financial assistance to the affected families."

Heads nodded and hands shot up, volunteers eager to lend their support. Samantha felt a flicker of hope, her heart swelling with gratitude as she observed the community rallying around her cause.

"Let's fight this darkness together," she implored, her eyes brimming with tears. "For our friends, our neighbors, and our loved ones who are no longer with us. Let us honor them, remember them, and ensure that they are never forgotten."

As the room erupted in applause, Samantha knew that the road to healing would be long and arduous. But with the community united in their grief and determination, they would face it head-on, rebuilding their lives one step at a time.

A single, harsh light illuminated Samantha as she sat before the cameras, her face a portrait of stoic determination. The reporters buzzed around her like flies, their voices a cacophony of questions and demands for answers.

"Chief Kingsley," one reporter began, "how has the community been coping with the knowledge that these heinous crimes were committed by one of their own?"

Samantha's gaze flickered briefly to her husband's empty chair, her heart tightening in her chest. "It has been a difficult time for everyone," she said, the words heavy on her tongue. "But we are coming together in support of the victims' families, and working tirelessly to ensure they receive the justice they deserve."

"Is there anything the public can do to help?" another reporter asked.

"Absolutely," Samantha replied, her voice laced with conviction. "We urge anyone with information about Edward's activities to come forward. Your courage may be the key to healing our community."

As the interview continued, Samantha found herself steeling her resolve. She would not allow Edward's dark deeds to cast a permanent shadow over their city. In the pursuit of justice, she would see to it that hope prevailed.

The courthouse loomed large before Samantha, its grandiose facade a stark contrast to the somber mood within. As she entered the building, the weight of her duty settled heavily upon her shoulders.

Inside the courtroom, she took her place among the grieving families, offering reassuring smiles and gentle touches as they faced the man who had torn their world apart. She knew all too well the pain of betrayal and loss and was determined to provide them with the support they so desperately needed.

"Order in the court!" the judge's voice rang out, commanding silence as the proceedings began. Beside her, a mother clutched a tear-stained tissue, her sobs barely muffled.

At that moment, Samantha made a silent vow. She would stand by these families, serving as their rock in the storm of Edward's trial. She would ensure their voices were heard, and that they found solace in the knowledge that justice would be served.

"Your Honor," the prosecutor began, his voice steady and unwavering, "we are here to bring a man to account for his heinous crimes against our community."

As the trial went on, Samantha's thoughts wandered to the media interviews she had given. She hoped her words had reached those who might hold the key to uncovering the full extent of Edward's depravity. And yet, even as she clung to hope, she couldn't shake the chilling thought - just how many secrets still lay buried beneath the surface?

"Chief Kingsley," a voice whispered, tearing her from her dark musings. It was the mother beside her, her eyes filled with gratitude. "Thank you for standing by us."

Samantha squeezed her hand, offering a small, determined smile. "I'll be here for you, every step of the way."

A cold wind whistled through the barren trees as Samantha stood before the families, her breath forming a misty cloud in front of her. She tried to ignore the unsettling feeling that something unnatural lurked just beyond the edge of their gathering. Grief hung heavy in the air, but she refused to let fear take hold.

"Thank you all for coming," Samantha began, her voice strong despite the chill that seeped into her bones. "The loss we've experienced is immeasurable, but together, we can begin to heal."

She motioned to the group of experts seated nearby, each a specialist in trauma recovery and grief counseling. "We've invited these professionals to guide us through a series of healing workshops and support groups. They'll provide us with practical tools and coping mechanisms to help us navigate our grief."

As the families listened intently, Samantha could see the weight of the past few weeks etched onto their faces. But within those eyes, she also saw a spark of hope – hope that they could find some semblance of peace amidst the chaos.

"Additionally," Samantha continued, "we will be creating a memorial garden to honor the victims. Each of you will have the opportunity to contribute to its design, ensuring that your loved ones are remembered in a meaningful way."

A murmur of appreciation rippled through the crowd, and one woman stepped forward, her red-rimmed eyes brimming with tears. "Chief Kingsley," she said, her voice shaking, "I think I speak for everyone when I say how grateful we are for everything you're doing for us."

Samantha nodded, touched by the woman's words. "It's my honor to stand with you during this difficult time. Together, we will heal and ensure that our loved ones are never forgotten."

As the first workshop began, Samantha watched the families slowly open up, sharing their experiences and emotions. She knew that their journey to recovery would be a long and arduous one, but it was a path they no longer had to walk alone.

Over the following weeks, Samantha worked closely with the families to bring their vision for the memorial garden to life. From the selection of flowers to the intricacies of the stone pathways, each decision was made with care, ensuring that every voice was heard.

"Chief Kingsley," a father said one day as they surveyed the garden's progress, "I just want you to know how much this means to us. My daughter loved flowers, and I can't think of a better way to remember her."

Samantha placed a reassuring hand on his shoulder. "Your daughter will always be a part of this garden, just as she'll always be a part of our hearts."

As the last rays of sunlight dipped below the horizon, casting eerie shadows across the garden, Samantha couldn't help but feel a chill run down her spine. The darkness seemed to encroach upon them, threatening to swallow up the fragile light they'd managed to nurture. But she refused to be deterred.

She would continue to fight, not just for the memory of the victims, but for the healing of the living – for in their unity and resilience, they would find the strength to face the horrors that lurked in the shadows. And though fear might grip their hearts, they would never let it consume them.

A haunting melody echoed through the dimly lit art gallery, as Samantha Kingsley made her way towards a group of local artists huddled in a corner. The eerie music seemed to dance on the edges of her consciousness as if to remind her of the tragic events that had befallen their community.

"Excuse me," Samantha interjected, her voice firm yet respectful. "I'm Chief Kingsley. I was hoping we could discuss a project that I believe can help our community heal."

The artists exchanged wary glances before one of them, a middle-aged woman with a kind face and tired eyes, replied, "We heard about the memorial garden you're creating. It's a wonderful initiative. How can we assist?"

Hesitating briefly, Samantha shared her vision of a mural dedicated to the victims, capturing not just their faces but also the essence of their spirits and the impact they'd had on the community. "Art has the power to heal," she said, her voice cracking ever so slightly. "And I want this mural to stand as a symbol of resilience and remembrance."

As the artists listened, their initial skepticism gave way to a quiet determination. They agreed to collaborate on the project, each bringing their unique talents and perspectives to the table. Over the next few weeks, Samantha watched in awe as the once-blank wall transformed into a vivid tapestry of colors and emotions.

"Chief Kingsley, I hope you don't mind my asking," ventured one of the artists, "but what inspired you to pursue these projects? You've done so much for us already."

Samantha paused, the weight of her husband's dark deeds pressing down upon her like an invisible shroud. "I... I believe that by investing in the future of those who have experienced loss, we honor the lives that were tragically cut short. These initiatives are my way of fighting against the darkness that threatens to consume us."

Later, as she stood before the completed mural, Samantha couldn't help but feel a sense of hope blossoming within her. Amidst the chaos and pain, they had managed to create something beautiful – a testament to the resilience and strength of their community.

With renewed determination, she set about establishing a scholarship fund in memory of the victims, providing educational opportunities for young individuals who had experienced loss. It was yet another way to ensure that the memory of those lost would live on.

"Though the darkness may try to engulf us," she thought, staring into the eyes of the painted faces that seemed to defy the shadows, "we will not let it win. We will rise above, stronger and more united than ever before."

As the haunting melody continued to play, Samantha felt the weight of her responsibilities bore down upon her. But she refused to falter, for she knew that with each step taken towards healing, the light would grow stronger, driving back the shadows that sought to claim them.

Samantha stood in the cold, empty living room of the Thompson family, the chill of the air punctuated by the faint scent of sorrow that lingered within the walls. Her breath clouded in front of her as she listened intently to their stories, her heart aching for each loss.

"Thank you for sharing," Samantha said softly, her voice strong despite the quiver that threatened to betray her emotions. "I know it's not easy to talk about, but please remember that you're not alone."

"Your support means a lot to us, Chief Kingsley," Mr. Thompson replied, his voice strained from the weight of his grief. "You've done so much already. We don't know how we would have managed without you."

Samantha offered a small smile and a nod, her thoughts focused on the promise she had made to herself: to stand by these families, to fight alongside them in their battle against darkness. Every conversation, every shared tear, only served to strengthen her resolve.

"Please, if there's anything else I can do, just let me know," she insisted, her eyes meeting each of theirs with determination. She knew that the road to healing was long and arduous, but she also knew that together, they could overcome any obstacle.

The sun dipped low in the sky as community members gathered together at the local park for the memorial service. Faces etched with pain and loss, they stood united in their grief, finding solace in their shared experiences. Samantha took a deep breath, steeling herself for the speech she was about to deliver.

"Friends, neighbors, and loved ones," she began, her voice carrying across the hushed crowd like a beacon of hope amidst the encroaching shadows. "We come together today not only to mourn the lives that were stolen from us but also to celebrate the indomitable spirit of our community."

"Every one of you has shown incredible strength and resilience in the face of unimaginable tragedy," she continued, her eyes scanning the crowd, connecting with familiar faces that had become like family to her. "It is this unity, this unbreakable bond that we share, which will guide us on our path towards healing."

"Let us remember those we have lost, not only for the pain they have endured but also for the love and light they brought into our lives." Samantha's voice wavered, but she pushed through, her eyes glistening with unshed tears. "As we move forward, let us carry their memories with us, drawing strength from the knowledge that though they may be gone, they will never be forgotten."

The silence that followed was pierced only by the mournful cries of a lone crow, its harrowing call echoing the somber mood that lingered in the air. But as Samantha looked out over the sea of faces before her, she saw something else – a flicker of hope, a spark of determination, a light that refused to be extinguished.

"Thank you all for being here today," she whispered, her voice barely audible above the rustle of leaves in the wind. "Together, we will move forward, stronger and more united than ever before."

And in that moment, as the sun dipped below the horizon, casting long shadows across the park, Samantha knew that no matter how dark the night was, they would find their way back to the light.

The moon hung heavy in the sky, its pallid glow casting an eerie light on the streets below. Samantha sat alone in her office, the dim lamplight flickering as a chill wind whispered through the window. The silence was oppressive, broken only by the ticking of the clock on the wall, each second punctuated by the sharp click of its hands.

"Another day," she murmured, her voice low and weary. "And still, so much pain."

"Chief Kingsley?" The door creaked open, revealing Officer Daniels, his eyes etched with concern. "Are you alright?"

Samantha looked up, her steely gaze meeting his. "I'm fine, Daniels. Just... reflecting."

"Understandable," he replied, stepping into the room. "It's been a long road for everyone involved."

"Longer for some than others," Samantha mused, her thoughts drifting to the faces of the families she'd come to know so well over the past months. She could see their pain, etched across their features like the lines of a map, each one leading to a new destination – a place of grief, anger, or despair.

"True," Daniels agreed, his voice softening. "But from what I've seen, you've made a real difference, Chief. You've given them hope."

"Have I?" Samantha's brow furrowed as she considered this, her heart heavy with the weight of responsibility. "Or have I merely forced them to confront their demons before they were ready?"

"Sometimes, that's the only way to heal," Daniels countered, his eyes locking onto hers. "By facing our fears head-on, no matter how painful it may be."

"Perhaps," Samantha conceded, her mind drifting back to the memorial service. She remembered the hushed whispers, the tear-stained cheeks, the hands clasped in shared grief. But she also remembered the laughter, the stories shared, the moments of connection that had forged new bonds between once-strangers.

"Chief," Daniels ventured hesitantly, "I know it's hard to see now, but I truly believe that this community will come out stronger for what they've been through. And that's thanks, in no small part, to you."

Samantha looked at him, her eyes searching his face for any trace of insincerity. Finding none, she nodded slowly, allowing herself a moment of quiet pride. "Thank you, Daniels. That means more than you know."

"Anytime, Chief." He gave her a reassuring smile before turning to leave. "Just remember – you're not alone in this fight."

As the door clicked shut behind him, Samantha allowed herself a rare moment of vulnerability. She knew that the pain would never truly disappear, that the scars left by Edward's crimes would forever mar the souls of those affected. But as she gazed out into the night, she felt a renewed sense of purpose and resolve.

I may not be able to erase their suffering, she thought, but I can make damn sure their voices are heard.

Chapter 23

Beneath the Surface

Samantha sat alone in her office, the dim light casting elongated shadows that danced on the walls like sinister specters. Leaning back in her chair, she stared out the window, her thoughts churning with the horrifying events that had transpired.

Her eyes, filled with a mix of sadness and determination, glazed over as her mind wandered to the moment she first suspected Edward's involvement in the murders. The memory was vivid, playing out in her mind like a scene from a dark, twisted film.

"Edward, what's this?" she had asked, her voice shaking slightly as she held up a bloodstained shirt she'd found hidden away in his closet.

He had looked at her, his expression unreadable, before he finally spoke. "I can explain, Samantha," he said, his voice unnaturally calm. But the fear in his eyes betrayed him.

"Explain? How do you explain this, Edward?" she demanded, her heart pounding in her chest. She could feel the ground beneath her feet crumbling as if it were trying to swallow her whole.

"Please, just listen to me," he pleaded, his hands reaching out for hers, but she pulled away, unable to bear the touch of a man who had become a monster in her eyes.

As she stared into the darkness outside her office window, Samantha's thoughts raced through the emotional turmoil of those days. The shock, the disbelief, the anger, and the crushing sense of betrayal – it had all felt like a raging storm inside her, threatening to tear her apart.

But amidst all the chaos, one thing had become crystal clear: she would not let this man, this monster who had once been her loving husband, continue to wreak havoc on innocent lives. She would bring him to justice, no matter the personal cost.

And so, her journey had begun. A journey that had led her down a path strewn with horror and despair, one that had revealed the darkest depths of human nature. But Samantha Kingsley would not be broken. She was a fighter, and she would face whatever challenges lay ahead with the same fierce determination that had carried her this far.

"Edward," she whispered to herself, her voice wavering with emotion, "I will stop you."

The flickering of the candle's flame cast eerie shadows on Samantha's face as she sat alone in her dimly lit office. Gone were the days when she wore her chief of police badge with pride, replaced now by a haunted expression that reflected her soul-deep weariness.

"Dammit, Edward," she muttered under her breath, the words like bile in her throat. "You've brought me to the edge of hell and back."

As she continued her descent into the abyss of darkness that Edward had created, Samantha's emotional and psychological transformation became apparent. No longer was she just a dedicated police chief – she had become a woman who had stared unflinchingly into the eyes of evil and emerged stronger for it. Her newfound resilience had been forged in the fires of adversity, tempered by a resolve as steel-hard as the cold metal of her gun.

"Chief Kingsley?" A voice crackled through the intercom, pulling Samantha out of her thoughts.

"Go ahead," she replied tersely, her mind switching gears from past horrors to present responsibilities.

"Detective Matthews is here to see you. He says it's important."

"Send him in," Samantha commanded, steeling herself for whatever new challenge awaited her.

The door creaked open, and Detective Matthews entered the room, his face etched with worry. "Chief, we've got another one. Same MO as the others."

Samantha felt a familiar knot of dread tighten in her stomach. "Where?"

"Abandoned warehouse on the east side of town. We need to get there ASAP."

"Let's go," she said, rising from her chair with determination.

As they hurried through the dimly lit corridors of the police station,

Samantha's thoughts raced, grappling with the conflicting feelings that swirled inside her. She used to love Edward with every fiber of her being, but now, that love stood in stark contrast with the knowledge of his heinous crimes.

"Damn you, Edward," she thought bitterly. "How could you do this? How could you destroy everything we had?"

The weight of that realization pressed down on her shoulders like a leaden cloak, threatening to suffocate her. But Samantha refused to let it crush her spirit. She would not allow herself to be consumed by the darkness that had ensnared Edward – instead, she would use her strength and resilience to protect others from the horrors she had witnessed.

"Chief, are you okay?" Detective Matthews asked, concern flickering in his eyes.

Samantha managed a tight smile. "I'm fine, Matthews. Let's just focus on stopping this monster."

As they stepped into the night, the air heavy with tension and uncertainty, Samantha steeled herself for the grim task ahead. She would bring Edward to justice, no matter the cost – and in doing so, she would ensure that the love they once shared would not be forever tainted by the darkness he had unleashed.

The full moon hung heavy in the midnight sky, its pale light casting a sickly pallor over the city streets below. Samantha leaned against the cold brick wall of an alleyway, her gaze following the movements of a suspicious figure on the opposite sidewalk. A bitter wind tore through the air, but she barely noticed the chill; her heart was ablaze with a fierce resolve that burned hot enough to warm her from within.

"Can't trust anyone these days," muttered Detective Matthews, standing a few feet away from her. "Not even your husband."

"Trust is a luxury we can no longer afford," Samantha replied quietly, her voice laced with steely determination. Her eyes never wavered from the shadowy figure across the street, her senses sharpened by the painful knowledge that darkness could lurk beneath even the most innocuous of facades.

As they watched and waited, the ache in Samantha's heart intensified. She thought of all the lives that had been shattered by Edward's crimes – not just the victims themselves, but their families, their friends, and entire communities left reeling in the wake of unimaginable horror. And she thought of herself, betrayed and tormented by the man she had once loved more than life itself.

"Never again," she whispered fiercely, her breath fogging in the icy air. "I will never be blind to the darkness in others. I will protect this city, its people, at any cost."

Matthews glanced at her, his expression a mix of admiration and concern. "You're one tough lady, Chief," he said gruffly. "But don't forget – you're only human."

Samantha looked him straight in the eyes, her gaze unflinching. "I am stronger now than I ever was before," she declared, her voice unwavering. "I have faced the very depths of human depravity, and I have emerged from that abyss with a resilience you cannot even begin to imagine."

"God help anyone who tries to stand in your way," Matthews muttered, and Samantha knew he spoke the truth.

As they continued their vigil, the heaviness in Samantha's chest seemed to grow, a leaden weight pressing down on her ribs, making it hard to breathe. But she refused to let it cripple her; she would carry that burden for the rest of her days if it meant preventing even one more tragedy like the ones Edward had wrought.

"Chief," Matthews said suddenly, his voice tense. "I think our guy's making a move."

Samantha's heart pounded in her ears as adrenaline surged through her veins. She leaned forward, every muscle taut and ready for action, her resolve as unyielding as tempered steel.

"Let's put an end to this nightmare," she whispered, her voice filled with equal parts determination and sorrow. And as she stepped out of the shadows and into the moonlit street, she knew she was taking the first step towards fulfilling her vow – a vow forged in the fires of pain and betrayal, and tempered by the strength of a woman who would never be broken.

The dim light from Samantha's desk lamp pooled around the framed photograph, the silver frame glinting in the shadows. Her eyes lingered on it, drawn to that captured moment of happiness. She and Edward stood side by side, his arm wrapped tightly around her waist, their smiles so genuine they seemed to leap out of the image.

"Happy anniversary, love," she heard his voice say in her mind, echoing through the caverns of memory. She remembered how he had whispered those words into her ear as they danced under the stars, their laughter mingling with the music that filled the air.

But that night felt like a lifetime ago now, swallowed up by the darkness that had descended upon them both. The man she had loved, the one who had been her rock and her refuge, was nothing more than a monster in human skin. And she, the chief of police sworn to protect her community, had been blind to the evil lurking within him.

"Edward," she whispered, her voice thick with emotion, "how could you do this?"

A tempest of emotions raged within her – grief for the life they had shared, anger at the lies he had told, and a deep, abiding sense of loss that threatened to consume her. But there, buried beneath it all, was something else: A flicker of determination that refused to be snuffed out.

Samantha closed her eyes for a moment, taking a deep breath to steady herself. When she opened them again, her gaze was clear and resolute. She would not allow herself to be defined by Edward's crimes, nor would she let the weight of the past crush her spirit.

"Enough," she said softly, her voice firm but tinged with sadness. "It's time to move forward."

As she stared at the photograph, Samantha knew that the scars of the past would always be a part of her – jagged, aching reminders of the betrayal she had suffered. But she also knew that she had the strength to rebuild her life, forge a new path through the darkness, and find a purpose beyond the pain.

"Edward," she murmured, her voice steady despite the storm of emotion raging within her, "I will not let your evil define me. I will rise above it, and I will make sure that no one else suffers as I have."

With that vow burning like a beacon in her heart, Samantha turned away from the photograph and strode towards the door, her steps strong and sure. She had a long road ahead of her, filled with obstacles and challenges she could scarcely imagine. But she would face them all with courage and resolve, for she knew that she was no longer the woman who had been blind to the darkness within others.

"Goodbye, Edward," she whispered as she stepped out into the night, the door clicking shut behind her. "I'm moving on."

Cold air seeped through the open window, causing Samantha's breath to frost as she inhaled deeply. The chill seemed to sharpen her resolve, steeling her for the challenges that lay ahead. She knew the road before her would be long and treacherous, yet she welcomed it with unwavering determination.

"Bring it on," she whispered to the darkness, a bitter smile playing on her lips. "I'll survive whatever you throw at me."

Closing her eyes, Samantha allowed herself a brief respite from the weight of her responsibilities. In that fleeting moment, she felt a strange calm wash over her – a glimmer of hope amidst the darkness. It was as if the universe itself was acknowledging her newfound strength, offering a subtle reassurance that she could overcome anything.

"Edward may have unleashed hell upon this city," she mused, her thoughts veering towards her former lover, "but he didn't break me. I won't let him."

Samantha's knuckles turned white as she gripped the windowsill, her inner turmoil manifesting in the tension that coiled through her body. She drew another deep breath, the icy air filling her lungs and invigorating her spirit. With renewed vigor, she pushed the window shut, sealing out the cold and ushering in a new chapter of her life.

"Time to face the world," she muttered, determination etched into every line of her face. "And woe betide anyone who stands in my way."

As she prepared to step back into her role as chief of police, Samantha knew that she had changed irrevocably. No longer was she the naive woman who had been blind to the darkness lurking beneath the surface of those around her. Instead, she had emerged from the crucible of betrayal and heartache as something far stronger – a warrior, poised to fight against the evil that threatened to consume her city.

"Edward, you may have brought darkness into my life," she thought, her pulse quickening with a potent mix of fury and determination, "but I will use that darkness to light the way for others. I'll ensure that no one else suffers as I have."

With those words echoing in her mind, Samantha strode from her office, ready to face the horrors that awaited her beyond its walls. She had survived her nightmare, and now she would use that experience to protect others from the evils that lurked in the shadows. No matter what obstacles lay ahead, she knew that she was strong enough to overcome them – and in doing so, forge a brighter future for herself and her city.

Shadows danced across the walls as Samantha stared out her rain-streaked office window, the city's murky skyline reflecting the storm brewing within her. A resolute sigh escaped her lips; she understood all too well that this was only the beginning.

"Edward... you've awakened something in me," she whispered to herself, the promise of retribution lacing her words like poison. She clenched her fists, her knuckles white with determination. "And I will use it to shield others from the darkness."

"Chief Kingsley!" a voice called from the doorway, interrupting her thoughts. It was Lieutenant Miller, his expression urgent and drawn.

"Have a seat, Lieutenant," Samantha said, her tone authoritative yet tinged with an unyielding edge. She knew what she had to do now – there was no going back.

"Thank you, ma'am," Miller replied, settling into the chair opposite her desk. His eyes flickered uneasily between Samantha and the window as if sensing the profound change that had taken root within her.

"Listen closely, Lieutenant," Samantha began, her gaze locked onto Miller's, ensuring he grasped the gravity of her words. "What we're facing is far worse than we could have ever imagined. We must be vigilant, and we must act to protect our people, no matter the cost."

"Understood, Chief," Miller replied, nodding soberly. As Samantha stood up, her posture straight and her gaze focused, he couldn't help but marvel at the transformation she had undergone. From the depths of despair, she had risen like a phoenix, fueled by the ashes of loss and betrayal.

"Good," she said, her voice unwavering. "Now let's get to work."

As they left her office together, Samantha couldn't shake the feeling that she was entering a new battlefield, one more treacherous than any she had faced before. But she was armed with the knowledge of her experiences and the strength she had gained from them. And no matter what horrors awaited her, she would face them head-on, for herself and those who couldn't fight for themselves.

"Edward's darkness may have marked me," she thought as they walked down the dimly lit hallway, "but it will not consume me. I will be a beacon of hope in this city, driving away the shadows that hide the monsters."

A shiver raced down Samantha's spine as she stood on the threshold of her office, staring into the gloom that lay beyond. The shadows seemed to dance and shift, taunting her with their elusive nature. But she was no longer a woman afraid; she was a warrior forged in the fires of loss and betrayal.

"Those innocent souls," she whispered, her voice barely audible, even to her ears. "Their memories will not fade into oblivion. I will make certain of it."

And with that, she stepped out of her office, the door closing behind her with a resolute click that echoed through the empty hallway. Her heels tapped a rhythm on the polished floor, each step imbued with a sense of purpose that radiated from her like an aura. She would face whatever challenges lay ahead, armed with the knowledge and strength she had gained from her harrowing experiences.

"Chief Kingsley?" A hesitant voice called out, breaking through her reverie. It was Officer Daniels, a young recruit who had only recently joined the force. His eyes were wide with anxiety, seeking guidance from the formidable woman before him.

"Officer Daniels," Samantha acknowledged, her voice steady and professional. "What can I do for you?"

"Uh, there's a situation at the old warehouse," he stammered, "We could use your expertise, ma'am."

"Lead the way," she commanded, her gaze never wavering from his. As they walked, she reflected on the weight of Edward's darkness that still pressed against her mind. Though the burden was heavy, she refused to let it consume her. Instead, she would channel it into her work, using it as fuel to protect others from suffering the same horrors she had witnessed.

"Chief?" Daniels ventured, his voice tentative. "Are you... Are you sure you're ready for this?"

Samantha paused for a moment, considering his question. The truth was, she could never truly be ready for what lay ahead. But she had come too far to falter now.

"Officer Daniels," she said, her voice resolute, "I've seen the face of evil, and I've looked it straight in the eye. It may have marked me, but it will not break me. If anything, it has only made me stronger."

"Understood, Chief," Daniels replied, his determination sparked by her words.

Together, they strode into the unknown, each step carrying them closer to the battles that awaited them. For Samantha Kingsley, this was just the beginning of a new chapter in her life; a chapter filled with fear and darkness, but also with strength and hope. And no matter how treacherous the path before her, she would walk it with unwavering conviction, guided by the memory of those victims whose lives were not lost in vain.

The empty hallway stretched before her like an abyss, its darkness swallowing the light of the flickering overhead bulbs. Samantha's footsteps echoed through the stillness as she walked away from her office, her posture straight and purposeful. The suffocating air hung heavy with a sense of foreboding as if the very walls were whispering their secrets to her.

"Never again," she whispered under her breath, her voice laced with determination and a touch of sadness. "I will never forget the darkness that can hide beneath even the sunniest exteriors."

As she continued down the hallway, the shadows seemed to cling to her, seeking to drag her back into their depths. But she would not be deterred. Her every step was a testament to her resolve and the vow she had made to herself and those who had suffered at Edward's hands.

"Chief Kingsley?" A voice called out, breaking the silence. It was Officer Daniels, his eyes wide with concern as he approached her. "Is everything alright?"

Samantha paused, taking a deep breath to steady herself. She allowed herself the briefest moment of vulnerability before steeling her resolve once more. "Everything is fine, Officer Daniels," she said firmly. "I was just... reflecting on things."

"Reflection is important," Daniels replied cautiously, studying her face for any sign of doubt or weakness. "But we can't let it consume us, Chief."

"Agreed," Samantha responded, her inner thoughts echoing his words. She couldn't afford to dwell on the past; there was too much at stake. "We have work to do, Officer Daniels. Let's get to it."

"Of course, Chief," Daniels agreed, his expression hardening as he fell into step beside her.

Together, they strode forward, each step carrying them farther from the darkness of the past and closer to the challenges that awaited them. Samantha knew that the journey ahead would be fraught with danger, but she was prepared to face it head-on.

Her mind churned with thoughts of Edward, the man she had once loved but now despised. She could still feel the icy tendrils of his darkness creeping into her heart, threatening to extinguish the light within her. But she refused to give in; she would not allow herself to be consumed by the same evil that had claimed him.

"Chief?" Daniels ventured, his voice tentative. "Are you... Are you sure you're ready for this?"

"Officer Daniels," Samantha said, her voice resolute, "I've seen the face of evil, and I've looked it straight in the eye. It may have marked me, but it will not break me."

"Understood, Chief," Daniels replied, his determination sparked by her words.

As they walked away from her office, each step echoing through the empty hallway, Samantha felt the weight of her vow settling upon her shoulders like a cloak. She embraced it, knowing that it would be a constant reminder of the darkness that lurked beneath even the most innocent of facades – and a testament to her commitment to never let such evil go unchecked again.

CHAPTER 24

A Pact of Darkness

The heavy mahogany door creaked open, revealing the dimly lit office where Samantha Kingsley, chief of police, sat behind her imposing desk. Daniel Thompson stepped inside, his eyes adjusting to the scarce pools of light created by the room's lamps. The atmosphere was tense and somber, echoing the gravity of their ongoing investigation.

"Daniel, I'm glad you're here," Samantha said, motioning for him to take a seat across from her. Her voice was weary but resolute. "We need to talk about the latest evidence we've collected."

"Of course, Chief" Daniel replied, his face etched with determination. He smoothed out his jacket as he settled into the chair, straightening his posture as if preparing for battle. "I've been going through the case files nonstop. Edward's left a trail of darkness in his wake, and it's growing more twisted by the day."

Samantha's jaw clenched at the mention of her husband's name, but her gaze remained steady on Daniel. "Your work has been nothing short of exceptional," she said, her voice measured. "You've managed to piece together information that would have slipped past most detectives."

"Thank you, Chief. The victims deserve justice, and I'll do whatever it takes to bring Edward down." Daniel's thoughts flickered to the faces of the lost souls they were fighting for - young women who had been cruelly taken from the world due to one man's sick desires.

Samantha nodded, appreciative of his unwavering dedication. "Edward's obsession with power and control is escalating," she said, her eyes narrowing as she recalled the chilling details of the case. "With your expertise, we've uncovered the extent of his crimes, and it's only a matter of time before we close in on him."

"His meticulous planning has made it difficult, but we're making progress," Daniel said, his mind racing with the various leads they were following. "The rental properties he owns have become a hunting ground for him. We need to keep digging until we find enough evidence to put him away for good."

"Agreed," Samantha replied, her voice carrying the weight of her inner turmoil. She knew that as Edward's wife, she had a personal connection to the case that complicated matters. Yet her loyalty to justice and the safety of their community outweighed any lingering affection she might have harbored for the man she once thought she knew.

"Daniel," Samantha continued, her gaze locked on his, "I want you to know how much I appreciate your dedication and skills in this investigation. Your efforts have been instrumental in uncovering vital information about Edward's crimes, and I'm grateful to have you on my team."

"Thank you, Chief. I won't let you down." Daniel's heart swelled with determination, bolstered by her admiration and his desire to make things right. Together, they would bring an end to the nightmare that had descended upon their city.

Daniel leaned against Samantha's office desk, the weight of the investigation pressing down on him like a leaden cloak. The room seemed to grow darker as if the shadows cast by the lives lost were creeping in. He studied Samantha's face, noting the lines etched from years of steadfast duty and hard decisions.

"Chief," he began, his tone somber yet firm, "I have to say that your leadership throughout this case has been nothing short of remarkable. You've managed to balance your connection to Edward with your responsibility as chief of police. It's not easy to walk that tightrope."

Samantha looked up at him, her eyes reflecting gratitude for his acknowledgment but also the burden of her pain. "Thank you, Daniel. That means a lot to me."

"Edward was my brother-in-law," she continued, her voice cracking slightly. "I loved him like family, but I can't ignore the truth of what he's done." Her fist clenched on the desk, knuckles white. "I must make sure he doesn't hurt anyone else."

Daniel reached across the desk, placing a comforting hand on her trembling one. "I understand how hard this must be for you. I've seen things in this line of work that haunt my dreams, but this... it hits close to home for both of us."

He hesitated for a moment, feeling the need to share his vulnerability. "My sister was one of the victims," he admitted, the words catching in his throat. "I've never told anyone, but it's why I became a detective – to protect others from suffering the same fate."

Samantha's eyes widened with sympathy, understanding the driving force behind Daniel's relentless pursuit of justice. "I'm so sorry, Daniel. We'll get through this together, and we will make sure their deaths are not in vain."

Their gazes met, and in that moment, they found solace in each other's strength and determination. The shadows seemed to recede slightly, the darkness held at bay by their shared commitment to bring justice to those who had been wronged. As they stood in Samantha's office, united in their resolve, there was no question that they would face the horrors ahead with unwavering resolve, determined to restore light to a world clouded by fear and grief.

The air in Samantha's office grew heavy as if the weight of their burdens had settled around them. Daniel looked at Samantha – her eyes reflecting a steely resolve, a fierce determination to prevent such tragedies from happening ever again.

"Daniel," Samantha began, her voice steady and resolute, "I believe we have a unique opportunity here. Our combined skills and experiences could be invaluable in stopping these horrific crimes from happening in the future."

For a moment, Daniel considered her proposal. The idea of working together to protect others appealed to him, but he couldn't ignore the doubts gnawing in his mind. He shifted uncomfortably, the chair beneath him creaking softly.

"Sam, I want to help, I do. But don't you think there might be potential conflicts of interest? We both have personal connections to this case, and our professional lives already face enough challenges."

Samantha leaned forward; her hands clasped on top of the desk. Her gaze never wavered from his, asserting her unwavering belief in their cause. "I understand your concerns, Daniel, but we can't let those challenges hold us back. If anything, our connections drive us to work harder, to ensure no one else has to suffer like we have."

Daniel's mind raced, weighing the pros and cons of joining forces with Samantha. He couldn't deny the strong chemistry they shared, both as professionals and as individuals who understood each other's pain. And yet, the fear of potential complications – of possibly jeopardizing their careers or even their safety – still lingered.

"Listen, Sam," he said slowly, rubbing the back of his neck as he grappled with his thoughts. "You're an incredible leader, and I do not doubt that together we could make a real difference. But we need to consider all the possible consequences, for ourselves and the community."

"Of course, Daniel," Samantha replied, her voice softening with understanding. "We'll approach this with caution and discretion. We won't let our personal lives interfere with our professional duties – I promise you that."

As the last words fell from her lips, a shiver ran down Daniel's spine. The gravity of their decision hung in the air between them, a chilling reminder of the path they were about to embark upon. Together, they would face the darkness, united in their quest for justice and driven by their desire to prevent further tragedies.

With a heavy heart but a determined spirit, Daniel met Samantha's gaze once more. "Alright, Sam. Let's do this. For the victims, and all those we can still save."

The dim glow of the moon cast eerie shadows across Samantha's office, turning the once-familiar surroundings into a chilling landscape of twisted shapes and half-seen horrors. Daniel's heart pounded in his chest as he listened to Samantha's words, trying to focus on their shared purpose amidst the creeping dread that threatened to consume him.

"Daniel," Samantha said firmly, reaching out to lay a reassuring hand on his arm. "We've both been in this line of work long enough to know how to keep our personal lives separate from our professional duties. I trust you – and I trust us – to do what's right for the community."

As her touch warmed his skin, Daniel felt a strange calm wash over him, a sense of resolve forged in the fires of their shared determination. He couldn't deny the truth in Samantha's words; together, they were a formidable force, one that could make a real difference in the fight against this insidious darkness.

"Alright," he conceded, his voice steady despite the lingering fear. "I'm with you, Sam. So, where do we start?"

"First, we need to tighten the background checks for property owners," Samantha said, her eyes narrowing in thought. "If we can weed out the criminals before they have a chance to rent out their properties, we might be able to prevent some of these tragedies from happening in the first place."

"Agreed," Daniel replied, his mind racing with the implications of their plan. "And what about surveillance? Maybe we can get a grant for additional security cameras in high-risk areas. That way, we can keep an eye on things and intervene before it's too late."

Samantha nodded, her expression darkening as she considered the potential challenges they would face. "We'll need to work closely with other departments, too. If we're going to tackle this problem head-on, we need all the resources and support we can get."

"Absolutely," Daniel said, his resolve strengthening with each passing moment. "We'll have to be strategic and efficient in our approach, but I believe we can make a real difference if we stay focused and committed."

As they continued to discuss their plans, the shadows in the room seemed to recede, pushed back by the light of their shared determination. They knew that the road ahead would be fraught with danger and uncertainty, but together, they were prepared to face whatever horrors awaited them. And as they stood side by side, united in their quest for justice, they felt the first glimmers of hope begin to pierce the darkness that had consumed their city – and their lives.

Daniel leaned against the window, gazing at the city skyline as twilight cast long shadows across the buildings. The dimming light reflected in his eyes, mirroring the darkness that had enveloped their once-safe community. His thoughts swirled with the weight of the investigation and the lives that had been lost.

"Daniel," Samantha began, her voice breaking through his reverie. "I've been thinking... We need a more targeted approach to handle these crimes. What if we formed a task force dedicated to rental properties?"

His brow furrowed as he considered her suggestion. "You mean, a team specifically trained to investigate and prevent the kind of atrocities we've seen lately?"

"Exactly," she replied, her eyes alight with determination. "And I want you to lead it. I'll oversee the operations, ensuring we have all the resources and support necessary to get this under control."

He hesitated, feeling the weight of the responsibility pressing down on him. But within that hesitation, he also felt the stirrings of hope – a chance to make a real difference in their community. He glanced at Samantha, noting the fierce resolve etched into her features, and knew that together, they could face anything.

"Alright," Daniel agreed, his voice steady and resolute. "Let's do it. Let's create this task force and put an end to this nightmare."

Samantha's expression softened, gratitude shining in her eyes. "I know it won't be easy," she admitted, "but with your expertise and our combined dedication, we can make a positive impact and save lives."

"Saving lives..." Daniel murmured, his thoughts drifting to the victims and their families. He swallowed hard, his jaw clenching with renewed determination. "That's what it's all about, isn't it? Preventing more tragedies like the ones we've seen."

"Exactly," Samantha affirmed, her resolve unwavering. "We owe it to the victims and their families to do everything in our power to ensure no one else suffers like they have."

Daniel nodded, his eyes meeting Samantha's with unshakable conviction. As the sun dipped below the horizon and darkness claimed the cityscape, he knew that this collaboration would be the first step toward reclaiming the light – for their community, and themselves.

The dim glow of a flickering streetlight outside Samantha's office cast ominous shadows on the walls, making Daniel shiver despite the warmth of the room. He stared at the scattered papers and photographs spread across the desk, each one a chilling reminder of the dark path they were about to embark upon.

"Okay," Samantha began, her voice steady and determined. "We need a solid plan of action if we're going to make this task force effective." She picked up a pen and started jotting down ideas on a legal pad, inviting Daniel to contribute.

"First and foremost, we'll need a team of skilled investigators who can look deeper into rental property crimes," Daniel said, his brow furrowed as he thoughtfully considered their options. "I have a few colleagues in mind who would be perfect for this."

"Good, let's aim to assemble the team within the next two weeks,"

Samantha replied, scribbling a note on the pad. "Once the team is in place, we can start by reviewing any unsolved cases involving rental properties and searching for patterns."

"Right, we'll also need to work closely with other departments to gather intelligence on potential suspects," Daniel added, feeling a renewed sense of purpose as the plan began to take shape. "With your connections as chief of police, I'm sure we can get the necessary support from other agencies."

"Definitely," Samantha agreed. "I'll reach out to my contacts and set up regular briefings with them. Meanwhile, we should establish a timeline for implementing our strategies – say, three months from now?"

"Sounds reasonable," Daniel said. This was happening. They were going to fight back against the darkness that had invaded their city. The thought both thrilled and terrified him. He looked at Samantha, the woman who had become such an essential part of this mission, and knew that together, they stood a better chance than anyone else.

"Another thing we should focus on is increasing surveillance in rental properties," Daniel continued, his mind racing with ideas. "We can work with property owners to install security cameras and other monitoring devices."

"Great idea," Samantha nodded, adding it to their growing list of objectives. "And I think we should also push for stricter background checks on potential tenants. It may not catch everyone, but it's a start."

"Agreed," Daniel said, feeling the weight of responsibility settles firmly on his shoulders. As they continued discussing their plan, the room seemed to grow darker, the flickering streetlight outside casting even more menacing shadows across the walls and floor.

"Alright," Samantha said finally, setting down her pen and extending her hand across the desk. "We have our plan. Let's make this task force a reality and ensure the safety of our community."

Daniel shook her hand firmly, feeling the strength of their commitment solidify in that simple gesture. They had taken the first step toward fighting back against the horrors that haunted their city, and together, they would face the darkness head-on.

"Let's do this," he whispered, steeling himself for the challenges that lay ahead. The shadows on the walls seemed to recede ever so slightly as if sensing the determination that now filled the room.

The flickering streetlight outside cast long, distorted shadows across the room as Samantha and Daniel prepared to leave her office. Silence hung heavy in the air between them. They knew that from this moment on, their partnership would be tested in ways they couldn't yet predict.

"Daniel," Samantha began, her voice steady but tinged with a hint of vulnerability. "I want you to know how grateful I am for your support in all of this. This case has hit close to home for me, and I couldn't have asked for a better partner in the fight against these horrors."

Daniel turned to face her, his eyes searching hers as he grappled with the emotions surging within him. He knew the gravity of the task they were undertaking and the potential consequences it could have on both their careers and personal lives.

"Thank you, Samantha," he replied, the sincerity in his tone evident. "But honestly, it's an honor to work alongside you. Your leadership and dedication to this case have been nothing short of inspiring."

Samantha's gaze never wavered. "We've both put a lot on the line here, Daniel. I promise you; I will do everything in my power to protect you and our partnership."

His heart pounded in his chest, the weight of her words settling into his bones. He knew she meant every word, and the knowledge that she had on his back filled him with a renewed sense of purpose.

"Thank you," he whispered, his voice barely audible over the hum of the office equipment. "I promise to give everything I have to this task force and our mission. We'll make sure no one else falls victim to these monsters."

"Deal," Samantha smiled, her expression softening momentarily before returning to its usual steely resolve.

They shared a final nod, each understanding the unspoken commitment they'd made to each other and the battle they'd soon face together. As Daniel turned to leave the office, he couldn't help but feel a glimmer of hope amidst the darkness that had engulfed their city. With Samantha's unwavering support and their shared determination, they would face the horrors that lurked in the shadows head-on, ready to bring justice for those who could no longer speak for themselves.

"Goodnight, Chief," he called out as he stepped into the dimly lit hallway.

"Goodnight, Detective," she replied, her voice strong and steady, the echo following him like a protective cloak as he disappeared into the night.

The shadows of the night seemed to reach out with grasping tendrils as Daniel walked down the darkened corridor. He couldn't shake the feeling that he was being watched, but he steeled himself against the paranoia that threatened to take hold. The horrors they had uncovered during their investigation were starting to get under his skin, but he knew that fear wasn't an option.

"Hey, Chief," he said, turning back towards Samantha's office, "I just wanted to say that I appreciate your trust in me. It means a lot."

Samantha stood at the threshold of her office door, the soft glow of the interior light casting an almost otherworldly aura around her. "Likewise, Detective. We both know how high the stakes are, and I'm confident we can make a real difference when we work together."

Daniel nodded, acknowledging the truth in her words. He knew that they were fighting against a depraved darkness, one that sought to consume innocent lives for its twisted satisfaction. But standing there, looking into Samantha's determined eyes, he could sense the hope that still flickered within them both.

"Tomorrow, we'll hit the ground running," he said, a newfound determination fueling his words. "We'll gather our teams, start implementing the changes we discussed, and begin making this city safer for everyone."

"Agreed," Samantha replied, her voice steady and strong. "We'll face these challenges head-on, and we won't let anything stand in our way."

As Daniel continued down the hallway, he couldn't help but feel a small spark of hope amidst the oppressive darkness. He knew the road ahead would be fraught with peril, but with Samantha by his side, they would form a united front against the evil lurking in their city. For the first time in what felt like ages, Daniel felt a renewed sense of purpose.

This is it, he thought, *our chance to make a difference, to protect the lives of others and bring justice to those who have been wronged. We will prevail. *

With that thought firmly in his mind, Daniel walked into the night, ready to face whatever challenges the darkness had in store for them.

CHAPTER 25

The Devils Verdict

Samantha Kingsley steeled herself as her hand gripped the worn brass doorknob, taking a deep breath before pushing open the heavy wooden doors of the courtroom. The scent of old wood and stale air assaulted her senses as she took in the somber atmosphere that hung over the room like a thick fog. A sea of faces stared back at her, their eyes filled with a mixture of curiosity, pity, and judgment.

"Chief Kingsley," whispered the bailiff, nodding respectfully as she walked past him to find her seat.

"Thank you," she replied softly, her voice barely audible over the pounding of her heart in her chest.

As Samantha scanned the room, her gaze fell upon the defendant's table where Edward sat with an unsettling calmness. He was dressed impeccably in a tailored suit, his well-groomed appearance a stark contrast to the monster he truly was. The man she had once loved and shared a life with now seemed like a distant stranger, his cold blue eyes devoid of any warmth or remorse.

"Order in the court!" called out the judge, snapping Samantha out of her thoughts. She took her seat among the spectators, her breathing shallow and rapid as she tried to center herself for the trial that lay ahead.

"Your Honor," began the defense attorney, rising from his seat and addressing the judge, "I would like to remind the court that my client, Mr. Edward Kingsley, is innocent until proven guilty."

"Of course, Counselor," replied the judge, his stern gaze sweeping across the room. "Let us proceed."

"Your Honor, I request permission to call my first witness," said the prosecution, a determined edge to their voice.

"Granted," the judge responded, nodding solemnly.

Samantha clenched her fists tightly in her lap, her knuckles turning white as she fought against the torrent of emotions swirling inside her. She could sense the hatred and sorrow that emanated from the families of Edward's victims, their presence a painful reminder of the lives her husband had callously destroyed. As each witness recounted their encounters with the monster that was Edward Kingsley, Samantha's resolve hardened.

"Miss Jackson," said the defense attorney, addressing a young woman on the witness stand, "Can you tell us about your relationship with Mr. Kingsley?"

"Objection!" interjected the prosecution. "Relevance?"

"Your Honor, I am attempting to establish my client's character through his interactions with others," replied the defense attorney.

"Overruled. Proceed."

"Thank you, Your Honor," said the defense attorney, turning back to the witness. "Miss Jackson, please continue."

"Edward was always charming and polite," she began hesitantly. "I never would've suspected him of... of doing what they say he did."

Samantha bit the inside of her cheek, struggling to control her disgust at the defense's attempts to paint Edward as a misunderstood man who had been driven to his actions by a troubled past. The man she had once loved now seemed like a stranger, a monster hiding behind a mask of charm and deceit.

"Your Honor, may I approach the bench?" the defense attorney asked suddenly, causing the judge to raise an eyebrow in curiosity.

"Very well," he granted, beckoning the attorney forward.

As the defense whispered fervently to the judge, Samantha locked eyes with Edward across the courtroom. A mix of hatred and sorrow passed between them, a silent acknowledgment of the shattered life they had once shared. And in that moment, Samantha knew that no matter the outcome of this trial, there could be no redemption for the man who had become a monster.

The prosecutor rose from his seat, a stern and imposing figure whose very presence seemed to demand attention. His eyes scanned the room before coming to rest on Edward, who sat unnervingly still at the defendant's table. Despite the horrors of the crimes he was accused of, Edward's expression remained one of eerie calm – a facade that only Samantha could see through.

"Your Honor, esteemed members of the jury," the prosecutor began, his voice resonating with authority. "Today, we will present irrefutable evidence that the man seated before you, Edward Kingsley, is not just a successful property owner, but also a ruthless predator."

Displaying an array of gruesome photographs on a large screen, the prosecutor continued, "These are the faces of the innocent victims whose lives were callously snuffed out by this man. And as we delve into the horrifying details of their deaths, remember that they were daughters, mothers, and friends – and that their families, like those here today, have had their worlds shattered by the senseless brutality of Edward Kingsley."

Samantha's gaze shifted to the families of the victims, their eyes brimming with tears as they clung tightly to one another for support. Their pain was palpable, and as she watched them stare at the photographs of their loved ones, she couldn't help but feel a crushing wave of guilt. She had been the chief of police during these atrocities – she should have protected these people, and yet, the monster responsible had been right beside her all along.

"Furthermore," the prosecutor pressed on, "the testimonies from several brave survivors will reveal the true extent of Edward's depravity. They will recount harrowing tales of abuse, manipulation, and fear, all orchestrated by the man sitting over there."

As witnesses took the stand one by one, their voices trembling as they shared their nightmarish encounters with Edward, Samantha found herself unable to tear her eyes away from him. He remained calm and composed, staring straight ahead as if the testimonies were of no consequence. It was as if the man she had once loved had vanished completely, leaving behind only a cold, heartless shell.

"Your Honor," the prosecutor concluded, "the evidence we have presented today leaves no doubt that Edward Kingsley is guilty of these heinous crimes. We implore you, on behalf of the victims' families and all those who have suffered at his hands, to deliver justice swiftly and without mercy."

The finality in the prosecutor's voice echoed through the courtroom, leaving a heavy silence in its wake. As Samantha looked back at the grief-stricken faces surrounding her, she felt a resolve forming within her. No matter what it took, she would ensure that Edward's reign of terror came to an end – not just for the sake of the victims, but for the broken lives left in his wake.

The defense attorney, a lean man with slicked-back hair and a calculating gaze, rose to his feet, his voice smooth and persuasive as he addressed the courtroom. "Ladies and gentlemen of the jury, I understand that what you have heard today is deeply troubling. However, I implore you not to let emotions cloud your judgment. You see, Edward Kingsley is not the monster he has been made out to be."

Samantha clenched her fists tightly, feeling a prickling heat rise within her. She watched as the defense spun a tale of a man broken by an abusive childhood, his actions the result of years of torment inflicted upon him.

"Edward was born into a life of hardship," the attorney continued, his voice imbued with false sympathy. "His father was an alcoholic who routinely beat him, while his mother stood idly by, unable to intervene. As a result, Edward grew up desperate for love and acceptance – something he sought in all the wrong places."

As the defense rattled off a list of Edward's supposed misfortunes, Samantha's emotions fluctuated wildly. Anger surged within her at the blatant manipulation, attempting to paint Edward as a victim rather than the cold-blooded predator he had proven himself to be.

"Your Honor," the defense attorney said, turning towards the judge, "We acknowledge the pain and suffering endured by those affected by Mr. Kingsley's actions. But we must consider the circumstances that led him down this path. Can we truly hold him accountable when it was his past that drove him to these extremes?"

Samantha fought back tears, remembering the warmth of Edward's touch, and the love they once shared. It was difficult to reconcile the man she had known with the chilling evidence presented by the prosecution. And yet, there remained a strange sense of detachment, as if she were observing the proceedings from afar, unable to fully grasp the surreal nature of it all.

The defense attorney paced the courtroom floor, his voice rising in fervor. "You must ask yourselves: Is Edward Kingsley truly evil? Or is he a man who has been failed by the very society that now seeks to condemn him?"

As the attorney sat down, a hush fell over the courtroom. Samantha's heart pounded in her chest; each beat was a reminder of the devastation Edward had caused. But even as she glared at him, his calm expression never faltering, she couldn't help but wonder if there was some truth to the defense's words.

"Your Honor," she thought bitterly, "the man I loved may have been a victim once, but that doesn't absolve him of the unspeakable acts he committed." And with that, she silenced her inner turmoil, steeling herself for the remaining trial and the cold, hard justice she longed to see delivered.

The air hung heavy with anticipation as the prosecution rose from its seat. Samantha couldn't shake the image of Edward's calm facade, his clear blue eyes the same shade as the waters that surrounded their Florida home. The man she thought she knew was a mirage, and the monster lurking beneath would soon be revealed by the witnesses about to take the stand.

"Your Honor," the prosecutor began, "I call my first witness to the stand."

One by one, the witnesses stepped forward, each face etched with the deep scars left by their encounters with Edward. They clung to the railing, knuckles white as they steadied themselves to relive the unspeakable experiences, they had endured at the hands of the man Samantha had once loved.

"Can you please describe what happened on the night in question?" the prosecutor asked each witness, guiding them through their harrowing tales.

A young woman's voice quivered as she spoke, her words laced with terror. "He... he broke into my home, restrained me, and... and whispered to me how helpless I was." She took a shaky breath, tears streaming down her cheeks. "I've never been so afraid in my life. I didn't know if I'd survive."

Samantha clenched her jaw, anger boiling within her. How could Edward have done this to innocent people? Her gaze fell upon him and for a moment, their eyes met. A surge of conflicting emotions washed over her – hatred, sorrow, and the faintest glimmer of longing for the life they once shared. Edward's impassive expression betrayed no sign of remorse or empathy, increasing Samantha's resolve to see him brought to justice.

The testimony continued with another witness, a middle-aged man, who recounted his ordeal. "He forced me to watch as he tortured my wife, laughing when she begged for mercy... We barely escaped with our lives." His voice cracked, the weight of his memories threatening to break him.

Samantha's heart ached for the victims and their families; their lives were forever altered by Edward's twisted desires. As she listened, a part of her couldn't help but wonder whether there was anything left of the man she had loved within this monster.

"Your Honor," she thought bitterly, "this is not the Edward I knew. That man is long gone, replaced by the terror that now haunts these people's dreams."

The prosecutor continued questioning the witnesses, each story more horrifying than the last. Samantha maintained her stoic exterior while her thoughts raced, grappling with the duality of the man who had once held her heart. She silently vowed justice would be served, determined to honor the lives he had shattered and the memories of those who had been lost.

The courtroom, once bustling with whispered conversations and hushed gasps, now lay silent as a graveyard. Samantha could hear the faint tick of the clock on the wall, its hands inching closer to their destination. She clenched her fists beneath the table, nails digging into her palms as she braced herself for what was to come.

"Your Honor, ladies, and gentlemen of the jury," the prosecutor began, his voice steady and resolute, "throughout this trial, we have heard the chilling testimony of those who have encountered Edward Kingsley, the man who has committed unspeakable acts of cruelty and depravity." As he spoke, Samantha watched the faces of the jury, her heart pounding in anticipation.

"Through photographs and firsthand accounts, we have been shown the depths of human suffering inflicted by this man," the prosecutor continued, gesturing toward Edward, who sat emotionless at the defendant's table. "A man who not only took pleasure in the pain of others but relished in the power it granted him."

Samantha's thoughts swirled like a tempest, memories of tender moments shared with Edward, now tainted by the horrors that had unfolded. She gritted her teeth, fighting back tears as the prosecutor drove his point home.

"Justice demands that we hold Edward Kingsley accountable for his actions, for the lives he has destroyed and the pain he has caused," the prosecutor implored, his voice rising with passion. "Ladies and gentlemen of the jury, I ask you to consider the evidence before you, and render a verdict that ensures this monster will never again have the opportunity to harm another soul."

As the prosecutor concluded his closing argument, silence descended upon the courtroom once more, the air thick with tension. The judge, his stern visage framed by the black robes that hung from his shoulders, turned to address the jury.

"Members of the jury," he began, his voice commanding and authoritative, "you have been presented with evidence and testimony in this case. It is now your solemn duty to weigh the facts and determine the guilt or innocence of the defendant." He paused for a moment, allowing the weight of his words to sink in. "You must decide whether Edward Kingsley is guilty of the crimes he stands accused of. The decision you make today will undoubtedly leave a lasting impact not only on the lives of those involved but on the very fabric of our society."

Samantha's heart raced as she listened to the judge's instructions, her mind consumed by thoughts of justice and retribution. As the jury filed out of the courtroom to begin their deliberations, she locked eyes with Edward one last time. The hatred and sorrow that passed between them spoke volumes of the shattered life they once shared, leaving Samantha to wonder if anything could ever be the same again.

The hands of the courtroom clock seemed to crawl at a snail's pace, their languid movement mocking Samantha's mounting anxiety. The dim afternoon light filtering through the tall windows cast eerie shadows across the room, sending an involuntary shudder down her spine.

"Your honor, the jury has reached a verdict," announced the foreperson, breaking the oppressive silence that had settled over the courtroom like a suffocating blanket.

"Very well," replied the judge, his voice a low rumble that echoed through the chamber. "Please proceed."

Samantha's heart hammered in her chest, threatening to burst through her ribcage as she clutched the edge of her seat. Her thoughts were a whirlwind, images of the victims - innocent lives brutally extinguished by Edward's monstrous urges - flashing before her eyes like a macabre slideshow. She could feel the weight of their unfulfilled dreams and stolen futures pressing down upon her shoulders, a burden she would carry for the rest of her days.

"Edward Kingsley," the foreperson began, their voice steady despite the gravity of the situation, "on the count of first-degree murder, we find the defendant..."

Time seemed to stand still as Samantha held her breath, the anticipation coiling in her stomach like a venomous serpent. She knew, without a doubt, that Edward deserved to pay for his heinous acts, but the thought of condemning the man she once loved filled her with a strange sense of dread.

"Guilty," the foreperson declared, and the word reverberated through the courtroom like a gunshot.

"Guilty on all counts," they continued, each affirmation driving another nail into the coffin of Edward's fate.

As the reality of the verdict sank in, Samantha felt a torrent of emotions battering against the walls of her soul. Rage at the man who had caused such unspeakable pain, sorrow for the lives irrevocably shattered, and an odd sense of detachment as she struggled to reconcile the loving husband, she once knew with the monster now exposed before her.

"Order in the court!" bellowed the judge, his gavel cracking against the wooden block like a clap of thunder.

Samantha's gaze locked onto Edward; his once-charming visage now marred by the dark truth that lay beneath the surface. She searched for any flicker of remorse or regret in his eyes but found none; only the cold, calculating stare of a predator finally cornered.

The hushed silence of the courtroom felt almost suffocating as Samantha stared at the judge, his stern faces an unreadable canvas. The weight of her badge and gun, nestled against her hip, seemed heavier than ever before.

"Guilty," the foreperson repeated, their voice steady and resolute, as if to make sure every syllable pierced the very air itself. It was a sound that echoed through the chambers, reverberating deep within Samantha's soul.

"Thank you," she whispered, the words barely audible even to herself. Tears streamed down her cheeks, hot and bitter, as relief washed over her like a tidal wave, crashing against the jagged cliffs of her emotions. For so long, she had fought for justice, for the countless lives Edward had destroyed with his twisted desires. And now, it seemed, their tormented souls might finally find some semblance of peace.

"Edward Kingsley," the judge intoned, his voice heavy with the gravity of the moment, "given the evidence presented and the jury's verdict, I have no choice but to sentence you—"

"Your Honor," Edward interrupted, his voice calm and collected, as if he were discussing the weather rather than the prospect of spending the rest of his life behind bars, "I'd like to address the court."

"Very well," the judge replied, his eyes narrowing in suspicion. "You may proceed."

"Thank you," Edward said, offering a charming smile that once would have melted Samantha's heart. Now, however, it only served to enrage her further. How could he still wear that mask after everything he'd done?

"First," Edward began, "I'd like to apologize—to my wife, Samantha, and to the families of those I've... wronged." His gaze flicked briefly toward the gallery, where the tear-stained faces of the victims' loved ones bore witness to his unfathomable cruelty. "I know that nothing I say or do can ever make up for the pain I've caused, but I hope, one day, you might find it in your hearts to forgive me."

"Forgive you?" Samantha thought bitterly as her anger roiled within her like a storm. "You don't deserve forgiveness."

"Second," Edward continued, his eyes locking onto hers with an intensity that sent shivers down her spine, "I want you to know that I never meant for any of this to happen. I was a... sick man, blinded by my darkness. But I'm not that person anymore. I've changed."

"Changed?" Samantha seethed inwardly, her thoughts a whirlwind of contempt and disbelief. "How dare he say that after all he's done?"

"Lastly," Edward added, his voice suddenly softening, "I want to thank everyone who has supported me through this ordeal—especially my wife, Samantha. I know I've put you through hell, Sam. And for that, I am truly sorry."

"Sorry, don't even begin to cover it," Samantha's mind screamed as she fought to maintain her composure. The tears continued to flow, a bittersweet testament to the heartache and loss that had defined this nightmare.

"Your words have been heard, Mr. Kingsley," the judge said, his tone icy and unyielding. "However, they do not change the facts of this case. You have committed unspeakable acts, and now you must face the consequences."

"Understood, Your Honor," Edward replied, his expression unchanged as the reality of his crimes finally began to sink in. For the first time, Samantha saw a flicker of fear in his eyes—a brief glimpse into the soul of the monster she had once loved.

Samantha's vision blurred as she took a deep breath, her eyes shifting from Edward to the faces of the victims' families. They were a mosaic of grief and grim determination, some with cheeks stained by tears, others with lips pressed firmly together, holding back a torrent of emotions. The courtroom had become a graveyard, haunted by the memories of those who had suffered at the hands of Edward Kingsley.

"Your Honor," the prosecutor spoke up, his voice cutting through the tense silence like a knife, "the people request that the maximum sentence be imposed on the defendant for his heinous crimes."

"Your request is noted, Counselor," the judge replied, his stern gaze never wavering from Edward. "Defense, any final words before I impose sentencing?"

"Your Honor," the defense attorney began, his voice trembling ever so slightly, betraying the weight of his task, "we acknowledge the pain and suffering caused by Mr. Kingsley's actions. But we must also consider the roots of his behavior—his troubled past and the dark forces that drove him to commit these unspeakable acts. We ask the court for leniency—for a chance at redemption."

Samantha's fists clenched beneath the table, her nails digging into her palms. Redemption? For the monster who had taken so much from so many? Her mind echoed with the screams of his victims, their voices raw and haunting—a cacophony of agony that would forever be seared into her soul.

"Mr. Kingsley," the judge addressed Edward directly, his tone devoid of emotion, "you have been found guilty on all counts. In light of the severity of your crimes, I am imposing the maximum sentence allowed by law: life without parole."

"Thank you, Your Honor," Edward murmured, his calm facade

betraying not a hint of remorse or fear.

As the gavel fell, Samantha's heart thundered in her chest, the finality of Edward's sentence resonating within her like a funeral dirge. She glanced at the families of the victims, their eyes filled with a mix of relief, sadness, and lingering despair.

"Your loved ones will not be forgotten," she vowed silently, her resolve hardening like steel. "I promise."

"Chief Kingsley," a young officer approached her hesitantly, his voice barely above a whisper. "There's a reporter outside who wants to speak with you."

"Tell them I'll be right there," Samantha replied, her tone firm and resolute. As she rose, her gaze fell on Edward one last time, the man she had once loved now a stranger—imprisoned behind the bars of his own making.

"Goodbye, Edward," she whispered, the words tasting like ash on her tongue. And with that, she turned away, ready to face the world beyond the courtroom doors—a world where justice had finally been served, but where the shadows of the past would always linger, a reminder of the lives lost and the darkness that had threatened to consume them all.